I0771206

INTERROGATION

By

Scott L. Miller

© 2017 by Scott L. Miller, Trenchant Press

Although the publisher has made every effort to ensure the grammatical integrity of this book was correct at press time, the publisher does not assume and hereby disclaims any liability to any party for any loss, damage, or disruption caused by errors or omissions, whether such errors or omissions result from negligence, accident, or any other cause. We take great pride in producing quality works that accurately reflect the voice of the author. All the words are the author's alone.
All rights reserved. Published in the United States by Trenchant Press. No part of this publication may be reproduced, stored in a retrieval system, or transmitted in any form or by any means—for example, electronic, photocopy, recording— without the prior written permission of the publisher. The only exception is brief quotations in printed reviews.
www. TrenchantPress.com

Jacket design and illustrations © Nyancept Art and Design

Edition: 1, ver 1.00

ISBN- 978-1-964289-03-8
ISBN- 978-1-964289-02-1

DEDICATION

To Rosemarie Modica-Kennedy,
from college at St. Louis University.
You were my Kristin; I made you taller.
I hope you're alive and well.

Whoever fights monsters should see to it that in the process he does not become a monster. And if you gaze long enough into an abyss, the abyss will gaze back into you.
Friedrich Nietzsche

INTERROGATION

PROLOGUE

Imagine what it must feel like to be treated like a piece of meat. To be fearful all the time and have no one to turn to, to be betrayed by the people closest to you. To misinterpret everyday events as plots hatched by an unseen enemy that's everywhere, waiting, just waiting for you to drop your guard and take a false step.

Imagine what it must be like to exist in an environment so toxic and unpredictable that each day could be your last. To interact with people who wear masks of many faces, none the same from hour to hour, never knowing the right thing to say or do or who, if anyone, you can trust, not even the one you grew up alongside.

Imagine never having a moment to relax, to just sit and be. To be wound so tightly you're always sick, or crying, or angry, and you dare not speak a word of this for fear of reprisal.

Now imagine you're only five years old and you think this is the way of the world because you lack another reference point.

Can you imagine this?

If you said yes, you're a liar. Only someone who survived that world could. If you're one of the few who have, how did it change you? Did you turn your rage inward? Did you become a monster?

I know someone who grew up this way. My life changed forever because of it.

AN AMATEUR JOB

When my phone rings in the middle of the night, I fear the worst and hope for the best. Let it be a kid asking if my refrigerator is running or if I have Prince Albert in a can rather than a client in crisis or a health problem with one of my parents.

Kris is on the other end, and when she tells me what happened a few minutes ago, I jump out of bed, dress, and run out the door like a madman. Through her sobs she says the police are on their way. I remind her to breathe and promise to keep the line open until help arrives. I reassure her that everything's going to be okay while the speedometer on my Solstice passes ninety on the highway.

When I arrive at her apartment complex, she sits on a green plastic lawn chair on the first-floor landing, a blanket wrapped around her slumped shoulders. She appears smaller, somehow withdrawn into herself. Disheveled hair clings to her face. Her eyes contain the same distant, withdrawn look I'd seen in hundreds of abuse and trauma survivors. A crumpled piece of paper rests between her legs while a uniformed officer sits across from her taking her statement. She maintains pressure on her elevated right foot, which is wrapped in a blood-soaked white bath towel and propped on a third chair. She seems calmer since the frantic call to me but looks to be in mild shock. A second officer and a technician trundle down the stairs as the interviewing officer finishes taking the statement and hands Kris his card. I kneel to hug her while they leave, then look at her foot.

"You didn't say you were hurt."

"I'm fine. I didn't know I was bleeding until it was over."

"What happened?"

"Some time before dawn I heard a tapping noise, like metal on metal, but I drifted back to sleep. Then something slammed hard into my front door, followed by a boom loud as a shotgun. I ran to the foyer and watched the door crack down the center, someone kept slamming his weight against it. I could hear his breathing; he was that close."

"What about the safety bar?"

She nods. "It stayed in place against the door knob, but each time he slammed into the door it bounced on the ceramic tile and nearly fell. I braced it with my foot while I dialed 911. When the door began to splinter, I yelled that the police were on their way. I called out that I had a gun, though I don't." She begins to shake. "He kept ramming the door. I turned on all the lights, ran into the kitchen, and grabbed the butcher knife. I ran back and gasped; the door stood open several inches. I saw a dark blur of movement outside, and thought I was about to die. He rammed the door one more time and I heard the whine of twisting metal, the hinge screws pulling out of the jamb. The door was about to collapse inward. I raised the knife, ready to fight."

She squeezes the crumpled paper tighter with her free hand, her knuckles white. "Then it got quiet. All I heard was my own shallow breathing. Two minutes went by that way. I closed the shattered door as best I could, repositioned the safety bar. I tried to look out the peephole, but it was black. There are blind spots on the front landing even when you can see through the peephole, so I wasn't going out there without the cops or you. I checked the back patio door, even though it's on the second floor. Its safety rod was in the track. Then I called you."

"How'd you get hurt? Let me examine your foot."

She slips the crumpled wad of paper into a front pocket of her jeans. "The loud boom was the Waterford bowl. It was on the table, but probably too far back against the wall. When he slammed into the door, it fell off the table and shattered into thousands of shards on the foyer. I must have stepped on some when I ran through the apartment, but I didn't notice the blood until he was gone."

The gash in her foot begins to ooze blood again when she eased pressure for me to have a look.

"You're going to need stitches. Let's go to the ER."

She nods again. "Go upstairs and take a look first, Mitch." Her tone suggests I should brace myself.

The sun crests the horizon and birds chirp happily outside by the time I walk the steps to her second-floor apartment. The cracked front door bows inward badly down the center. It almost looks like two pieces of splintered wood held together by a coat of paint. Somehow it still hangs on the strength of two tiny, twisted brass screws. The jamb shows multiple marks and gouges from a jimmy. Fingerprint residue left by the lab tech on the jamb reveals scores of prints and smudges. The wannabe intruder used a magic marker to blacken the peephole so she couldn't see out. Inside, bits of broken bowl sparkle like red and white diamonds in the advancing sunlight. Her blood stains every floor of the small apartment. The carpet will need to be deep cleaned. The butcher knife lays on the landing. The mangled safety bar is bent and missing one of its rubber end caps.

She must have been scared out of her mind.

Back downstairs, she tightens the towel. "The cops said it was an amateur job. Most likely a random kid looking to boost jewelry or electronics or cash for drugs. They said there's been a rash of nearby break-ins. The neighbors were asleep; nobody saw or heard anything unusual. If the intruder had used a bazooka, sweet old Mrs. Wilson next door wouldn't have heard it. They lifted prints but they'll be mine, yours, or other second-floor residents and visitors. I think I saw surgical gloves on his hands."

"What else are the cops going to do?"

I wrap her foot in some gauze and an Ace bandage I'd brought down.

"Patrol the area more often. Some extra drive-bys each shift for greater neighborhood presence, but that won't last long. They contacted my landlord. He's supposedly going to buy and install a new door and deadbolt. They recommended he rethink the intercom system. If a burglar rings all the doorbells, someone eventually buzzes him through the outer security door without asking who's there, or he can follow someone else on through and act like he lives here, no questions asked. They suggested I put my lights on timers and get a guard dog." She laughs sardonically. "Pets aren't allowed in the building."

She winces when she tightens the wrap past her tolerance level. Her body stiffens. "He didn't stop when I yelled that I had a gun. He hit the door again and again. He wanted to get to me. I can't prove it, but I know it. I had this creepy feeling that he was laughing at me, getting off on my fear. I think he was operating on some internal clock and felt his window of opportunity close as more time passed, so he left. He wanted me, not my TV, Mitch."

A sudden chill slices through me. Based on what I'd seen, I can't argue the point. "Come stay with me."

A tired smile appears. "I thought you'd never ask. Help me get upstairs to pack a bag."

Surprised she'd want to try the steps, I help her to her feet and pull her to me, her warm body against mine. She wraps her arms around my neck and manages a smile. "You're a tough cookie in a crisis," I whisper into her ear.

She pulls back and looks up at me. "I grew up in the Bronx. I survived gangs in the subway and rats the size of dogs in the alleys. I was there when the towers fell on 9-11. This won't stop me. I don't back down from a fight." I notice her touch the front pocket of her jeans and think of her boss Dr. Warren Green, head of the Gateway University Medical School and the creep who harassed her at his party the other night.

"I'll go upstairs; tell me what to pack."

This time she flashes a broader smile. "Honey, I love you, but men have no idea what women need with them, or where everything is. It'll go much quicker with me."

She wraps her arms around my neck again and I carry her upstairs.

I place her down on the bed and she tells me what to pack in a bag and suitcase before we stop at the ER for stitches. On the drive to my townhouse, I ask about the crumpled piece of paper, but she'd fallen asleep in the passenger seat, so I let her be. I never saw it again.

FLASHBACK TO SATURDAY

The Saturday evening before the break-in, Dr. Warren Green had ruined what had otherwise been a great day. In the morning, we'd hiked seven miles of twisting trails along the Meramec bluffs that wind through Castlewood State Park. At the top, we soaked up the sun and ate a light picnic lunch sitting on a colossal limestone ledge that overlooks the river valley. Hawks hunted, gliding in slow wide arcs high in the cloudless sky. The distant rat-a-tat tat of pileated woodpeckers echoed across the valley. A cooling breeze combed the tops of the maple and ash trees. Kris never looked so beautiful. I was happier than I'd ever been. All was right with my corner of the world.

Kristin Gray is a full-time executive secretary and part-time student working on her master's degree in social work. She's the most sensual woman I've ever known. Intelligent, stubborn, and independent, she divorced her husband a year and a half ago, and we've been together for the last six months, my personal best. I felt like we've known each other forever, and when I think of the other women I've dated, women my male friends can't believe I left behind, I wondered what I'd ever seen in them. A former Miss Missouri, an Italian resident at Barnes with a trust fund equal to the GDP of a small nation, executives, a couple of local actresses and dancers, and a few socialites. None of them could compare with Kristin Gray.

I'm smitten. I'm in love.

We followed the hike with two sets of tennis and a shower until it was time to get ready for the party Green had invited Kris and her hospital co-workers, and apparently a chunk of St. Louis, to attend. We drove to his estate in Huntleigh Hills where we planned to make an appearance, schmooze, and then enjoy a late dinner on The Hill.

"We'll see how the other half lives tonight," Kris had joked as the size of the homes quadrupled along Lindbergh Avenue.

"Looks more like the top one percent of the other half," I said as we turned onto a tree-lined, meandering road. We joined a slow procession of cars winding past an entrance manned by electronically controlled iron gates.

The crunching of the perfectly round stones in the driveway under my tires sounded like the breaking bones of tiny animals. A Japanese garden of raked rock rivers and large mugo pines paralleled the curving pathway and culminated at a huge two-story fountain in the circular drive, where valets in tuxedos stood at the ready. I handed over the keys and we walked toward the covered entryway. Past the slate roof of the three-story stone and stucco estate, I could see the corner of a lighted tennis court and what appeared to be an Olympic-sized pool. Beyond the pool stood separate living quarters, a freestanding sauna the size of a two-car garage, and a cedar shake gazebo. A temporary burgundy canopy erected near the gazebo provided additional relief for the guests from the evening heat. Prolific rose and grape arbors, maintenance buildings, and a stable complete with steeplechase occupied sections of the rolling expanse of lawn. Men in dark suits and reflective sunglasses patrolled the grounds, denying public access beyond the living quarters.

Kris tugged at my sleeve and pointed to our right. "Look at the cars."

Busy valets worked feverishly, parking Toyotas, station wagons, Camrys, and Kias in a remote grassy area while BMWs, Mercedes, Jags, and Corvettes received preferential parking near the fountain at the front entrance. Parking by class.

I glanced back at my cherry-red Solstice, the top still down. "I wonder where they'll park her."

She ignored me. "Local sports stars and other celebrities will be here," she said as she hooked a bare arm into mine. She wore a full-length black dress slit up the right side, her low-cut top adorned by a string of white pearls. Local celebrities be damned, Kris will be the most stunning woman in the building.

I looked over my shoulder again and saw the valet park my car next to a black Porsche turbo on the opposite side of the fountain. "Yes!" I said and pumped my fist. "They know class when they see it."

She rolled her eyes.

"It's a guy thing."

"I figured as much," she said with a smile and patted my arm. We neared the arched entrance when a stretch limo pulled up across from us. "I'm asking for a raise."

"Did he marry money? The salary of a hospital medical director with ties to a Midwestern Catholic college run by the Jesuits didn't buy all this."

A Hummer limo discharged a former St. Louis Rams lineman wide as a battleship and bedecked in a deep purple tux, with a foxy young woman draped on each of his ham hock arms.

"I have no idea," Kris said as we were ushered into the main reception room, two stories tall, where guests stood or sat chatting in small groups and munching hors d'oeuvres. Hundreds of voices filled the great room along with clinks of crystal, silverware, and china while a string quartet played Vivaldi next to a grand piano polished a deep glossy obsidian.

A statuesque woman in a full-length, red silk kimono, her jet-black hair woven in a tight chignon, welcomed us and introduced herself as Elizabeth Green. I caught a trace of jasmine perfume behind a tan lobe studded with a diamond the size of an M&M. "Warren makes the most wonderful comments about you, Kristin."

The women shook hands. "Don't believe a word he tells you."

An older couple entered behind us and called to Elizabeth, interrupting our time with her. The smiling mustachioed man reminded me of the portly Community Chest character in the Monopoly board game while his younger wife looked every bit the matron weighed down by jewels. I guess he doesn't like waiting in lines.

She returned their smiles and turned back to us. "University benefactors. If you will excuse me, I must play hostess. You two make quite the handsome couple. Please mingle and help yourself to food and drink."

Kris looked at me somberly while we entered the main room arm in arm. "Ah, such trials. The life of a hostess is never done."

She introduced me to her work friends, and we drank some decent Asti and chatted for an hour or so without a Warren sighting. We decided to take a tour of the mansion before leaving for our dinner reservation. The main room with its massive stone fireplace, large Turkish rugs, Italian marble floor, cathedral ceiling, and stained-glass windows reflected generations of wealth—or, at least, the appearance of it. Expansive spiral staircases on each side of the great room led, I assumed, to living quarters and additional rooms upstairs, but red velvet ropes cordoned them off to foot traffic.

We walked a flagstone path to the greenhouse. Two stories tall, it contained assorted fan palms, water lilies, orchids, Australian Tree Ferns, large Chinese taro, and banana trees. Impressive, they had their own miniature version of the Missouri Botanical Gardens without the entrance fee or the bother of all those pesky commoners getting in the way.

Our next stop was the den, which housed an impressive library of leather-bound first editions of the classics, mahogany furniture, gold leaf crown molding, and a wet bar complete with a walk-in humidor and wine cellar. "Do you know I've counted seven fireplaces so far on this floor alone," Kris said with a mixture of awe and disgust. "The gas one in the main room seems big as my kitchen."

"Two people live here," I said. "This is overkill, even for the uber-rich. What I need right now is so basic."

"What do you need right now, handsome?" She came closer, smiling.

"You know exactly...." I bent down to kiss her and then excused myself when I saw a bathroom off the billiard room.

"Tease," she pushed me. "I'll be somewhere down this hallway," pointing off to the left. In a haughty voice, she added, "If I get lost, dispatch a St. Bernard with brandy."

I bowed. "As you wish, Miss Daisy."

When I found her sometime later, she was standing, arms folded, opposite a tall man in a quiet alcove. From her posture, I could tell she was angry. The space between them thick with tension; she was seething.

I moved closer to her. "What's going on?"

A servant entered with a canapé tray and eyed the dapper-looking man. He, too, immediately read the mood in the room and said, "Excuse me, sir," before executing a quick about-face retreat. The pianist in the nearby main room began a light and happy piece that wafted our way even as a heavy silence hung in the air here like trapped sewer gas.

"Kris, what's wrong?"

"We're leaving. Now." She made a beeline in the direction of the front door, leaving me to face the man. He was in his forties, lean and fit, with a trace of premature gray at his temples, and a smirk on his face.

He called to Kris, "See you next Tuesday."

I frowned. "You must be Warren Green. Your reputation precedes you."

He turned to me as if I'd disturbed him. "And you must be the Swinger."

Swinger. So he'd seen Friday's Channel 4 interview and already knew who I was. "No woman deserves to be called that. You need to apologize to her. What did you just do or say to her?"

"I don't believe that's any of your business."

The blood started to pound in my temple. "Whatever just happened isn't over. Count on it."

A faint smile danced across his tanned face, and he lifted his glass as if in mock toast or agreement, I couldn't tell which. I left to catch up with Kris. On my way out, I passed a familiar face among the party guests but didn't and couldn't stop to acknowledge his presence. I wondered if the evening could get any weirder.

I found her in the passenger seat of the Solstice. She'd been crying.

"Take me home. I'm okay, just take me home."

"What happened?"

Silence. More sewer gas.

She's a grown woman. She doesn't need saving. I knew she'd talk when she was ready.

I cancelled the dinner reservation and drove us to her apartment on Laclede. She changed into an over-sized St. Louis Cardinals T-shirt and we sat in silence on the couch. Before midnight we were hungry, and I phoned in a delivery of pot stickers and stir-fry.

She pushed a dumpling around her plate. "Thanks for being patient. I just wanted to get out of there. Warren's a major player. He's hit on me before, but never tried anything physical until tonight."

The tension instantly seemed to leap from her and burrow into me. "What did he do?"

She bit her lower lip and put the chopsticks down. "He cornered me. He was excited, almost euphoric, about some business deal he's about to close, probably the one he's been so secretive about lately. Then he got flirty, and I attributed it to the scotch on his breath." She paused, as if to steel herself for what she was about to say. "He grabbed my breast. I batted his hand away and he tried to reach through the slit of my dress to my panties. I hit him with a well-placed knee. You arrived not long after."

"I'm going back there."

"No, you're not. He'd have security toss you out on your ear. Discreetly, of course." She laughed sardonically. "He's used to getting his way and thinks he can take whatever he wants." She made a face, looking a bit steadier. "I won't let him fondle me or call me the C word. If I feel the same way about it in the morning, I'm going to file a complaint. The Psychology Department has an opening for a secretary. No need to work for a sexist pig if I don't have to."

"Did anyone witness it?"

She shrugged. "It happened so fast he caught me off guard. I don't know, I don't think so, but…."

"What?"

"There was something else. I only saw him for a second. There was a man walking on the upstairs balcony. I only noticed him because he seemed to be watching us, but he shielded his face from me. I could be wrong, but it looked like Steven."

"Your ex-husband?"

She nodded almost imperceptibly. "I've had no contact with him since the divorce. I assumed he moved back to New York. Right when I thought I saw him, Warren grabbed me."

I'd been wrong, the evening could and did get weirder.

"Are you sure it was him?"

"I'm not certain, but … I don't know. It seemed like him. It's not easy to mistake someone else for the man you grew up with, the man you were married to." She rose and dropped her half-eaten plate in the sink, turning to face me. "I feel like being alone tonight. If you don't mind."

So I drove home with the leftovers on the passenger seat wondering why she never told me her boss had hit on her before and why a man in his lofty position would risk assaulting her, drunk or sober, with over two hundred guests milling nearby. A few hours earlier, I'd called her Miss Daisy as a joke, but as I drove, I thought of *The Great Gatsby*. Instead of seeing the road before me, I felt like Jay Gatsby staring at the green light at the end of Daisy's dock.

II   II   II

After we'd dated for some time, Kris told me about her ex. They'd been childhood sweethearts in the Bronx, marrying right out of high school, and they both attended college in the city. After graduation, he received a full scholarship to Gateway Medical School in St. Louis with aspirations to become a neurosurgeon. Kris put her plans for her Master's in social work on hold, going to work full-time as a secretary to pay the bills. At the end of their first year in St. Louis, he'd become Warren Green's protégé, on the fast track to greater things. Then something changed, as imperceptible and insidious as the lengthening of an animal's claws. His normal outgoing mood turned introverted, sullen. His rational approach to the world shifted to wariness, then paranoia. The self-absorption needed to get through the grind of med school developed into ugly arrogance. He became hypercritical of everything she did, picked fights with her over little things. His library study sessions stretched to days at a time. He lost weight and color.

"What type of speed was he doing?" I'd asked while she refilled her glass the night she told me about their relationship.

She looked at me, stunned. "How'd you—?"

"I'm in the helping business. I've pretty much seen it all."

"It started with uppers, then coke."

"Was he seeing another woman during those long library sessions?"

She did a double take. "You just gave me goose bumps. How on earth—?"

"Drugs and infidelity often go hand in hand. I'm sorry."

"He was a no-show, no-call for my birthday that year. I'd fallen asleep on the sofa waiting for him and woke the next morning to the screech of tires. I looked outside and saw him exit an old blue Monte Carlo driven by Stephanie, his study partner and fellow med student. She was pleasant the one time we met—intelligent, outgoing, and attractive. She has fiery red hair almost to her waist. I watched her fondle the crotch of his jeans while he leaned in to kiss her goodbye. Five minutes later he looked me in the eyes and denied he was sleeping with her."

She tapped a finger on the table and exhaled.

"He admitted to using drugs. I suggested he seek help. He said he didn't need it, that he'd quit when he was out of med school. He called me a stupid bitch. A stupid bitch! When I asked him what he called

Stephanie late at night, he slapped me so hard my teeth rattled. He grabbed my hair and rammed my head into the side of our china cabinet. I inadvertently caught one of his thumbs in my eye and saw nothing but stars. He screamed for me to leave, saying he'd kill me if I returned. I ran barefoot to campus, filed a police report, and obtained a restraining order. By nightfall, one eye had closed and I had a mild concussion. I stayed with a girlfriend from my family therapy class."

II   II   II

I thought about that conversation while I drove and found my fingers drumming the steering wheel just as hers had drummed the tabletop that night. She said she'd tried to contact him later, but he never returned her messages. He hadn't responded to her notes in his mail slot at the med school. Friends told her he was living with the redheaded study partner. Kris filed for divorce two weeks later and Steven didn't contest it. She'd asked for and received the apartment, and the only words he'd said to her at court were, 'Thanks for filing, it saved me money.' A month later he and the redhead washed out of med school together. He disappeared and left no forwarding address. He had rocketed off campus like a missile, and Warren Green never mentioned his name in her presence again.

Had Steven returned and, if so, why? Why was he at Warren Green's party? And if she chose to file a complaint against Green, how would it play out, given the man's Olympian status at Gateway? Lastly, why was one of my clients at the party and how did he know Green?

As I pulled into my driveway, I reached over and cracked open a fortune cookie, crunched half of it, and read the small folded message by the dashboard lights. *What you don't know can hurt you.* I considered opening Kris' fortune but let it be.

THE WOLF

We spend a quiet Sunday and Monday of the Labor Day weekend reading, watching old movies, and generally trying not to dwell on what happened Saturday night. We chill and binge on television shows and reminisce about our summer vacation to Maui. We relive the helicopter ride to the waterfalls and sheer cliffs of Molokai, the pig roast, the evening sailboat cruises, and watching a massive school of sailfish leap from the waters while they fed on smaller fish.

Monday night, I ask Kris if she still thinks Steven was the man on the balcony, and her answer remains the same. I don't like the idea of him resurfacing so suddenly, especially at Warren Green's place. I give her space to think about whether she plans to pursue a harassment charge.

Tuesday morning rolls around and it's time to face reality.

I make Kris breakfast and take it into the bedroom. I see she's made a decision; a set of folded clothes lays on the bed, health and beauty products line the sink, and she holds a bath towel in her hand.

"You sure you feel up to work today?"

She takes some quick bites of egg and toast. "I have to. I need the money. Besides, I can't file a complaint from here."

"You're welcome to stay here as long as you want. Any word from the super about the apartment?"

"He hasn't returned my message. It probably means the door wasn't replaced over the holiday weekend."

She kisses me and turns for the bathroom. "Thanks for the food. It was sweet of you."

After breakfast and our showers, I drop her off at work and then drive to my Clayton office.

II   II   II

I wave to Gus the security guard and park in my underground space beneath the Clayton building that houses my office. It's been seven years since I started the private practice, five since I quit my day job. Some are surprised to learn I'm not a psychologist or psychiatrist. My Doctorate, like my Masters, is in social work. Most graduate students in my field hop off the academic bus at the master's level to pursue work in a myriad of public and private settings, but I accelerated through the extra two years in a year and a half, completed my practicum, and published my dissertation. I wanted to be my own boss, so I started a part-time practice at night in addition to my day job, and now I've got seven other therapists and therapy providers on staff.

In the eyes of the state of Missouri, social workers are 'therapy providers,' because psychologists legally coined the word 'therapist' for themselves. It's a distinction without a difference to the public, but a potential peril in the pecking order for us in the mental health field. Use the wrong word on a business card and you can be sued. But when we're not worried about the pecking order, most of us just use "therapist" as shorthand because "therapy provider" is too clumsy and our clients call us therapists, anyway.

Most of my current clients are motivated to change, middle class, employed, and pay their bills. Many struggle with depression and anxiety unrelieved by medication; some are schizophrenic or have Axis II personality disorders. My first client of the day is not truly motivated to change, nor is he middle class. But he was the man I noticed at Warren Green's party the night before.

Sam Paxton strode into my office today wearing a simple white form-fitting cotton shirt and black twill pants with black Ferragamo boots. Built like a bulldog and with the demeanor of a pit bull, he'd boxed and run numbers as a youth for a well-known St. Louis organized crime family, and his flat nose bears scars from those halcyon days. He wears hats to help him look younger and hide the plugs in his bald spot, indicators of a vain man. His brown eyes seem to be ever on the lookout, hunting.

Sam is a self-made millionaire in his mid-forties and owner of one of the largest trucking companies in the Midwest. He takes pride in the fact that he mauls the trucker's union at the negotiating table every year, destroys or absorbs his competition, and finagles sweetheart deals with local politicians to pay little or no corporate taxes in exchange for keeping his businesses in town, which he plans to do anyway. And he holds his head high at the mention of his nickname, The Wolf.

Until his wife Rita developed advanced Multiple Sclerosis at an early age, he had been master of his domain. As the main fabric of his highly organized and structured personal world slowly unraveled around him, he was powerless to prevent it so he howls at the moon and at other people, and sometimes strays.

I spend the first part of our session trying to convince him to a trial of an anti-depressant, but he won't agree. He buys into the false notion that people on meds are weak, flawed, or crazy. Now he sits across from me twirling his fedora in his powerful hands as if he fingers a worry stone. He takes advantage of a lull in the conversation to change the subject.

"Saw you at the fundraiser last Saturday."

I played my cards right. I let him acknowledge the chance encounter.

I keep it low-key. "Oh, that's right, you were at Warren Green's house. It looked like a party to me. What was the cause?"

The lines on his face ease as his comfort level rises. "With a man of vision like Warren Green, business is as constant as Democrats wanting to raise taxes. Business is business whether it's completed in a boardroom, on a country club fairway, or a downtown restaurant over a plate of Kobe beef." He pauses, his mouth curves into a grin. "I hope you enjoyed yourself."

A man of vision if your vision leans to the predatory. "How long have you known him?" I ask casually, aware he didn't answer my first question.

He raises his eyebrows, as if surprised by the follow-up question and pleased the focus is off him. "We go back years. We met on the board of a local firm. I introduced him to influential people who recognized his potential and helped him realize it." The sly grin returns. "To think I only have a high school education. It's not always what you know, is it?"

All too often it's who you know. I didn't want to validate his statement, so I said nothing.

He clears his throat and changes the subject. "I saw you there with his girl." He does a double take and adds, "I didn't mean it that way. I mean his secretary." He continues to backpedal. "His executive assistant. The attractive and smart young woman with the long brunette hair. Damn these days of political correctness, you can't carry on an everyday conversation without the worry that you might offend someone or some civil rights group."

"It does urge one to think before speaking."

The Wolf's eyes narrow again as the black fedora spins again in his powerful hands. "I saw that beautiful woman storm out the front door with you hot on her heels. I hope you were able to corral that feisty filly."

So, you're a cowboy now, Wolf? "Kristin. Her name's Kristin."

He cocks an eye toward me. "I take it she's not a fan of fundraisers."

"She also thought it was a party." I decide to push. "History teaches us that some 'men of vision' believe the rules don't pertain to them, that their station in life entitles them to multiple outlets for their passions. What are your thoughts on the subject? Does too much power corrupt, or is that stance too simplistic?"

He glares at me like he did so often during our previous sessions, only this time he remains in control. He stirs uncomfortably in the leather chair. "We're all human, even you, Dr. Adams, though I'm not sure you realize that yet. I don't know how that pertains to the party, but I witnessed what everyone else saw, she left the party upset, with you trailing in her wake. People thought, as I did, that you two had a disagreement, a lovers' spat. Warren remained into the wee hours of the morning entertaining select guests, me included."

I hadn't asked him to provide Warren Green with an alibi for Saturday night, but that's what he did. Is that coincidence?

In our previous session, I'd challenged him about his wife, now bed- and wheelchair-bound and a total-care patient at home. His attention to Rita had flagged over recent months to almost total delegation of her needs to twenty-four-hour, private duty nurses. When I pressed him, he unleashed a verbal barrage that stopped just short of becoming physical. At the height of his tirade he shouted, "Maybe something like this should happen to you!" The Wolf admitted to having affairs with other women after Rita became too sick to have sex. We eventually began to discuss his feelings about it, what the affairs meant to him, the impact on his relationship with Rita, and what he planned to do about them.

He'd been enraged then, but not now. He seems pleased, for some reason, that now I know he's part of the Warren Green pack. And that Warren Green's pack had power, and I didn't.

When our time is up I feel a slight relief to watch him leave and eager to see my next client.

SWINGER

My grad school professors taught us that therapists aren't supposed to have favorite clients because such feelings cloud the therapeutic relationship and impede client progress. Nevertheless, my favorite client, Bob Vale, is a chronic schizophrenic in his late twenties. He lost his Medicaid insurance coverage years ago thanks to the governor of our not-so-progressive state, so now I see Bob pro bono. The prodromal symptoms of his schizophrenia appeared when he enlisted in the army as an under-age recruit and worsened while he struggled to complete basic training. A social and emotional runt, he occupied the role of whipping boy most of his adult life. When his thought disorder turned acute, he believed enemies lurked everywhere and he suffered incapacitating terror, body shakes, and feelings of impending doom.

A researcher named DaCosta labeled Bob's nervous condition 'Soldier's Heart' when he observed it in shell-shocked Civil War soldiers. Today we call them panic attacks. Now we know anxiety existed before man learned to walk upright. The earliest recorded reference to anxiety is 5000 years old. 3000 years before Christ, it was believed the afflicted had made the gods angry and the victims simply had to bear the brunt of it. Early mankind relied on a supernatural model, pray to feel better or sacrifice something (a cow or goat) or someone precious (sometimes a virgin) to the gods. Later, Hippocrates came along and coined the ancient Greek term melancholia, or black bile, which enjoyed a long run of popularity before eventually giving way to various early concepts of depression. Recent years have brought forth a virtual biblical flood of newly coined psychological conditions and syndromes plentiful enough to make one's head swim.

We've come a long way, but the bar wasn't set too high from the beginning.

When command hallucinations ordered Bob to line his helmet with foil so the enemy couldn't read his thoughts, he ceased being a reliable tool for the army and received a medical discharge.

Over the last nine years I'd guided him through the deaths of both his parents and informally became a surrogate mentor on his rocky road to independence. He's eked out a meager existence on psychiatric disability while living in his dead mother's bungalow in the city. He suffers relapses when he stops taking his medication or gets intoxicated or comes under intense stress.

But Bob's progress has literally come to a crashing standstill. In fact, he'll be lucky to see his next birthday.

I park my Solstice in a visitor lot and walk a flight of steps to see him.

Bob Vale currently occupies a hospital bed, he's connected to a ventilator with chest tubes running to the floor that drain blood. So far, he's lost a testicle and his spleen. He has a lacerated kidney and bilateral subdural hematomas severe enough to warrant an induced coma. Multiple orbital fractures and massive swelling make it too early to know whether he'll lose vision in one eye. He has six rib fractures and a broken collarbone. He has no surviving family, no one to speak for him. I'm his lone visitor. During one brief lucid moment after admission, he gave me a general description of his attackers, which I passed on to the cops. As details from the police report trickled in, it became clear that unless he recovered to identify those who robbed and beat him, their involvement in the case would end.

I check in with the nurses, and, as anticipated, Bob's condition remains unchanged.

"I saw the interview on the Friday evening news," one of the nurses said. "Thank you for taking a stand for him. I'm glad you did what you did. He deserved it. It breaks my heart to see him in there all alone," another chimed in.

It broke mine but it also made me angrier than hell. And that's why I did the interview at Channel Four the previous Friday, to tell Bob's story since no one else would.

The three major local television stations periodically interview area mental health professionals when they believe breaking news stories contain psychiatric issues. I'd filled the role of unpaid consultant for this station many times, but the interview about Bob was the first time I'd decided to pull a few strings and call in a favor, even though the topic was a bit of a stretch.

After a make-up artist in the studio applied pancake makeup to my face, I thanked Debbie Macklin, the paper-thin blonde Channel Four news reporter, for the airtime. If I had a sandwich, I'd have given it to her.

"I should be thanking you. What happened to that poor guy is news. You gave me the idea for a story that I will turn into an exposé."

She listened briefly to the Bluetooth in her ear then made a quick circling motion with her hand for the cameraman to start filming. She cleared her throat once and smiled into the lens. "Good evening, St. Louis viewers. This is News Channel Four's Debbie Macklin with the first of a three-part series on area massage parlors. Should they go the way of the old-time bathhouses? Why are massage parlors sometimes associated with the seamier side of urban life, and is this a fair characterization?"

Her face turned somber as she continued, "Tonight a young man lies in a coma at a local hospital fighting for his life after a vicious beating, allegedly by employees and/or patrons of Dolly's Delight, a massage parlor in rural Jefferson County. With us tonight is Dr. Mitchell Adams, an area Ph.D. social worker in private practice. We've asked Dr. Adams to lend his expert opinion before on a variety of mental health topics and tonight we ask him to comment on massage parlors, pro or con in our society today, Doctor?"

Out of the corner of my eye, I watch a cluster of men the size of dinosaurs enter the television station from a side door while I stood next to the waif-like reporter. "Debbie, there are chains of licensed therapeutic massage businesses and there are *massage* parlors. Accredited massage businesses are staffed by trained professional masseuses who've completed hundreds of supervised training hours to learn the art of massage. Even the most cursory look inside Dolly's Delight reveals its tarnished underbelly. There are racks of adult magazines and videos, along with sex toys and drug paraphernalia for sale. Their walls display no diplomas or certificates because no licensed massage therapists work at Dolly's."

Shouts of disagreement rained down on me from the cadre of men who'd just entered the television studio. I turned and saw an entourage of behemoth body builders surround a dark, handsome man in his thirties. His jet-black hair was slicked back into a short ponytail and a gold cross studded with diamonds dangled from his left earlobe. His coal-colored shark eyes glared at me. He stood defiant in a tailored London tweed black suit; gaudy gold chain bling gleamed from his neck. Frank DeLuca owned and operated Dolly's Delight, among several other businesses with questionable reputations.

Debbie Macklin nervously shifted what weight she had from one foot to the other and quickly nodded for me to continue.

I furrowed my brow at her briefly. "Dolly's is like the tanning salon 'business' that made the news one year in Dallas—the entire operation had only one tanning bed but many 'special' customer rooms behind a curtain guarded by a burly gatekeeper. A hundred dollars bought you entrance to the back room with a bed and a female employee. Businesses such as these are simply fronts for prostitution—"

Curses spewed my way from the bodyguards while DeLuca shouted at me, "What's the point of this? You want your fifteen minutes of fame and your face on television? I'll be back in business tomorrow and you know it."

So much for the controlled interview, but I too can improvise. I turned to him and said calmly, "You robbed and beat an innocent man. That's felony assault. Manslaughter if he dies. If that's how you treat paying customers, you should be out of business and behind bars."

The most massive bodyguard took a step toward me, but DeLuca stopped him with a hand on his meaty forearm. Behind me Debbie called for security.

Best idea I've heard all day.

Cool and calm, I forged ahead. "If Dolly's isn't a front for prostitution, show us your massage licenses. Where are your certificates from the Department of State Health Services? These records should be displayed for all to see."

He pointed a finger at me. "Are you calling me a pimp? I'm a legitimate businessman. I ought to sue you, you little shit!" Seeing him tug at his stiff French collar made me smile; I was getting under his skin. At times I antagonize clients, to a lesser degree, of course, to motivate them or prompt them to express anger when it's therapeutic, but I felt a satisfying guilty pleasure when I got under his skin.

Sticks and stones.

"Be my guest, sue me." I calmly pointed to his entourage. "Why the bouncers, the goons with no necks, if you're a legitimate businessman as you claim? I wasn't aware the art of massage was so dangerous."

DeLuca had to shout at the biggest behemoth to stop in his tracks. He dramatically waved his gold ringed hands in the air. "Talk, talk. You're all talk. Where's your proof?"

That was my problem, but I wasn't about to admit it.

Desperate times.

"You're a panderer. You feed off human weakness."

His laugh rose an octave behind his cocoon of protection; he put his hands on his hips. "You do the same. People pay you to listen to their neurotic little sob stories. How pathetic!"

I lowered my voice to draw him closer. "Quit hiding behind your henchmen. Come talk to me. Man to man."

The four musclemen stared at him, looking for direction. DeLuca nodded and the sea of muscles, tattoos, and faded denim parted.

He stood next to me while I spoke in an even softer whisper.

Exasperated, he leaned in closer. "What the fuck you say?"

I'd drawn his face next to mine. I smelled Axe cologne and mouthwash as the studio lights glinted off the heavy gold chain around his hairy neck. I whispered, "I don't care about busting your girls. I know your goons hurt Bob. I want to know one thing, were you part of it?"

His smile showed white, capped teeth. "Your retard friend lives in a dangerous and crazy world. He will return to my girls; people like him always do. And yes, I am a very hands-on boss." His smile turned to a leer and slowly spread across his darkly handsome face. Those soulless dark eyes showed delight as if he revels in doling out pain.

I remembered how Bob looked in his hospital bed. He wasn't smiling.

I landed a straight punch hard to his square jaw that dropped the big man to the floor and knocked the grin off his face. He stood up, swinging awkwardly in retaliation as I backed away from his fists which caught nothing but air. Chaos reigned, people ran helter-skelter throughout the news station. DeLuca's bodyguards toppled station staffers like dominoes while they worked their way toward me. Moments before I became a splat on the news station wall, station security arrived with guns and batons drawn, mace at the ready.

Sometimes I do stupid things.

"I'll fucking kill you! You'll be sorry!" he screamed, wild-eyed, his unraveled ponytail dangling in front of his startled face as security restrained the big boss man. He stabbed the air between us like he was wielding a knife. His torrent of threats persisted as security slowly obtained control of the situation and escorted DeLuca and his reluctant goons from the studio.

He didn't need to say it. I already regretted what I'd done.

He baited me and I fell for it. I'd never punched another person before, not even in grade school. I guess there's a first time for everything. Security let go of me and I rubbed my stinging hand. It felt good at the time, but now I just wanted to put this behind me and sneak out of the building with my tail between my legs. I adjusted my coat and tie, looking for the nearest exit.

What I saw next was a glowing red light. A handheld studio camera followed me while another trailed DeLuca and his Bunyanesque entourage. The bearded cameraman gave a quick thumbs-up and called out, "Got it, Deb," as station security whisked her through a metal fire door to safety.

Great.

Back at Kris' apartment after the interview fiasco, I sat on her old yellow couch waiting for the news with a sense of foreboding. I told her the interviews were supposed to be separate. DeLuca wasn't scheduled to appear for an hour.

"Do you think that smarmy blonde toothpick set you up?"

I nodded. "That's what I'm afraid of. She didn't return my call. Let's hope she has a heart."

Kris raised an eyebrow and shook her head. "Any woman that skinny has to be mad at the world from lack of food. Don't hold your breath."

She handed me a Tanqueray and tonic. "Better drink up. It's all about ratings. Their mantra is: *If it bleeds, it leads.*

As if on cue, a smiling Debbie Macklin came on the screen to introduce part one of her three-part exposé on area massage parlors. Her intro ran pretty much word-for-word as I remember it when the camera cut to me prepared to answer her question. Then, with my voice-over as background, roving pictures from Dolly's Delight filled the screen, showing racks of porn movies and sex toys, the video sex booths, until one of the long-haired, steroid-enhanced bouncers denied the cameraman entrance past a certain point. So far, so good.

It was good the public got to see Dolly's interior. Debbie returned on screen and reminded viewers of a man's beating, allegedly by security at Dolly's. This served as lead-in to my confrontation with Frank DeLuca and concluded with my punch and the subsequent studio melee. When the piece ended the blonde broomstick called me, "The Swinging Social Worker."

Good God.

With DeLuca's angry, wild-eyed, disheveled look caught on freeze-frame, her final voice-over promised part two would include the latest developments on the legal case and an update on Bob's condition, plus what to look for and where to go for a therapeutic massage by a licensed massage therapist.

We took our eyes from the TV and looked at one another. "I hope none of my clients watch the news."

Kris smiled and pointed to my half empty glass. "Want a refill, Swinger?"

I leveled my eyes at her. "Very funny."

At the time I thought, I hope that moniker doesn't stick. But it had. At least with the Warren Greens of the world.

THE SMELL AND THE COLOR OF

PAIN

I woke in the middle of the night because the bed was shaking. Kris tossed and turned, mumbling 'no' in her sleep, with increasing intensity until she sat up, her tiger eyes fixed with terror, beads of sweat clinging to her face and hair.

My heart sank. "Wake up, hon! You're having a bad dream. You're at my place. You're safe!" I tried to hold her but when she saw me, she flailed her arms and scratched me below the left eye, drawing blood. I held her until the terror subsided and her breathing slowed.

At last she came awake. "I'm sorry. This has gotta stop." She ran her fingers through her tousled hair and padded off naked toward the kitchen. I rolled over, turned on a light, and waited. She'd been staying with me since the break-in and had been plagued by nightmares.

In the first dream the safety bar in her apartment gave way and the intruder was her boss. "You're coming with me, slut," he snorted, his nostrils flared like those of a bull. His red eyes bore down on her as wisps of steam shot from his nose in warm spurts, his fetid breath smelled of Scotch and blood. Warren the bull-figure drew circles on her red nightgown with a black magic marker, outlining her areolae and dotting the silk where her nipples touched the fabric. He fondled her breasts. "Away from your bleeding-heart social work program, away from your therapist boyfriend." She fought back but he was too strong. She woke from the dream in a sweat when he dragged her from the apartment.

In the second dream it was her ex-husband, or more accurately the ghost of her ex, who was the intruder in her second nightmare. The safety bar gave way to a disheveled Steven dressed in rags, his handsome features now sallow and gaunt. He pointed a bony, gnarled finger at her. "Because of you, I never made it through medical school. Now I live in an abandoned blue Monte Carlo in the projects and sell my blood to survive. A good day for me is if I avoid gang rape. Have you ever had three or four drunken hobos run a train on your ass? It's a feeling that's hard to describe. Pleasure and pain, two sides of the same coin. We gave each other our fair share of both." The Steven-thing raised his flesh-eaten arms for her inspection while he ogled her. "If only you'd stood by me when I needed your support the most, I wouldn't have to offer you to my Sterno friends now. They'll love you, my darling." The Steven-thing grabbed her wrist while a dozen homeless men with ragged beards and rheumy eyes burst into the foyer, fighting one another to be the first to have at her. She woke up in a sweat, crying out for help.

She returned from the kitchen with a glass of water.

"Did the safety bar give way again?"

She nodded and placed her glass on the bedside table.

"Who was it this time?"

She looked me straight in the eyes. "You."

I felt as if my skin had sloughed off my body and slithered under the bed.

"You picked up my present, the Waterford bowl, and threw it to the floor. When you spoke, it was with my father's voice: *That was for Steven. This is for me.* You removed a wide cowboy belt with blue-and-orange colored diamond patterns."

Visibly shaken, she took a sip of water.

"I don't own a wide cowboy belt with blue-and-orange diamond patterns."

She seemed to shrink in the bed. "It was the belt Dad used on my sisters and me."

She appeared to debate whether she wanted to continue. I let her decide.

"I tried to run but fell because of the glass shards in my foot. You stood over me and I saw you were—aroused. I kept saying no, I begged you, but you refused to listen. You raised the belt overhead and said: *A good soldier would have stood by her husband. She would have made it work, and she damn sure wouldn't have run off with the next man who came along.* I woke as the brass buckle whistled toward my face. Then I found myself here with you." She lowered her head. "Again, I'm sorry I scratched your cheek."

"You dad was strict?"

"He was an ex-Marine and a big control freak. Much more of a hard case than I let on before. You know when I ... never mind. I'm cold." With that she left the bedroom again.

I found her sitting naked in the living room by the fireplace, poking at a small fire she'd started. The room gradually filled with flickering ambient light as shadows danced on the walls. There was no need for a fire on such a mild night, but if she wanted a fire, so be it. We sat hunkered together like two people seeking shelter in a cave from a storm. She stared into the slowly growing flames and hugged herself tight.

I fashioned a makeshift bed by the hearth from oversized pillows and a blanket. We lay that way while sap from the newly added wood hissed and popped. Tension crept into the room.

She leaned against me while the shadows from the flames played across her worried face. "What have we done?"

"What do you mean?"

"Us." She spread her arms wide as if to include the room and me. This."

"You can't pick and choose when to fall in love."

She gave a brief start as thin blue flames shot from the ends of seasoned wedge-split logs, dancing and popping in quick succession. Compact and noisy jets of fire released their gas pockets and flamed out. The first section of ember dropped through the grate onto a thin bed of gray ash, pointing at me like a human finger glowing bright red. I felt a tug of guilt. The room grew hot, the air oppressive.

She stared into the growing flames. "I love you so much, but does this ever feel weird or in some way not right to you?"

I knew what she meant as our pasts collided with the present, but I refused to believe we did anything wrong. We hadn't broken any rules. "To hell with that. It's not like either of us planned this."

"We didn't plan it, but I'm not so sure anymore." She hung her head. "I don't want to drag you into this."

I asked what she meant, but she stared silently into the fire. She drifted to sleep, tossing and turning the rest of the night next to me. I watched the fire slowly die, eager to know more, and slept fitfully.

The next morning, I woke to the pungent smell of coffee brewing and the sight of hummingbirds flying and darting over my backyard deck overlooking the wooded common grounds. The multi-colored birds chased one another through the trees in their constant war for dominance over the feeders, though there were more than enough to go around.

I worked the kinks out of my back from sleeping on the carpet while Kris paced the living room. Freshly showered, she wore one of my white dress shirts while she rattled off instructions to someone on the phone. Ending the call, she entered the master bedroom, ran a bath towel through her hair, and reached for the dryer.

"The new door and deadbolt are installed. I want you to drive me home. I have to buy textbooks, prepare for my family therapy class, and start a new job."

"Okay."

She tossed my shirt on the bed and began to pull herself into her jeans. "I have to go back," she said, her jaw set.

"I understand. You want me there for moral support? To check the door and bolt?"

She frowned as she wiggled into a lacy red bra. "Don't. Don't do that." She wagged a finger at me and threw the unused hair dryer onto the wet towels. Apparently she'd go with the wet look today.

An occupational hazard of mine is that people may think they're being psychoanalyzed or treated like a client when they're not. It can be a nuisance. I thought of the hummingbirds fighting for the illusion of control. "It was just an offer."

She turned away to cram things into her overnight bag. "I have to face it alone sometime. New Yorkers aren't supposed to be afraid of anything. It pisses me off that I am." She turned to face me. Her anger softened and she whispered into my chest, "I'm sorry." She didn't answer when I asked what the apology was for.

II II II

I dropped Kris at her apartment and headed to the office for my next appointment. Lisa Carter was a tall, young TWA flight attendant. Her face was red and puffy when I greeted her in the waiting room. Once I closed the door behind us, she walked up to me and sobbed against my chest. Our first physical contact felt like I held a bird with a broken wing. I couldn't help but notice a liberal dose of perfume, Samsara? Before her crying slowed, I broke off contact and directed her to a chair. She fussed over the mascara she'd left on my white dress shirt, brushing at it with

French manicured nails, the gold hoops on her wrists jangling. She apologized and promised to have the shirt laundered. I said not to worry about it and asked what's going on.

She took a deep breath and with trembling hand passed me a yellow sheet torn from a legal pad. She fumbled in vain for a tissue in her purse. It appeared an angry hand had scribbled the note, judging from the pressure of the strokes and occasional holes punched through the paper, which read:

> Miss Know-it-all,
>
> You don't understand me and never did. Everything I do is dirty and repugnent to you. I will be free You cannot win by resisting me bitch if you try I will take all you love and smash it to shreds. I know what pain is I know its smell, its color, its power. It's a dark, cold mistress that must be fed. I will teach you of fear and rage and pain You will bow down to me and beg me for mercy and for death. I have distroyed stronger enemies than you and I will distroy you. I will rape you. I will tear out your heart and eat it I will gut you like a peace of venison and set fire to your entrails You cannot possibly understand what you are dealing with nor can your precious Therapist doctor 'the-rapist' get it? The rapist you see all the time. May you have an interesting death and life in Hell. My will be done as it is in heaven Amen

"Harold wrote that. To me."

She rose from the chair and paced. She wrung her hands and hyperventilated. She pushed out her next words in staccato bursts, "I can't go home … he'll kill me … I'm so afraid … I have nowhere to go!"

A hand rose to her forehead before her legs went out from under her. I caught her before she fell. She quickly wrapped an arm around my waist and raised her eyes to meet mine. It felt contrived, like we were actors in an antebellum melodrama while Atlanta burned in the background.

"You're okay. People faint when their blood pressure goes down, not when they're keyed up."

I led her to the client chair, positioned a box of tissue within reach, and sat opposite her. Between me and the other therapists in the office, we went through a barge of tissues a year.

"Did you have any other contact with him today?" I asked, placing a bottled water on a side table within her reach.

She fished a cigarette out of her purse and tapped its end twice on the chair arm before sliding it between full, pouting lips. It was an automatic move made under stress. Then she remembered. "I need it. Can you bend the rules once?"

A minute into the session and we faced a full agenda. I produced a small ashtray from a drawer in the table and slid it toward her. "One. If it doesn't help, I will talk you down from your anxiety."

She lit up, calming after the first few puffs.

Hail to the quick fix.

"I found it," she said, as she eyeballed the note in my hand, "on the kitchen table this morning. The phone rang while I was reading it. It was Harold. He said he hoped to see me after work because he 'really wanted' to kill me. Like he'd enjoy it," she said, making a face at her last words. She took another inhale.

I allowed her time to continue if she wished.

"We had a fight last night. He hated the dinner I made. I know I'm no gourmet cook in the kitchen, but he accused me of poisoning him. I thought it was a joke, but he said I make him weak, that I want to take control of his mind. He said dinner tasted like iron and phosphorus. How can pot roast taste like phosphorus, whatever that is?"

I shrugged and waited for her to continue. I knew when she was on a roll.

"If you're thinking drugs, Harold's body is a temple. He keeps himself in great shape. He doesn't even take aspirin. Anyway, Dave told me that Harold's parents had big-time mental illnesses and spent chunks of their lives in a sanitarium. Harold lied to me. He said his parents led a normal boring life together until they passed away five years ago."

"Who's Dave?"

She wiped away a tear. She regrouped and considered her answer. "Back in the hot seat. He's a mechanic at the dealership, a co-worker of Harold's. Last night Dave said that another grease monkey recently borrowed a tool of Harold's without asking. When he returned it, Harold broke his nose with the wrench. Dave had to pull him off the guy."

Nighttime talks with her husband's male co-worker. Does it end there?

Lisa crushed her cigarette in the ashtray and let loose a sardonic laugh. "What am I supposed to do? Leave and start my life over again?"

Her face changed from a Deer-In-The-Headlights look to one of Make-Everything-Better-Right-Now that I've seen many times.

"Don't make snap decisions about your marriage. If you make a major life decision now it's likely to be a knee-jerk one and those are often wrong. Your emotions are in almost as much turmoil as Harold's. His psychosis or delirium is treatable. It can go into another long-term remission just as it has during the years you've been together. More than likely he kept his mental illness from you because he didn't want to scare you away. It still carries a stigma.

She blew her nose and nodded.

"Here's what can be done. He can be involuntarily committed up to 96 hours, excluding weekends and holidays. To do this, someone with first-hand knowledge of his recent mental state must complete and sign a notarized affidavit describing the thoughts or behaviors that make him a danger to himself or others. Harold's handwritten note is also evidence, even though it's unsigned. Then the county police locate Harold and escort him, hopefully with his cooperation, to a psychiatric unit that accepts his insurance."

She dabbed at a corner of an eye with a tissue. "What happens when he refuses?"

"He'll go against his will. It usually doesn't come to that. Most people defer to an armed show of force."

She shook her head and smirked. "Harold's not most people."

"Maybe not, but he will be admitted one way or another. If he still refuses treatment when the time expires and the treatment team thinks he needs additional inpatient care, the hospital takes him to court. A judge hears testimony and rules whether he remains a danger. If the judge thinks he is, Harold could be committed up to twenty-one more days. Family members rarely need to testify because by then there's plenty of input from hospital staff. What do you think about this?"

She fumbled for the tissue box again and sighed. "He'll know I put him in a psycho ward. He'll be madder than hell."

"He may be. With medication, treatment, and time, his psychosis will lift and the anger will subside. He should return to his former self after he receives help."

She tugged at the hem of her skirt, a lightweight blend of spring colors that rode six inches above the knee, accentuating a dark tan. Her free hand absently tugged at a diamond-studded ear lobe then brushed back a misbehaving brunette bang. She sat straight up in her chair as if she were leaning into a stiff wind. "He needs more help than I can give him. I'll do it, but I must warn you. You don't know him."

"Warn me?"

She leaned back in her chair, lips parted. "He'll know we were behind this."

We.

I looked at her.

"He'll blame you for putting me up to this."

Your precious doctor 'the-rapist.'

"He's insanely jealous of other men. Dave, our neighbors, and guy who looks at me when we go out."

A third reference to Dave. The man gets around.

"He's especially jealous of you."

Her body language betrayed her.

She leaned toward me and as she did her white cotton blouse hung forward from her shoulders. She wasn't wearing a bra. Her blue-gray eyes rose to see whether mine strayed, her lips parted to ask a question as a sly smile played on that full mouth.

She reminded me of a Barbie Doll.

A six-foot tall, brunette Barbie of the Friendly Skies.

She simply said, "Why?"

"Why what?"

Those big doe eyes widened. "Why can't he be more like you?"

"Your husband has good qualities. They're what attracted you to him in the first place. You're unaware of what I'm about to say on a conscious level, but you're redirecting your feelings for Harold to me. You're bestowing Harold's good traits onto me while he retains the negative ones."

So goes the Cliffs Notes version on the concept of transference.

She rose again and strolled about the room. She stared out the picture window toward downtown St. Louis. A 747 slowly dumped its white wake of pollutants across the blue sky.

The white trail looked pretty and harmless from a distance. Like Lisa.

"What attracted me to Harold was the fucking—he's hung like a porn star." She walked back in the direction of her chair but instead made a detour to look at the framed picture on my desk.

"I want more than that now, intelligence, compassion, stimulating conversation. Your wife is very pretty, but I don't see a ring on your finger."

"Lisa, please sit down."

She shifted a hip slightly toward me, tugged at a diamond stud in her ear, and sat.

"You came to me initially for marital help, even though Harold refused to attend the sessions. You said last week you've learned more about yourself and that the relationship had moved forward. Now you face another test. I can help you better understand what your husband is going through. Harold is in crisis now. Let's get him the help he needs and you the time and knowledge to make informed decisions about what you face as a married couple."

"What if the cops can't find him? What if he comes home and kills me? I can't go there. Where am I supposed to stay? I have no family here."

The what if game … What if Harold's suspicions are grounded in reality?

I suggested she call friends right now. After several calls, she talked with someone who agreed to put her up for a few nights.

"Good, long as that friend isn't named Dave."

She made a face and scribbled on a piece of paper. "Cheryl is another flight attendant. She lives in Maryland Heights, between here and Lambert Airport. This is her number. Plus, you have my cell phone."

"I will call. Count on it."

Her ears perked up.

"To let you know when Harold is safely in treatment and where. So you can return home. At some point a hospital therapist may ask you to participate in his treatment and later someone will call to notify you of his release date. I can walk you through the process."

The notification part is called Duty to Warn. If Harold still harbors anger toward her, at least she will know when he's been released.

I dictated my notes after the fifty-minute session and saw the other client on my schedule that morning, a depressed housewife with self-limiting social phobias. By then it was lunchtime. I called Kris to check in, but she didn't pick up. So I changed into a pair of shorts and prepared to do battle with my best friend.

STREET RULES

Heat waves rose from the asphalt courts as the temperature hit ninety-five. The birds had more sense, as they perched under the protective shade of nearby trees and chirped at us. No breeze stirred on the playground as I palmed the ball at arm's length from Tony Martin, my former private practice mentor turned police psychologist who does ride-a-longs for the city of St. Louis. A solitary lady tennis player resolutely volleyed a yellow fluorescent ball against a weathered green backboard a court away. Each solid thud of ball striking wood matched my heartbeat.

Sensing fatigue in my larger opponent, I wanted to take the ball out quickly and go for the kill.

I grinned. "I've taken away your legs. Your heart is next, big man."

He's set up for a crossover move and drive to the basket.

He wiped sweat from his brow. "You done talking trash, Slick?"

"You ought to know me by now. Game point. You're buying after I bury this fade away."

We were about the same height, but the older Tony outweighed me by thirty pounds. He'd banged me around pretty good under the boards today, using his girth and strength to control the boards, but the longer the game continued I sensed I was wearing him down. Hands on his waist, a telltale sign of fatigue, he fought to catch his breath. "You haven't won shit yet, Junior."

I dribbled to the right of the key and eyed the front of the rim, feigning to pull up for a quick jump shot. When he rushed forward to put a hand in my face, I made the crossover dribble to my left hand and blew past him. He cursed and swiped at the ball in desperation when I drove into the lane. He sprinted to catch up and got between the basket and me as I left my feet for the shot. The contact sent him flying to the asphalt.

"Foul!" he shouted.

I landed on my feet and arched my back to watch the ball carom hard against the backboard, dance along the rim, and rattle through the steel net.

"Game, buddy," I said, smiling at my fallen friend.

He sat with his back against the chained link fence, wiping blood from a scraped knee. "Are you deaf? That was a foul!"

"You weren't set."

"Bullshit! Look where I am. You knocked me into West County."

"You were moving. If you were set, you'd have gone straight down in a heap."

Tony extracted a pebble from his hairy shin, still breathing hard. "You're kidding. If that's not a foul, nothing is."

"If anything, it was a blocking foul on you."

"The game ends on that? That's nuts."

"I made the shot. Street rules."

A trickle of blood slowly snaked its way into his sock. "Man, you are one competitive bastard. I'm too tired and hungry to argue. Let's eat."

I extended my hand and helped him up. "We both are, but you gotta get off the couch and push yourself away from the table."

"I used to have a body like yours. And I used to be handsome like you. Wait till you hit forty-five and have a wife who loves to shop and two hungry teenagers to feed. Life changes you, pal."

"You more than hold your own, but you need more exercise, Tone."

"Now you sound like Cindy. By the way, what happened to 'bury this fade away' a minute ago, you dog?"

I grinned. "Opponents misdirect and play mind games. Just like clients."

"Just the ones who hate to lose."

I laughed, picked up the ball, and sank a reverse lay-up as we walked off the court toward Uncle Bill's Pancake House on Kingshighway. "Clients lie. They lie to their spouses, families, themselves, and most of all, to us."

"You're especially cynical today. What's going on?"

"The usual." Our evenly matched ritual involved more than basketball. For years, we'd play whenever one of us needed a fresh set of ears to bounce something off the other, usually a difficult case or a personal problem for Tony. Tony had committed his share of mistakes over the years, but he was my best friend and mentor. Smart, compassionate, and the owner of such a reassuring, silver-tongued voice and warm demeanor that I've heard him talk jumpers off ledges and convince numerous suicidal callers to enter treatment. Women routinely turn their heads when he speaks. If James Earl Jones were white, he'd sound like Tony. To colleagues he's known simply as "The Voice."

We followed the hostess. "Don't eat a lot, okay? I have four mouths and a fat Golden Retriever at home to feed."

We scored the last available booth shortly before a church bus pulled into the lot and discharged a large flock of hungry people. I ordered my usual grapefruit juice and asiago cheese bagel. Tony slurped a Coke while he waited for his steak and egg combo plate with hash browns, and a side of blueberry pancakes. The fronds of the Boston ferns on the ledge next to us swayed when the air kicked on as if they were dancing to the piped in Muzak. Nearby, a customer's portable radio forecast today's high to top the century mark.

He adjusted his napkin. "I want to pick your brain for a minute about private practice."

I raised an eyebrow and took a sip of water. "I'm flattered. You know more about it than anyone I know. Pick away."

"What's the break down these days?"

"You thinking of getting back on the horse?"

He shifted slightly in the booth and the vinyl squealed beneath him. "At last I think I've put the whole nightmare behind me. And the burnout."

Not to mention time for the bad publicity to die down.

"You never took time off, never said no to anyone, and you worked fourteen-hour days."

He nodded. "You only know half of it. There were nights I slept at the office, weeks when I hardly saw Cindy or the girls. I let the clients consume me. Toward the end it felt like they were eating my brain." His mood darkened. "Then *she* came along...."

We looked up when our smiling young waitress brought our food and departed.

He produced a nervous cough. "The twins are off to college next year. I don't want to tag along with these police knuckle-draggers the rest of my life. I know a therapist in his sixties who's about to retire. I may buy his practice if the price is right."

I knew he'd never want to work for anyone else, especially someone he once tutored, so I didn't offer. He asked about how running a private practice had changed since his affair with a patient put him out of business and into the seat of a squad car doing ride-alongs with the city police to defuse domestic disputes. I told him my business break down, that I keep 25% of the income the other therapists bring to the practice in exchange for rent, advertising, and office equipment. He took it all in with just a question or two and then grew quiet. I spread butter on a bagel half and the scraping of the knife on the toasted bagel mirrored the sudden change of mood at our table.

He poured more syrup on his dwindling stack of flapjacks. I could almost see the second thoughts swirling in his big brain. "I thought I was ready for this."

"You are. The hardest part should already be in place, as long this guy can show you numbers that substantiate his client base, you nurture and grow that foundation by taking good care of the clients. Then they take care of you. You won't be riding in the back seat with cops calling the shots, you'll be steering your own car."

He thanked me for the info and nodded as he dipped a hunk of steak into his fried egg. He caught the eye of our young waitress, requested a Coke refill, and turned back to me. "Now I have something for you. Remember Cindy's friend, Gretchen, the blonde real estate agent with the killer bod? I think you two met at our pool party last summer. She broke up with her veterinarian boyfriend last month because he treated her like a dog. She asked Cindy about you the other day. She wants to hook up, you lucky bastard."

I looked across the table at my grinning friend. "Not interested."

He stared at me, a look of disbelief on his face. "Shut up! I'd trade my left nut for a crack at that."

I put down my juice, pushed away my plate, and smiled. "No, Cindy would crush both your nuts and your little Willy. Besides, I think Kris is the one." In this moment I didn't think Kris was the one. I knew she was. Speaking to my best friend here at Uncle Bill's after a one-on-

one game, I realized I was all-in with Kris. I was in love for the first time in my life. I had no interest in this other woman. The idea didn't hit me during our vacation—strolling along the beach holding hands in Maui, or swimming under a waterfall, or on a sunset booze cruise, or driving the road to Hana in a convertible. Not when we flew home and she returned to her apartment and I ached for her. Not even when I wanted to protect her after the attempted break-in and from Warren Green's harassment. I knew I was in love when the prospect of another woman meant nothing to me. From here on out I wanted to be with Kris and make her happy.

His fork stopped in mid-shovel. A tiny glob of egg yolk clung to his bushy black mustache while he sat with a stunned look on his face. "You're shitting me."

I shook my head.

"Dr. 'Love-'Em-And-Leave-'Em' has finally been trapped in a woman's web? This is the same Mitch Adams who broke it off with a former Miss Missouri when things got serious, right?"

"Last time I checked."

He leaned forward in the booth and the vinyl screeched again in protest. "The same guy who dumped that rich and gorgeous Italian resident at Barnes Hospital without so much as a 'Ciao, Bella' when she mentioned commitment?"

"I regret how I handled that. I like to think I'm not the same guy."

He poured the last of the syrup on his pancake stack. "You're not seeing anyone else?"

"Not for months. I don't think I realized it until now."

"You're not pulling my leg?"

I smiled. "This is getting old. No."

He leaned back on his side of the booth and patted his belly. "Cindy's going to have puppies when she hears this. Our friend, one of St. Louis' most eligible bachelors, is taking himself out of circulation. Who the hell am I going to live vicariously through anymore? You talking marriage?"

"I want to live together first. Then we'll see." I wanted to tell him about the break-in, about the possibility that her ex had resurfaced, but I didn't.

"What does she want?"

I was hoping he wouldn't ask.

I was stalling, but I really couldn't stand it anymore and pointed out the egg on his mustache. "The jury's still out, her first marriage crashed in flames and shook her world. Committing a second time terrifies her. She wants to complete her master's degree first."

He finally pushed away his plate and drained his second refill of Coke. The glass in front of his face couldn't conceal his spreading grin. "The worm has indeed turned. Sounds like you fell for someone who's more commitment phobic than you." He pointed at me. "Let's hope this doesn't end with egg on your face. I see why you're smitten. She's a stunner and she's smart. She's the whole package."

"But?"

He leaned back while he made his point. "You two have met at a time when you occupy vastly different worlds."

I tensed. We've gone on double-dates. Does he know how we met? Working with the police, does he know about the break-in, did he read the police report? "What do you mean?"

"You're a happy-go-lucky boogie boarder gliding along, sailing smooth dating waters and she's a kayaker upended in the rapids, still righting herself from a failed marriage. You've never allowed yourself to get close enough to anyone to have your heart broken. You don't know the sting of abject, unrelenting pain. Sooner or later, love teaches everyone about suffering. You're an only child and your parents are alive and well. You've yet to lose someone super close to you. That's influenced your therapeutic style. I sensed her withdraw a bit when Cindy prodded her about your relationship the last time we went out. You two haven't known each other that long. Giving her more time couldn't hurt. You know what they say," he said with a mischievous grin behind that mustache, "time wounds all heels."

Good, he doesn't know.

"Very funny. Have you finished stuffing your face, Mr. Butterworth?"

"Touché. Congratulations about Kris. If you two eventually tie the knot, my gift to you will be a set of scruples, Mr. Fade Away."

I smiled and returned the good-natured barb. "Where are you going to find any?"

"No hitting below the belt. You're the only person who can say that to me and get away with it."

"I know. Gotta get back to see another client. Time is money."

A LITTLE GRACE

People enter therapy for different reasons—the boss says enter treatment or start to look for another job, the spouse gives a similar ultimatum, some seek relief from mental or physical pain, while others long for a human connection to lessen feelings of isolation or loss. Whether the motivation is external or internal, clients expend time and energy explaining themselves, often vigorously defending or justifying their behaviors, thoughts, and feelings.

It turns out the only client scheduled that afternoon fit no such cubbyhole.

His employer received a complaint about him and sent him to me. The initial complaint snowballed into others with similar accusations. If proven true, the charges could cost him his reputation, his profession, and change his life forever. My task is to determine whether this new client is a sexual predator and make treatment recommendations to his employer, the Roman Catholic Church.

'Father James,' is a tall and handsome priest in his early forties who teaches religion and conducts retreats for college underclassmen and women. Ditch the black shirt and Roman collar for a Polo shirt and white shorts, and he could pass for a tennis pro or personal trainer. His facial features reminiscent of a young but more muscular Richard Chamberlain with an even tan, thin straight nose, and a shock of wavy brown hair that dangled over the center of his forehead. He presented himself after Gateway University placed him on administrative leave pending an evaluation.

Father James stared out the picture window for several minutes, his broad back to me before he finally spoke. "This," he said with a dismissive wave of his hand, "is the archbishop's idea. Mother Church is thorough yet discreet in what she shares with those outside Her auspices. I believe she wants me cloistered. The exact extent is to be determined. That's where you come in, an independent arbiter for the sufficient level of my punishment."

I never had a client go into such detail to explain my role in his therapy before it starts, especially when he gives the impression he doesn't care about the consequences. Is this surface bravado real in the face of such serious allegations? His comments seemed practiced, rehearsed, and intellectualized beyond everyday conversation.

"Why don't we get started?"

Father James studied the wall decorations and my diplomas while he slowly made his way to the chair opposite mine. "I see my Church file on your desk, so you must know that I have a master's degree in counseling and completed my training at Menninger Clinic and Johns Hopkins. I was a therapist at Gateway University for several years and treated graduate and undergraduate students there, primarily individual and couples counseling. What qualifies you to play a role in determining my fate?"

Great, he wants a pissing contest.

"The diplomas you inspected are my Ph. D. and master's degrees from the Gateway University of Social Work. I've worked on psychiatric units at the River City State Hospital on Arsenal. I have ten years post-doctorate work, the last seven in private practice. I've conducted therapy with priests before. I've worked with sexual predators and abuse survivors for years. Anything else?"

"Did River City prove to be a good training ground?"

And people call me a control freak.

"Yes, it was."

He steepled the fingers of both hands, closed his eyes and thought for a moment, as if he were considering a follow-up question about my experience. "I see. Is your approach Freudian, Rogerian? Are you a disciple of mindfulness, or heaven forbid, Cognitive-Behavioral therapy?"

"I prefer an eclectic approach, whatever works for each client based on their diagnosis, life experience, and current situation."

At last Father James walked to the chair opposite mine. He studied it as if he were checking for something hidden. He finally sat and nodded. "A pragmatist. I thought so. Fair warning, I know all the tricks of the trade as well as or better than you. I will not assist the Church in my own crucifixion, nor does Her judgment concern me. I will tell you what I want you to know when I want you to know it. My version of reality."

"That sounds like a challenge, Father. As a counselor you know that what you say here is held in strict confidence, safe from the ears of the Church, the archbishop, and the Pope. It's as sacrosanct as the confessional unless you tell me you plan to harm yourself or someone else."

"That will not happen," Father James smirked briefly and then controlled his body language. "You present no challenge to me. I'm merely stating the facts before we start. The Church shall deliver Her will upon me in due time, but I can already tell you will serve a useful purpose."

You have your own agenda and you're trying to establish the ground rules. I'll play along for now. You're a slippery one, replete with double entendres and a smoldering intensity below that rocky surface.

"Isn't that what any honest client provides in therapy, Father, their own version of reality?"

His eyes narrowed and he paused a beat. He shrugged, as if there was no harm to concede the point. "You could say that. People, you included, aren't honest with themselves, much less with others. You have prejudices, biases, and leanings. You are trained, like me, to be an arbiter of societal disputes. What assurance do I have that you will hold yourself accountable to the same rigid standards I hold myself?"

Back to me again, what is it with this guy?

"You have none. You know therapy doesn't occur in a vacuum or come with a guarantee. I'm not the one accused of sexual misconduct. All I can promise to give is my best fair and impartial assessment."

Father James smiled at me. "Of course you will."

"Are you above therapy, Father?"

He laughed. "Heavens, no." Then added: *We can all use a little grace now and then.*

I tossed him a soft curveball. "That was an onion."

He shifted his weight in the chair, suddenly on guard. "I don't follow."

"An onion seems a simple thing but has many layers before you reach its core. You admitted being in need of grace. The word has multiple theological meanings. Grace can be the free, unmerited love and favor of God. Grace can also be a state of reconciliation to God. Or it can mean God's divine influence that acts in man to keep him from sin."

I allowed a brief silence to pass between us. "Which state of grace are you in need of, Father?"

He rose from the chair and walked to the window.

My carpet's getting a workout this week.

A minute passed before he turned back to me. "I don't like to sit, and your chair is uncomfortable."

"Counseling is a strange career path for a man who doesn't like to sit, Father."

"Do we choose our paths, or do they choose us?" He pointed his right index finger at me. "I've underestimated you. That won't happen again. You're a smart pragmatist and a quick thinker. I bet you've been quite successful to this point using the tricks of our trade to wheedle your way around most of your clients' defenses. Back to me. Find the answer to that question and you'll have the whole story, won't you?" He smiled, Sphinx-like.

The tricks of our trade. Enough already.

"I'm not the enemy, Father." This isn't the time for games.

He stared at me, lost in thought. "I apologize for the attitude. Step into my shoes and tell me if you still feel the same."

The surface anger and intellectual distancing aside, I gave him the benefit of the doubt. He's frightened, under intense stress, and faces many unknowns.

"Are you undeserving of therapy, Father?"

"That is the least of my concerns," he said as he inspected the chair again before sitting down.

"So, you have concerns. Do you doubt you're worthy of forgiveness?"

He didn't answer.

"Forgiveness from the survivors?"

No reply.

"The families of those you molested?"

Still no answer.

"The Catholic Church?"

More silence.

"From God?"

Nothing.

"Father?"

He flushed slightly and his facial muscles tensed. For the first time I noticed the tiny white scar near his mouth, the lone flaw to his movie star good looks. He steadied himself. "Your ploy won't work. I won't allow it. The Church can do what she wants to me."

"Yet you're here, Father, spending energy and time, wanting to talk and not wanting to talk. Why would you be here if you don't plan to respond to the allegations? This is your chance to tell what really happened, to defend yourself."

"The Lord works in mysterious ways."

"Can you be less cryptic, Father?" And less clichéd.

He did not answer. Our remaining time elapsed in a silent battle of wills, we engaged in a stare-down contest. Having worked as a counselor, the protracted therapeutic silence between us didn't seem to faze him as it did other clients.

My watch beeped, signaling the end of our fifty minutes. I let the time drag on another five to further test his resolve, but he didn't waver.

On his way to the door I said, "Maybe next time you'll tell me why you're here, Father."

He turned his torso just enough so I could see his face and the smile reminded me of the Mona Lisa's. "If it's God's will, you will find out."

I used the few remaining minutes in the hour to organize my thoughts and first impressions before I dictated my notes on the mysterious priest.

THE FIGHT

Kris had insisted on staying at her place Wednesday night, but Thursday after work, I picked her up and we decided to do something we hadn't done in a while, we toured the Science Center across from Forest Park and the Planetarium. Then we drove south for a burger and onion rings at O'Connell's Pub on Shaw. She took the last empty stool and I squeezed in next to her, standing, at the crowded bar while we waited for a booth. Her friend John Chang tends bar there part-time and greeted us with a smile and Kris with a wink as he made our Tanqueray and tonics. John's a biology major who lives on campus and was the friend who first suspected Steven was on drugs. He placed our drinks on colorful paper napkins and walked to the other end of the bar to fill a large drink order for a waitress.

I stirred my drink. "I have an idea. What do you think about moving in with me? You could take a full class load and graduate a year sooner."

Kris squirmed in our tight confines and turned to face me. "No. I am putting myself through grad school, no matter how long it takes. I put my life and career on hold for Steven. Look where that got me."

I thought we were ready for the next step, perhaps I thought wrong. "I understand. It was a bad idea." I wanted to say more but left it at that. She looked at my watch. "How long is the damn wait?"

"The hostess said ten more minutes."

She squirmed on the barstool and rubbed her forehead. Her color had paled. "I have to get up at five in the morning to meet my ride to the Family Therapy workshop in Columbia."

"So let's skip dinner here and pick up something on the way home." I touched her shoulder.

She grabbed her purse. "I don't have time for this shit."

Now I was perturbed. "What's going on? What exactly is 'this shit' you speak of?"

She raised her voice. "I have a class to prepare for. I can't be here at your beck and call."

From the other end of the bar John Chang watched us intently while he pretended to polish a glass, his bartender radar on alert. The big man in a pinstriped suit near us at the bar shot me a dirty look.

"I've never asked that of you," I said, lowering my voice.

"Not in so many words," she said, loud enough for the group next to us to hear.

I didn't want to cause a scene, but I didn't want to drop it, either. I threw a twenty on the counter. "You want to go, we'll go."

"Enough with the macho act, Mitch."

I was missing something. This was somehow related to the attempted break-in or Warren Green. My mind flashed back to it and to the night of the party. "What was in that note you put in your pocket when I took you for stitches?"

She turned toward me, looking scared and on the verge of tears. "Stop it!"

"What are you—?"

She stood and tried to put some distance between us by pushing me away but lost her balance and toppled backwards on her heels. She reflexively grabbed the sleeve of the big man in the pinstriped suit before she hit the floor tailbone first.

"Jesus Christ, buddy. Leave the lady alone," the man in the suit shouted while he stood. His friends also pushed back their chairs, sending a series of shudders and shimmies against the hardwood floor that seemed right out of a Clint Eastwood spaghetti western. John

Chang's back was turned to fill another order for a waitress; he hadn't seen the slip. He stood at attention now, along with everyone else in the crowded bar area, staring at the two of us and waiting for resolution. Anything could happen and anyone could fuel it.

"Are you alright, Miss?" the man in the pinstriped suit asked.

"No, I'm not," she whispered, eyes welling with tears. "My heart's breaking."

With every eye in the place on her, her anger returned. "That's it," she said, to no one in particular. Then she called out, "John, call me a cab, please."

In tears, she turned and kissed me long and hard. "I have to. For you," she whispered. Then, loud enough for the other tables to hear: "You're being an ass."

Before I could say a word, she grabbed her purse and headed for the door. The last I saw of her was her back as the crowd gave her a wide berth. She shook her head in anger and then I lost sight of her in the mass of people. I tried to follow but the parted sea of customers became a solid wall of men blocking my way, led by the man in the pinstriped suit and his friends. They'd reached a verdict—that I'd knocked a woman to the floor and was harassing her. They told me to calm down and give her some space. By the time I reached the street she was gone.

I drove to her building and parked on Laclede. Even with the city lights, stars shone in the cloudless night sky. Flashing red and amber lights from the electric signals reflected in rhythm off the hoods and windshields of the parked cars along the street. A shaggy brown mutt angled away from me across the street and scuttled around the east end of the complex toward the Dumpsters.

A light was on in her second-floor apartment. I pressed her doorbell at the security entrance, but she didn't answer or hit the buzzer.

I waited and tried them all. This time no one buzzed me through. The intercom on the wall stared back at me, its round black mouth mute. I returned to the car and scanned the top floor. Her drapes were now drawn, the window darkened. I took out my cell phone but didn't call. Whatever was going on, I knew she wouldn't answer.

Down the street a black Cadillac Escalade was parked facing me, its engine idling. A solitary figure watched me through the tinted windshield, the driver's face a dark silhouette in the shadows. On impulse, I walked toward the high-riding Caddy when the driver threw the SUV into gear and executed a tight U-turn, laying rubber before I could see what I believed to be the face of a male. I got a partial on the Missouri plate; it ended in 820 or 828.

Is someone following me or Kris?

Or was the solitary driver merely spooked by the sight of a stranger approaching his expensive car late at night in the city?

No messages awaited me at home on the landline. I stared at the silent phone and then made myself a drink and played a classic cd by The Who. Neither the gin nor *Behind Blue Eyes* helped.

I shouldn't have brought up the subject in a crowded place. I should have led with my heart, not my head. I shouldn't have attached mere practical reasons for why we should live together. I lost my cool and now I'm being childish because I want her to be the one to call. But the more I thought about it, the more it sounded like she broke up with me. Somehow for my own good. I couldn't make sense of that.

I have to. For you.

Do the right thing, dumb ass. Call the woman. But my stupid male pride won out.

I walked outside and saw no black Escalade anywhere in the cul-de-sac. I'm being ridiculous, but I still didn't call. Instead, I poured myself another drink, stewed some more, and then went to bed angry, something we swore we'd never do.

THE LOADED COTTON BALL

I woke with a pounding headache, reached for the phone to call Kris, but then remembered she was on her way to Columbia for the Family Therapy workshop. I'd wait till she was home to call. We would talk about what prompted her anger and I could learn the meaning behind the cryptic comment she whispered to me before she stormed out of O'Connell's.

I dragged myself to the office and thanked my lucky stars that my first appointment was a no-show. I chewed a couple more aspirin and busied myself with reviewing client notes and going over bills until it was time for my session with Rick Arno.

Rick is a borderline, also known as an anti-social personality. Borderlines are to psychiatric clients as great white sharks are to fish— they glide through life for all intents and purposes looking like normal fish until something sends them into a frenzy. They divide the world into black and white, with no shades of gray in between. Their rigid belief system isn't wired to deal with the nuances and differences of other people—their relationships disintegrate because they view people as objects and societal rules as challenges to be broken. They are often impulsive, often abuse or torture animals as children, and display severe mood swings with fits of intense rage. A cunning and charming borderline on a psych ward will pit staff against staff or patients against staff. A local hospital in the not-too-distant past opened a unit solely for these clients and it failed miserably in large part because they couldn't retain staff. Put bluntly, borderlines use, alienate, and provoke people.

There is no pill for borderline personality disorder.

Some commit suicide.

Some are murdered.

Some are fortunate to mature out of the illness if they reach age forty.

Prisons claim many.

While others, like Rick Arno, are ordered by judges and parole officers to see therapists like me in a last-ditch effort to ward off reincarceration.

He plopped down in the leather chair opposite me, grinning like he'd hit the Powerball. A tight Kurt Cobain shirt and faded jeans covered his lean, wiry, thirty-two-year-old body. Stringy brown hair reached his shoulders and his stubble looked four days old. His right boot tapped the carpet to a lively beat in his head when he looked to me. "This week has been heaven, man. It felt so fucking good to get that ankle bracelet off my ankle. Went anywhere I wanted. Did what I pleased without having to report to my p.o. all weekend."

"What did you do with your newfound freedom from your probation officer?"

He leaned back and put his hands behind his head. "Went to Tiny's after my set with the band. Hustled some pool, got a beer buzz. Met this fine young thing at the bar. By closing time I'd sweet-talked her into my new ride, a fiery red Camaro with two white rally-stripes right down central and a 5.7-liter V8. Turned out she came there with some dude who tore out after us, but once I unleashed those three hundred plus ponies, the power kicked in and never stopped. The lame dude became a gnat in my rearview." Rick grinned. "He was no match for me in the sack, either."

"What was the girl's name, Rick?"

He smirked and crossed his long legs, one boot now tapping an even faster beat against the other.

An anxiety tell.

"She may have said her name, but between the shots and the beers I forget."

"What *do* you remember about her?"

He thought for a moment. "She liked the throaty growl my Camaro made. Being chased by her boyfriend turned her on. The minute I lost him her hands were all over my crotch. She said I must have some big cojones, taking off with another man's girl like that. Chicks dig that element of danger. We parked off-road behind some woods near a lake and climbed in the back."

"And after?"

His dishwater gray eyes narrowed; his mood darkened. "I lit a Camel but she started ragging about the smoke. Who the hell doesn't smoke after sex? So I say, 'You don't like it, don't let the door hit your ass on the way out.' She whined about her asthma, called me a bastard, and punched me. I pushed her out of the car, told her to calm the fuck down, but she pounded the roof and kicked the door. '02 was the last year for the great Camaro line. It's a classic. Nobody does that to my ride. I told her to 'get a grip or I'm gone.' She kicked the door again, and I drove off. Bitches, they spread their legs and think they own you."

Typical Rick behavior.

"Fresh off house arrest, you leave a bar with another man's woman, with him in hot pursuit, you elude him, strand the girl in the woods once she's satisfied you, knowing she has a medical condition—"

"No, I left a crazy bitch with two working legs and thumbs near a highway. She probably had a cell in her purse and called her pimply-faced boyfriend. If not, she hitched a ride."

"You don't know whether she had a phone, and you don't know if she made it safely home. She could have suffered an asthmatic attack while walking along the side of the road and died, far as you know. A young woman hitching alone at night is at high risk for rape."

He squirmed in his chair, frustration in his face. He walked to the ninth-floor picture window, staring into the bright sunlight that flooded my corner office. If I didn't hold a modicum of leverage over him, he'd probably be cursing me by now. He watched the street activity below as the air conditioner rumbled to life and rustled the palm tree fronds in the brass pot near the window. Another sticky St. Louis day in the upper nineties to get the blood boiling. He completed his self-imposed mental time-out and sat back down.

"I hate being in this chair. Look, I picked up a chick in a bar. I didn't meet her at her parents' house with a corsage. She chose to get in my ride, there were no promises made and no expectations stated. I laid out the consequences if she dented my ride again. She decided to push the envelope. She'd tell you that herself."

"Maybe, but we'll never know."

"She got what she wanted. We both did," he said with a sly grin.

"I bet any trace of satisfaction for her quickly vanished into those dark woods."

The vein that pumped noticeably in his forehead when under duress worked overtime. "Why are you making a big deal out of this? I didn't do anything wrong. I didn't even have to tell you about it." He ran his hands through stringy hair and pointed a finger at me as another thought hit him. "What about my p.o?"

"What about him? If you treat people like they were your parole officer, you'd be in far less trouble. You say you didn't do anything wrong. You didn't do anything right. This is a perfect example of how you get in deep shit. The girl's boyfriend could have shot you or totaled your Camaro. The girl could say you kidnapped her. More likely, she could have your plates run, claim rape, and you're back in federal prison facing strike three. You put yourself in needless danger for a twirl in the back seat. I bet you didn't even use a condom. Your body could be a Petri dish incubating the clap or worse—"

"Shoulda, coulda, woulda. Like I said, I met a chick in a bar. You say I didn't do anything right. I say I didn't do anything wrong. I call that a push."

"One day you're going to mess with the wrong man's woman and you're going to wind up dead, or worse, Rick."

He shrugged it off with a wave of his hand. "We all die someday. Speaking of chicks, who was that drop dead gorgeous babe I saw you with last Saturday? Man, what a knockout!"

Had he seen Kristin with me? Where? I hadn't noticed him. I decided to see where this went or if he'd drop it, so I didn't answer.

A smile spread across his long narrow face, assuming he regained the upper hand by shifting the focus away from himself. With a gleeful look, he said, "I played bass last week in a band called Head Games over near Gateway University. When the band took five, I headed out for a smoke to clear my head and saw you walking this babe to your car. Great tits, great hair. Is she a model? She sure filled out that low-cut black dress. I could tell she enjoyed showing off that body. Hell, she damn near flaunted it. She had a confident swagger to her. Bet she's a handful, in more ways than one. Before she got in the car, she went on her tippy toes to kiss you, and I swear you copped a feel. Wow! She was a righteous hottie."

He *had* spied on us and gotten off on it. I didn't answer or appear uneasy.

My silence clearly annoyed him, so he switched tactics. "Is your ride a GXP? Does it have overdrive?"

I'm not getting into a pissing contest with him over engine power. I'd lose, he knows it, and it wouldn't lead anywhere productive.

"And then what, Rick?"

"What?" he said, looking bewildered, squirming in his chair.

"The babe."

"Then you drove off," he said, still perplexed. Then added, "Oh, I get it. There are a thousand apartments nearby. I have no idea where you or the gorgeous girl live, so don't blow a fuse. I'm not stalking you."

Charming. Enough already. Why had I let this go so long? The break-in?

"Do I look worried to you?"

He didn't answer. His right leg bounced, restless.

"Why'd you go to prison the first time?"

He shifted uneasily in his chair. "You know. The cops pinned an arson charge on me."

"No. You went to jail because you let your other head do your thinking. You had an affair with the trophy wife of an older man. She conned you into believing she'd run away with you, but only after you arranged a tragic accident late at night in her husband's office. You fell for one of the oldest schemes in the book, the grieving widow inherits his money, and you take the old man's place. How many times did she visit you in jail?"

He looked away.

"I thought so. She used you. You're lucky that older man made it out of the building you torched, or you'd be doing life, maybe on death row.

"Your behavior at Tiny's the other night was no different. You allow women to lead you around by your Johnson. Instead, you need to treat people like equals or how you would like others to treat you."

The alarm on my watch beeped twice, signaling the end of our time. Rick was one of my clients who anticipated it, like an ADHD kid fixated on the bell for recess.

"Until next week. Remember, use the privacy door on your way out." This lets clients avoid revisiting the waiting room as they exit.

He rubbed a bony hand across his horse-like face. "I don't care if people see me here. I'm not nuts."

I pointed to the privacy door. "Respect the boundaries of others. And I don't want to see you again in the waiting room after today's session. Or any future one." Two weeks earlier when I went to bring in my next client, he had returned to the waiting room to hold court with a small group of wide-eyed clients listening to his gritty street-life philosophies.

Before he could protest, there was a rap on the waiting room door, and it swung opened to reveal two men in the doorway. Arno seemed to know what they were before the introductions. He hugged the wall like a man on a ledge.

One was thin and white, mid-fifties; maybe five feet eight standing on his tiptoes, with chiseled facial features softened by thin wire-rimmed glasses. His conservative suit matched his closely cropped salt-and-pepper colored hair. Next to him loomed a Black man in his mid-thirties, well over six feet with broad shoulders and no neck. A wide scar serpentined around his left eye, skirting the socket before it tapered near his earlobe. He had the cauliflower ear of a heavyweight boxer. His bright green sport coat looked ready to burst at the biceps any minute, making him look like a gargantuan parrot on steroids. The small man introduced himself as St. Louis City Detective LeMaster and the giant as his partner, Detective Baker.

They've come to arrest Rick. What'd he do this time? Was it about the girl he left to hitchhike home? But they didn't give Arno a second look.

The small man spoke in a booming voice that belied his size. "Dr. Adams, we'd like a word with you, in private."

I invited them in. Arno breathed a sigh of relief and beat a hasty retreat out the back way. At last he used the right door. Scared straight works sometimes.

The little man stepped forward. "Dr. Adams, we work City Homicide. The body of a young Caucasian woman was found this morning. Late twenties, early thirties. No missing persons' report matches her facial features or body type. She was dressed nicely, like someone on her way to work or an appointment. There was no identification on the body."

"What does this have to do with me?"

Massive Detective Baker stirred. His manner was cool and unhurried, the antithesis of LeMaster's. He answered in a soft voice, setting his bushy Fu Manchu in motion. "We found a business card on the body. Your business card. Right now it's the only lead we have."

Oh, no. Lisa Carter. Had Harold made good on the threats in his letter?

"Was she a tall, attractive brunette?"

They paused to exchange brief knowing looks until LeMaster spoke. "Do you have a recent picture of this woman?"

"I don't keep pictures of my clients."

"In that case, we'd like to see if you could identify the body. Time is a critical factor in a case like this, Dr. Adams."

So she was a murdered, good-looking brunette. "Did the card have an appointment date and time on the back?"

"Nothing on the back, just a plain card."

"Give me a few minutes to bump back my afternoon schedule."

The detectives escorted me on a leisurely fifteen-minute car ride east on Highway 40. I sat in the back of a nondescript city car with bad AC, sweating. Dark clouds scudded and thickened across the afternoon sky. They brought the city hope of a pop-up thunderstorm and temporary rescue from another scorching, sticky day.

I care about my clients and don't want any of them in pain, much less dead. A few clients had died from natural causes or accidents, but never murder or suicide, far as I knew.

"Maybe she was the friend of a client. Maybe she was about to make an initial appointment. Maybe she was a client of another therapist in the practice. Maybe she—" I said, hoping against hope it wasn't Lisa.

Baker executed a smooth illegal left turn against traffic and ignored the angry honks of other drivers. With a perturbed look, LeMaster half-turned toward me from the front seat. "Doctor, I understand you hope she's not a patient of yours. Let's not speculate. We'll see what you see and then it is what it is."

The unmarked police car passed a small gathering of homeless men and women camped in stairwells in an area shaded by towering downtown buildings. They existed invisibly in the shadows of these steel and glass monuments to money, forgotten pariahs unwanted near the cathedrals to capitalism where executives wore three-hundred-dollar ties and women carried six-hundred-dollar Dolce & Gabbana purses. LeMaster radioed for a patrol car to roust the squatters. Baker's jaw tensed and he squeezed the steering wheel just a bit harder.

I felt the need to respond. "The city has three times as many homeless people than shelter beds, and with this heat wave, the one shelter is full. Where are they supposed to go?"

LeMaster sat impassive as a stone wall in the front seat. Baker's eyes met mine in the rearview. Did they soften behind the shades?

A stray plastic grocery bag tumbled end-over-end in the hot breeze like a Catharine wheel until it snagged on an orange temporary construction fence. The cooing of nesting pigeons on the limestone rooftop greeted us once we parked in front of the city morgue. LeMaster flashed his badge to a security guard. We gained access to the hallway, our footsteps echoed in the Spartan emptiness.

The door handle to the morgue refrigerator made a loud clacking sound, followed by a whoosh of cold air in stark contrast to the outside heat. LeMaster removed his glasses to wipe the fog from them. A dead foulness hung in the air, impossible not to notice. Breathing through my mouth helped. LeMaster instructed the attendant to show them the Jane Doe that arrived earlier this morning. LeMaster and Baker stood unfazed, but I was a newbie in this Valley of the Dead. I found myself itching to put highway between me and this place. My breathing turned shallow.

Please don't let it be Lisa Carter—or any client of mine.

The attendant, a slight man in his twenties, wore horn-rimmed glasses and a wrinkled, dirty white lab smock. He put down his sandwich and ran a hand through tight black curls thick as a Brillo pad. His bushy eyebrows moved up and down like those of Groucho Marx. The look of boredom became a sour stare in the direction of LeMaster's order that interrupted his lunch.

There was no way I could eat food in this room.

The hirsute attendant directed us to the far end of the freezers near a brick glass wall. He rolled his eyes and began whistling *Knockin' on Heaven's Door* in a somber and soulful manner as he rolled the cadaver from the pigeonhole wall-freezer marked Number 6.

LeMaster frowned. "Show some respect, Thompson. That'll be you under the sheet one day."

I saw my breath in the air, while the cloying medicinal smell reminded me of fetal pigs, frogs, and butterflies from biology class. I hated to watch the death throes of a butterfly or the last frenzied gasps of frogs in a jar, sentenced to death with a chloroform-soaked cotton ball. I wanted to rub my hands together and blow into them.

Thompson sensed my discomfort. "They warn you about this one?"

I shook my head.

He smirked. "Didn't think so. Looks like you're a virgin, too. Somebody did a number on her. It isn't pretty."

LeMaster took one big step forward. "Enough. Do your job without another word."

I assume Thompson resumed his deft whistling of the classic Dylan melody to further irritate LeMaster.

I steeled myself for the prospect of seeing Lisa in some horribly beaten state. Harold, what have you done?

When Thompson turned back the sheet, the swollen face, neck, and upper shoulders eventually came into view of what could have been the remains of a young woman, but the colors no longer belonged in the human spectrum of skin tones. The cadaver's neck, engorged to twice its size, appeared made of some bizarre plastic or rubbery material from an alien world. The neck looked like twisted gutter tubing. Someone in the grip of an uncontrolled rage had pummeled this young woman's face into a pulpy mass of gray, purple, red, and yellow tissue. I looked for Lisa Carter in the carnage, but her face wasn't there.

It took time for it to sink in, but my wish had been granted. It wasn't a client of mine. What at last helped make the ID was the wavy hair.

My mind fought my eyes while I studied the upper body on the slab; it refused to accept what my eyes registered. I looked up and then away. The nearby glass reflected my face, now distorted into a rictus of horror.

Thompson abruptly stopped whistling.

I was transported back in time to that biology class. *I* was the butterfly in the slick glass cage. The loaded cotton ball landed next to me. My breath left my body. My arms flailed but found no purchase on the smooth brick glass wall.

The bruised and shattered face on the morgue slab was Kris's.

A KAFKA NOVEL

She's in Columbia for a Family Therapy workshop. She got up before dawn today to walk to another student's apartment and bum a ride. That couldn't be her lying on the morgue slab.

And denial is oh so much more than a river in Egypt.

I don't remember many of the events that followed, likely from amnesia caused by emotional blackouts after I identified her body. I think the detectives sat me down and asked hundreds of questions ten different ways for the rest of that afternoon and into the evening. I don't recall a quarter of what I said. It felt like some huge beast had seized hold of me, shook me about the room, banged me into the walls and refused to let go, its jagged teeth punctured my head and heart. The detectives must have driven me home because my car wasn't in the garage.

I do remember waking up alone this morning with a mammoth headache. Bile and the taste of vomit crusted my mouth. Papers, clothes, and empty bottles littered my once immaculate living room. A bag of ice continued its melt down on the black quartz countertop while a steady trickle of water snaked down the kitchen sink cabinet into the growing pool on the ceramic tile. Water beaded on the hardwood floor in the hallway and gradually inched toward the living room carpet.

Who made this mess?

Now I remember. LeMaster and Baker had driven me home. They told me to get some sleep, but I couldn't. My mind raced. I grabbed the Tanqueray bottle from the freezer and a bottle of Bitter Lemon. I had a drink. Then another, and another. I wanted to shut down, to erase all memory of that frozen room from my mind.

Sights and smells from the morgue forced their way back, branded into my brain. Kris on a slab. Her broken face flashed into my mind; my stomach roiled.

I remember brief flashes. I stood there demanding to see the woman's back. Kris has a flat birthmark on the back of her left shoulder. I know its exact location and shape. The unrecognizable mass of destroyed tissue—lower lip cleaved in two, eyes swollen shut and neck so ravaged it seemed scarcely human—resembled Kris but couldn't possibly be her. It won't be there and that'll end this nonsense. She's in the middle of the state at a seminar.

I remember the suddenly serious morgue attendant Thompson froze at my command. He deferred to LeMaster, who nodded his consent. Thompson moved to the other side of the slab as if in slow motion and raised that side of the torso. Every pair of eyes locked on mine.

There it was, shouting and screaming bloody murder at me.

I need another drink.

Loud knocking on my front door startled me back to the present. LeMaster and Baker entered, and from their grim looks I had an idea what was on their minds. Baker wore the same green sport coat from the other day; his biceps stretched those sleeves to the max. LeMaster wore a tailored light blue seersucker jacket and white pants.

They eyed the mess in the living room and made a show of searching to find a clean area on which to stand.

"Do you have any leads?" I asked, trying to stand without wobbling as the floor kept moving beneath my feet.

"What we have," LeMaster replied, "is an irate boyfriend. Your latent fingerprints were the only ones found at the crime scene, other than those of the deceased. We lifted your partial right thumbprint from the belt Miss Gray wore when she was murdered and we found your right index print on one of her shoes. I think that's very strange, Dr. Adams, how do you explain that?"

I'm their suspect. How can this be?

"How do you know they're mine?" It sounded churlish and defensive. I immediately regretted my words. LeMaster asked the question like any competent interrogator would, one he already knew the answer to, and I fell for it.

"The latents were identified as yours, with one hundred percent accuracy, by our central computer. They're a perfect match to the set you provided the State of Missouri when they hired you nine years ago to work for River City State Mental Health Hospital." LeMaster studied me closely. "From the look on your face, I gather you forgot that all new state hires are fingerprinted, Doctor." The subtle sarcasm tacked onto the last word wasn't lost on me.

He was right. A burly stranger had manipulated and rolled each finger into a cold black inkwell, pressing them on a blocked sheet of paper before I started my practicum. I remember the ink was tough to wash off.

Baker took a step toward me. "This puts you at the crime scene. You struggled with her. She said somethin', made you lose control, and you just snapped. She break up with you? Was she seein' another dude? There anything else you wanna tell us about that day, somethin' to get off your chest? You sho' feel better if you do," Baker worked a toothpick in the corner of his mouth while he grinned down at me.

I backed away from him. "We saw each other almost every day. I stayed at her apartment four or five weekday nights, and she usually spent the weekends here. We shared laundry duties, put away each other's clothes, and kept clothes at both places. I'm sure my prints are all over her apartment and hers are in every room here. She wasn't murdered in her apartment, or you wouldn't have needed me to identify her. Did you find my prints anywhere else at the murder scene?"

LeMaster removed his spectacles and took his time wiping them clean before he looked at me, smiling. "So, the game is on."

He produced a worn notebook from his coat pocket. "The night before the murder witnesses overheard you argue with Miss Gray at O'Connell's Pub. They said she broke up with you and you took it hard. They heard you exchange heated words; they said you struck her, causing her to fall to the floor. She asked the bartender to call her a cab and left without you. Bar patrons had to physically restrain you so she could leave in peace."

"That's not true," I said, defensively. I must have looked like a guest on Jerry Springer—dressed in a wife beater T-shirt and slept-in chinos, hair rumpled, face unshaven, half in the bag—adrift among the remnants of an all-night drunk fest in my living room.

Had she really broken up with me? It's all a blur.

Baker took another step forward, brown toothpick bobbing up and down. "You been drinkin', your inhibitions all loosey-goosey, and this smokin' hot mamma suddenly breaks up with you in a bar full of people, makin' you out to be a chump. People makin' faces, laughin' at yo' ass. That's a recipe for revenge. Sometimes revenge goes too far. You hunt her down after that embarrassin' melodrama at the bar, try to talk some sense into her, but it all goes to shit. You go crazy and next thang you know you standin' over her and she be dead. You prob'ly didn't mean to kill her, but things got out of hand. That's the way it went down, right?" The toothpick suddenly stopped in the right corner of his mouth. "You the jilted boyfriend, my man. You can't fuck her no mo', nobody else ever gonna tap that sweet thang, right? Bitch had it comin', didn't she? Playin' you to be the fool."

It was repulsive, the way he talked about her. I wanted to yell at him to shut up, but all I could think of was the supposed breakup. What did she tell me before she left?

I considered several answers, but they sounded inadequate or lame. My lone corroborator was dead. I said Kris and I had talked about living together, which wasn't resolved that night. I described her accidental near slip to the floor at the bar. I spoke of Warren Green's unwanted sexual advances and the recent attempted break-in at her apartment the morning after the party. I mentioned her abusive ex-husband/junkie who may have resurfaced at Warren Green's party.

LeMaster referred to his notes. "How convenient. It's funny you should mention that. Dr. Warren Green has multiple alibis for the times of the attempted break-in and the murder. You didn't observe this alleged attack, yet you are the only one who claims it happened in the middle of a party with hundreds of guests present. Guests we interviewed saw Miss Gray leave upset, with you trailing behind. Again. I see a pattern emerging, with you as the controlling, abusive boyfriend."

Now I remember what she whispered, "I have to. For you."

"She filed a harassment charge against Green the next day. She quit and found another job at Gateway University because of him."

LeMaster took some time to scan his notebook. He stared at me with what looked like pity. "Were you with her when she filed?"

I shook my head.

"There's no record in the Human Resources Department of Gateway Medical Center or HR at Gateway University of any charges filed by her, or anyone else for that matter, against Dr. Green. There's nothing to back your claim. I can think of scenarios in which she would tell you she planned to lodge a complaint and then did not, but I doubt you want to hear them."

I was speechless. A new nightmare unfolded in front of me. "You're wrong. The University's made a mistake. It's there, somewhere. She told me she filed." I tried to recall exactly what Kris had told me. Had I heard what I wanted to?

I was a patsy in their eyes. I felt like curling up into a ball.

"It doesn't exist, Dr. Adams. She did change jobs, but she didn't register a complaint."

I'm sure Green buried it, but to claim cover up with no proof would dig a deeper hole and make me sound like a conspiracy theorist.

LeMaster closed his notebook. "There is one odd detail. We can't locate Steven Gray. He has not used his Social Security number since he left the university, which is unusual if he's living the straight and narrow. However, we have no reason to believe he's had any contact with Miss Gray since their divorce.

"Which brings us back to you. Do you have an alibi for early Friday morning?"

I'm trapped inside a Kafka novel.

"No. Kris went home and I drove back here."

"How do you know she went home if you drove to your townhouse?"

"She asked John the bartender to call her a cab. I assume that's how she left. I still wanted to talk, so I drove to her building. The light was on in her apartment. I rang the buzzer. She didn't answer. I went home. End of story."

"You lied. Just now you said you drove straight home. You were stalking her, weren't you?"

This must be how Rick Arno feels in my chair.

I bit my tongue. "We had an argument. Couples do that. We didn't break up."

"So you keep saying. How long were you at her apartment building?"

"A couple minutes, maybe five."

"Did you stop for gas or use a credit card on the way home that night or early the next morning?"

He's trying to recreate a timeline. He wants to catch me in a lie; he already knows the answer. "No."

"Did anyone see you at home that night or the next morning, a neighbor or delivery person? Did anyone see you pick up the morning paper or the mail?"

I thought of the shadowy silhouette in the black Escalade speeding away from me that night. I considered mentioning it. "I don't think so."

"You hesitated. Why?"

"No reason."

His eyes narrowed. "You're lying."

He's pretty good.

"Did you telephone Miss Gray later that night?"

"I considered calling many times. No."

LeMaster looked puzzled. "Why not if, as you claim, you two were still together and so much in love?"

She was crying when she kissed me. It was a goodbye kiss. That piece of paper.

"That's a regret I'll have to carry around with me."

LeMaster reopened his notebook. "Where were you during the attempted break-in of Miss Gray's apartment?"

"Sleeping alone at home in bed. She called me after she dialed 911. I dressed and came right over."

"Funny, you claim the two of you spent nearly every day together, yet your absences from her stand out like open sores, with no one to corroborate your story."

"Funny is the last word I'd use to describe it."

LeMaster remained impassive as an Easter Island statue. "Do you know who Miss Gray planned to ride to Columbia with the morning of her murder?"

I flashed back to her body on the slab again and forgot LeMaster's question. Another blackout. I've got to get my act together or they're going to pin this on me.

"I'm not saying anything else until you tell me why she's dead. Was she robbed, raped? Where did it happen? I love her. I have a right to know."

Baker moved in closer to me. "Temper, Doctor." His huge bulk seemed to suck the air out of the room. Staring at me but talking to LeMaster, he said, "Dr. Adams is a smart, confident guy. I think we about to find out just how smart and cocksure he is. He knows the consequences for murder. He knows he can do time for withholdin' evidence. He gonna cooperate with us. He don' want the neighbors to see him hauled away in handcuffs and then be tossed in a city holdin' cell. Half an hour there can be a lifetime, not to mention general population after that," Baker stuck his battle-scarred face next to mine and grinned, revealing a shiny gold upper tooth. The stink of pork rinds hit me.

LeMaster said, "The first forty-eight hours of a murder investigation are critical and often make or break a case. You may possess a crucial piece of the puzzle that helps us catch her killer. Who is the classmate Miss Gray planned to ride with that morning? You can save us time and legwork."

"I think they're a married couple in her family therapy class, possibly with the last name of Hudson. They live in an apartment on Lindell west of the university."

"Thank you, Dr. So, you knew the route she took that morning."

Back to me, again. "What can you tell me? Give me something, some information."

LeMaster surveyed my living room. "Careful what you ask for, you just might get it. We will talk again, soon. You need to come to the station to provide hair and blood samples. Our lab techs also need cloth and fiber samples from your townhouse, possibly your office."

"Where was she found?"

Baker cleared his throat. "Pull yourself together and clean this mess up before the cockroaches arrive. They be a bitch to get rid of," he said, grinning.

LeMaster faced me again. "By the way, love entitles you to nothing. My training, experience, and instincts tell me this was a crime of passion. I've seen smarter people than you lose control and commit impulsive, monstrous acts in the name of love. We see murder disguised in the name of love every day. You may be the latest poster boy for it. Don't leave town without my permission."

OTHERWORLDLY

Cockroaches. I couldn't close the door on them fast enough. I leaned against it for support and shut my eyes. The world in freefall, it no longer made sense and I ached for Kris. I considered cleaning up the place, to start with the beer bottles that I didn't remember buying much less drinking, but the thought of it felt overwhelming. Nothing mattered anymore.

I picked up a crumpled section of newspaper from the leather sofa and sat. Apparently, I'd circled a filler article in yesterday's Post-Dispatch near the back of Section A that read:

BODY FOUND

The body of an unidentified young woman was found near a Dumpster on the Gateway University campus early this morning. Any motive for the killing is unknown at present and police have no current suspects. This brings the city homicide count to 173 in St. Louis to date, up thirteen percent from this time last year.

I don't remember scribbling a red question mark on the right margin. Kris was no longer Jane Doe Number Six in the city morgue freezer. Now she was this year's murder victim number 173. I brought in today's Post and scanned the news section until I found the following article:

STUDENT SLAIN

The body of the young woman found yesterday on the Gateway University campus was identified as that of Kristin Marie Gray. 32, of the 3200 block of Laclede Avenue. Miss Gray was a graduate student in the Gateway School of Social Work and a university employee. She is survived by her family in New York. Police have no suspects in the case but are pursuing leads. Robbery may have been a motive, as there was no identification on the victim. The university is offering a reward for information that leads directly to solving the case. Anyone with knowledge about the crime may call the City Homicide Unit at 314-555-1200.

She was attacked during the pre-dawn walk to her classmates' apartment. Like many city neighborhoods, hers had its share of crime. I always reminded her to be careful on her solo travels downtown, but she'd laugh and brag about being 'Bronx, born and bred, baby.' When she sensed my concerns for her safety, she'd kiss me and say: *I have you to protect me.*

If I hadn't brought up living together, we wouldn't have fought, I would have spent the night and driven her safely to her classmates' apartment. She would have made it to Columbia in one piece, attended the workshop, and come home. If I hadn't been so damned pig-headed, she'd still be alive.

If—

If I don't stop this, I'll go insane.

I saw her picture on top of my television and tried to will her to climb through the silver frame and into my arms, but nothing happened.

Stop it. Stop it now.

My hand held an open beer I don't remember grabbing. More emotional blackouts. I poured it out and noticed the red light on my answering machine flash beneath a section of crumpled newspaper. I pressed the round button and shut my eyes, struggling to find a reason to do anything other than crawl into a ball and let the wind scatter me.

"Good morning, Mitch," Kris announced warily. My eyes snapped open.

Her hesitation indicated that the next words would be difficult for her to say.

"I wanted to let you in last night, but my stupid Sicilian pride won out. I thought you'd come out and talk with me before the cab came, but you didn't. I didn't want to do this over the phone, but I couldn't bear to look you in the face. The break-in has terrified me. Maybe I'm being silly, but I think somebody followed me home last night in the cab from the pub. I can't let anything bad happen to you—"

CLICK.

Had the Escalade followed the cab or was she having post-traumatic paranoia?

BEEP.

Her crying burst through the machine. She blew her nose and sniffled. "I'd grown up with Steven all my life but it turned out I didn't really know him. You know that better than most, don't you? I...." Her words caught, emotion choking them back.

CLICK.

Damn this old machine. Let there be more.

"C'mon," I said to the machine. "Where's the ..."

BEEP.

She exhaled air, calmer: "I want us to be together more than you'll ever know, but we can't. You're a good man. I've wasted your time. We were *so* close to the next step. You deserve someone without all my baggage." Her voice cracked again and the tears returned. "Try not to hate me. I will always love you." She tried to say goodbye but couldn't get past the G-sound through her tears.

CLICK.

"Is that it? Why—?"

BEEP.

"Good morning, sir. This is Tracy with the Post-Dispatch. Do you currently have the Post delivered directly to your door? If not, we're running a special this week, for—"

No more messages.

She just added fuel to LeMaster and Baker's case against me. I hope they don't delve too deeply into the past.

I can't let anything bad happen to you. What did that mean?

I erased the last sales message and replayed the others again. Why'd she break up with me? What was she talking about? Nothing made sense. I stretched out on the sofa.

The next thing I knew I was running down a dark and narrow alley, a black Escalade blared its horn and bore down on me. Its high beams blinded me when I glanced back at it and the constant honking stung my ears. The expansive silver front grill snapped at the backs of my legs like a pit bull. I woke from the dream with a start, opened my eyes, and found myself on the couch in my darkened living room. More pounding rattled my front door. If a tall, hooded figure greeted me at the door holding a scythe, I was okay with that.

LeMaster and Baker stared at me and I laughed. "Close enough, c'mon in."

They looked at one another in silence and walked in.

"Let me guess, you caught the killer, have a video-taped and signed confession from him, and you're here to apologize, right?" I laughed again. I knew I must look and sound crazy, but I didn't care.

LeMaster took the lead. "Phone records show several calls made from Miss Gray's apartment to this townhouse yesterday morning, the morning of her murder. You failed to tell us this. I want to know why before we book you.”

I walked to the table and touched the play button on my answering machine.

Afterward, LeMaster held his stoic façade. “She ended the relationship. You lied to us. Why?”

“I didn’t lie. I heard the messages for the first time shortly after you two showed up this morning.”

“You weren’t home early in the morning when she made these calls?”

He was smart. “I was here but couldn’t sleep after the argument. I drank too much and went to bed. She must have called then. I don’t remember much about yesterday. I was dead drunk this morning, and it was only after you left that I noticed the red light on the machine.”

“Still, she ended the relationship,” LeMaster said.

I repeated our conversation at the bar. “It sounds crazy, but I think she felt coerced into breaking up with me. Why and by whom, I don’t know, but she was.” I thought back to our last kiss and her words: *I have to.* “Read between the lines.”

LeMaster set his square jaw. “I see another scenario. You missed her calls because you were waiting outside her apartment to follow her, hidden by the darkness. You knew the route she’d take. You try to win her back, it goes badly, and she rebuffs you a second time. Things get physical, she fights back, and the struggle gets out of hand. You don’t mean to, but you kill her. You return home and hear the messages. What a Greek tragedy. Then you drink to forget.”

“I thought she was on the road to Columbia by six.”

Baker stepped up. “What’d you do when you woke up, Swinger?”

While Baker took his shot at me, I saw LeMaster pick up her picture from my table. He stared at her face, whispering to the picture almost as if he expected her to respond, like I had earlier. LeMaster looked like he was off someplace far away.

I took a deep breath. "I chewed some aspirin, tried to clear my head. I sat on the sofa and napped some more. Like I said, she was on her way to a workshop. It was the start of another day, except that I had a hangover."

LeMaster focused on the picture in his hands. "That's enough for now, Baker. We'll take the answering machine with us," he said, sounding distracted.

"You can't do that," I told them.

LeMaster put down the picture and turned to me. He held two fingers an inch apart as he walked up to me. "You are this close to coming downtown in cuffs with us. We need hair and blood samples. Will it be the easy way or the hard way?"

"If it helps clear me, lead the way."

Baker eclipsed the light in the room as he approached. The grin gone, the toothpick ominously still, he held out his meaty hand. "The machine, Doc."

"No. You need to get a warrant."

LeMaster dropped the warrant on the table. "Detective Baker, bag the machine first."

"I want that back, with all the messages intact."

Baker walked around me and produced an evidence bag for the device.

LeMaster ignored my remark. "What size shoe do you wear, Doctor?"

"Why? I've answered your questions. Tell me something."

"What size," LeMaster repeated with no trace of exasperation.

"Twelve. Why?"

"The plot thickens. We need to have a looky-see in your closets then," Baker said.

LeMaster told Baker to begin a thorough search of the rest of the townhouse.

Baker bagged and tagged an old pair of tennis shoes into a second evidence container. He placed carpet fibers into tiny plastic folders, marking and logging each one. They escorted me to the hospital where staff took blood and hair follicle samples. When they were done, they dropped me at the office so I could pick up the Solstice.

They had me next in line to be bagged and tagged.

A STRANGER DRESSED IN BLACK

The cops had already wasted precious time targeting me, but I wasn't about to give Warren Green a free pass. I remembered that more than once over the past several months, Kris had raised questions about a project Green was spending a lot of time on. She thought it strange that the executive secretary would know nothing of the boss's major project. She'd described a series of circumstantial incidents and segments of overheard conversations that could amount to nothing, but nevertheless had piqued her curiosity. Hushed snippets of what sounded like clandestine meetings, involving advanced medical research, high-tech equipment, and computer purchases. One day at the end of work, she chanced upon a massive invoice destined for Green's estate. The delivery date was several months ago. She had no proof of wrongdoing or impropriety, but when I added her suspicions with everything else that had happened in the last week, it sounded like a worthy lead. Kris also said that Green was euphoric over a deal he was about to close, which led me to wonder if there was a connection between the deal and Kris's murder.

Had she stumbled onto something that cost her her life? Was she seen as a potential whistle blower, a threat to the project, and eliminated? What of Steven Gray—her abusive ex-husband and Green's former protégé, who LeMaster admitted had likely gone underground? Had he resurfaced at Green's party? Was it coincidence or does a connection remain between Steven and his former boss? If so, and Kris had seen Steven at the party, did she have to pay for that with her life?

If the cops weren't going to do anything, I would.

At two in the morning the glimmering moon hung low and fat in the sky until a bank of fast-moving clouds rolled in to conceal it. I parked the Solstice in a secluded area a block away from the perimeter of the walled estate and gathered my tools and gloves. I'd scouted the layout of the grounds earlier and decided that the southwest corner, farthest from the guard station, offered the best-concealed entry. I'd seen no prior evidence of guard dogs and hoped like hell none were on the grounds because I'd be at their mercy.

Iron grillwork topped the ten-foot brick wall boundary on this corner of the estate and could not be breached without a ladder. I had made an earlier trip to an arborist supplier and with my new tree-climbing spurs, I scaled the straight trunk of a large pine tree near the wall. A branch that looked heavy enough to support my weight traversed the wall. Immediately above that lowest branch, however, forked several other large and gnarly branches, preventing me from simply walking along the branch to the wall. I'd have to swing hand over hand across the ten feet of thick, knotted branch to reach the iron grilling. From there I planned to maneuver my dangling body over the iron spikes and drop silently like a Ninja inside the security wall. *Like a Ninja* should have been my first clue about my plan.

With my gloves on and a pocket Mag light in my mouth for vision, I easily negotiated the length of the branch and reached the wall. So far, so good. As I prepared to pass directly above the iron headers, noticing that the keen-edged points looked sharp as razor-wire, something crawled up my bare left arm and scared the crap out of me. I shuddered, my left hand slipped from the rough bark, and I nearly impaled myself on the jagged wrought iron as I shook off the daddy longlegs. Beads of sweat trickled into my eyes, and the Mag light slipped out of my mouth, skittered off the top of the wall, and plunged me into total darkness. After I regained a two-handed grip and my heart resumed beating, I pressed on. As I traversed the spikes, my shaking hands lost control and the spasms in my arms sapped my remaining strength. Above the iron barbs, I let go. The back of my head scraped iron and I hit the ground hard, tumbling and sliding to a stop inside the estate, completely un-Ninja like. My knee ached from the blind fall and for a minute I saw stars not in the sky. I crawled to where I hoped the flashlight had fallen, although I wasn't even sure it landed inside the wall. My shaking hands grabbed something, but it was a stick. After I fumbled for minutes in the blackness, I found the light leaning against the brick wall, but it didn't work. I jiggled the housing in the flashlight base until it finally flickered to life. I gathered my bearings in relation to my three optional exits. My ankle was on fire. I waved the light on it, a gash bled above my left ankle, where the climbing spur on my right leg had dug into it during the fall.

Twenty minutes into my break-in and I'd nearly skewered myself, lost my light source, sliced my ankle, and almost broken a leg. This seemed like such a good idea in the light of day.

I inspected several smaller outbuildings. Nothing but lawn and garden tools, mulch, outdoor furniture, or other grounds keeping equipment. Water cascaded in the fountain on the far side of the estate; the sound carried clearly in the still darkness. When I saw the first lights ahead, I approached with caution, using the cover of trees. Light spilled from below the closed, double stable doors and a bright shaft of light angled from an open window frame. Still no sign of dogs. I crested the last gentle rolling hill south of the barn and crouched behind several giant tufts of pampas grass. I waited five minutes, then began to cross the fifty feet to the barn when I noticed a tiny orange-red arc of light swing briefly in the air six feet off the ground. It fell to the gravel in front of the door, sputtered, and died. Then I saw him. Concealed in the shadows of the front of the barn, a burly man wearing a camouflage hunting jacket had flicked a cigarette butt, crushing it with a boot. He appeared to be standing guard. When the man turned sideways I saw the rifle and scope.

What the hell? What have I gotten myself into?

After some time he opened the door and walked inside. I crept toward the south side of the stables to the open window. The fat and sassy moon emerged between the clouds to leer at me just as I stepped on a dead branch, cracking in the still air like a snapped bone. I froze in the open expanse of turf, an easy target for someone with a flashlight, or rifle.

Do I go forward or run away?

I tried to run, but thick patches of weeds wrapped around my ankles and threatened to take me to the ground. I kicked through them and pressed up against the east wall of the barn.

This was a bad idea.

Reminding myself to breathe, I edged along the weathered cedar wall toward the open window frame. A wide wooden trough rimmed the interior walls of the one-story barn and the faint, sweet smell of damp hay filled my nostrils. It looked and smelled like a barn, but a humming, electrical sound came from within. I peered inside. There were no horses. The only remnants that this had once been a stable were some empty stalls and hay that lined the inside feeding troughs. Instead, the place brimmed with laboratory equipment. The was likely the equipment listed on the invoice Kris stumbled upon at work. The humming came from a generator and other machines. A man sat hunched at a long table, his back to me, while he adjusted a microscope and viewed slides. Computers and racks of test tubes filled the remainder of his work area.

The man briefly glanced up at the guard before returning his focus to the microscope. "Jesus, you guys make me feel like a prisoner.

Why must the Nazi have you patrol the grounds? And he calls me paranoid."

"You are," the guard said.

"Damn! Another failure," the man said to himself. Then to the guard: "There's no need for all this cloak and dagger."

The muscular guard lit another cigarette, the light from below turning his skull into a scary Jack-o-lantern. "Maybe you should focus on your job and leave the rest to us."

The man stretched in the chair and rubbed his forehead. "This thing's becoming part of my cranium. I've been at this for weeks. Cold pizza, Red Bulls, and a tinny radio aren't enough to keep me going. I need a massage and some good weed, minimum. I gotta get out of this straw dungeon before you or one of your soldier friends burn it down with your cigarettes."

"Then quit whining and complete your job."

"I need more equipment. Faster computers, analyzers, and lab animals. There's only so much I can do under these conditions."

I saw a handgun tucked into the guard's belt buckle when he turned to the doors. He smiled at the man. "Then ask him for it. He'll be here soon. He's in a mood; something happened."

The man at the microscope waited to make sure the guard's back was turned before he lifted his middle finger.

The armed lookout left the barn. Would he stand sentry at the door or patrol the perimeter? Was I safe here? This was the dumbest idea I've ever had.

The man at the microscope produced a pill from his jeans and washed it down with the dregs of a Red Bull. "Now I know what you're up to, you sonofabitch," he said aloud to himself.

He wolfed down a slice of pizza, cranked up the volume on the small portable radio, and a heavy metal song flooded the converted stable with discordant noise and lyrics that promised annihilation. He adjusted the eyepiece and returned his attention to a glass slide.

I heard a noise in the darkness behind me. Was it the guard or an animal?

Then something else. The sound of a car approaching, closing fast. The faint glow of headlights appeared over a gentle rise, growing brighter by the second. A sleek limo crested the hill, headed toward the stables. In seconds the ground I stood on would be illuminated once the vehicle negotiated the winding road and angled back to the barn.

This keeps getting better and better. If I can't retreat….

Between the roving guard and the oncoming car, I had little choice. I climbed into the wooden trough, praying it would support my weight and hoping the man at the table couldn't hear me over the apocalyptic music. A warped board creaked loudly under me, but the man with his back to me didn't seem to notice. I crawled inside the trough, leaving a blood trail on the barn wall while the beams lighted the east side of the barn. I frantically covered myself with the sweet-smelling yellow hay and peered over the rim of the trough, fearful of capture. At least my hiding spot was in a darkened corner of the interior. I was a trespasser hiding in a manger and Warren Green certainly wasn't the Prince of Peace.

I heard the solid thud of car doors shutting and the crunches of approaching footsteps. The barn doors swung open with a creak and the guard escorted four passengers inside. The two largest new arrivals appeared to be additional security. The third man was shorter, mid-forties with a buzz cut, and the stiff deportment of a military man. The other man I knew. Security focused their attention on the tightly wound man.

Warren Green turned to the hunched man at the table. "Status report?" Green looked GQ dapper in a tailored black evening tuxedo.

"More failures. Two virulent strains that may cause permanent sterility."

"I want every finding, even those." He extended a hand for the man's work.

Green scanned the work briefly. "Keeping accurate records and documenting everything, *John*?" The way he said the man's name made it appear they were privy to an inside joke.

The man at the table snickered at mention of his name. "Each and every study a double-blind procedure."

The military man frowned, and a facial tic appeared. He gestured stiffly with his arms. He spoke with an Israeli accent. "This man is an underling who labors in a barn. You allow him to treat you as an equal? He lacks discipline and character. Plays music at his work station. You make some kind of joke with him. He won't be laughing if he doesn't finish his job, and soon. The time for us to act is now. Deliver on your promise, and I guarantee we will be the highest bidder."

A board beneath me groaned and the wood beneath me shifted, then held. All heads turned in my direction. I held my breath in the darkened area of the barn and awaited the inevitable flash of light to shine so the guards would haul me from my hiding spot, but they returned their attention to the boss.

Green placed a hand on the visitor's shoulder. "Patience, my friend. Rome wasn't destroyed in a day. We must fly below the radar here, which is why we're in a barn on private property. You insisted on touring the facility and I'm aware this doesn't look like much, but solid science backs up every test we run here. We will be ready to conduct business soon. Now if you'll return to the limo with my staff, I want to talk to this underling."

The tense little man glared a final time at the man now spinning test tubes and followed the guards out the door.

Green stepped closer to the man with his back to me. "You hear the news?"

The man with his head buried in the microscope didn't move a muscle and simply said, "Uh-huh."

"We don't need any unnecessary attention."

"Whose fault was that?" the man answered.

"I wouldn't know. Would you?" Green said, apparently trying to read the man's face behind the microscope. He looked like he was seeing the man in a new light, as if he were sizing him up.

The man kept his face buried in the microscope. "Tragic," he said, deadpan.

Were they referring to Kris? If so....

Then the man pushed himself away from the table. He walked up to Green. "I need better equipment to do this job right. Tonight, you brought in a military whack job and last week's visitor was a towel head. Nocturnal visits under heavy guard? I get the feeling that we're not working on the same project here. This isn't about a morning-after pill. You're interested in the hot strains. You can't shut me out. I got clean for this. You could get me killed or life in a federal prison. I need a bigger slice of the pie for that kind of risk."

Green flicked a tiny piece of something from his tuxedo lapel. "Lose that tone with me. You're in no position to make deals." He grinned down at the man. "You'll get everything you deserve."

That led the man to pause before he answered. "You're damn right I will," he said, but with less conviction.

Green smirked and left the barn. The younger man standing at the table turned to me for the first time. Seeing his face confirmed his identity from a picture I'd seen earlier, though he now looked thinner and paler. He paced and cursed, throwing a chair the length of the makeshift lab that banged against the trough, rattling and shaking the boards. The trough sank another inch but remained intact. He pulled a joint from his boot and sparked it. "Ha!" he said to himself. "They never check the shoes." He gave the barn door the finger. He settled back at his work table and cranked up the volume on the small radio.

I heard the limo slowly back up and turn around.

I turned off the Dictaphone and returned it to my pocket. After five minutes of relative quiet passed outside, I carefully backed out of the trough. I assumed the muscular guard still patrolled outside, so I didn't use the flashlight. The moon chose not to help, likely smirking at me while it remained obfuscated by clouds. A pant leg of my black jeans snagged on a protruding nail and that same board creaked loudly under my shifting weight while I exited the hiding place. As my weight was divided between the trough and window frame, the trough sunk another inch, groaning, but the chair helped keep its place. The going was painstakingly slow. I could only hope the guard wasn't standing there ready to put a gun to my head the second I backed out of the open window frame.

I never felt so naked in all my life.

I managed to retreat from the barn window without a gun being pressed against my head. Minutes passed. The driving, nihilistic song on the radio gradually took a back seat to chirping crickets. Not knowing where the guard was terrified me. I considered my escape routes. The first was too well lighted. On the way to plan B, I passed near the estate. An outdoor floodlight suddenly flicked on, not thirty feet away. I hid behind the trunk of a wide oak. The security man from the party strode purposefully down the steps, his dark sunglasses perched atop his head, coming straight toward me. His jacket swung open, revealing a handgun at his side in the dim yellow light as he neared. His younger partner followed, also headed straight for my hiding place.

This was it; I must have tripped some silent alarm and they're here to capture me. If what I think is being engineered in that barn, I won't be able to talk my way out of this and I may not be alive much longer.

The first man abruptly stopped short of the tree. I heard a brief grunt followed immediately by the squeal of metal. Two patio chairs I hadn't seen in the dark faced the mansion opposite the wide trunk I hid behind. The second man took the other chair and lit a cigarette. From five feet away I heard the inhale of his first puff and hoped they couldn't hear the pounding of my heart.

"I don't know about you, but I'm ready for this job to end. No smoking inside, no butts on the steps, no TV, and no drinking. Too many rules, man."

"I hear that," the older guard with the sunglasses said. "It'll be over soon and you temps will be on your way. The man pays well if you walk the straight and narrow."

The younger man leaned back and stretched. "Trophy wife arrives any minute from Lambert. Great eye candy. I'd love to play Hide the Salami with that. I wonder what she'll be wearing. Have you seen how her ass molds into those tight horseback-riding pants?"

"They're called Jodhpurs and don't even think about it. If by some miracle you nailed her, you'd wake up next morning with your pecker in your mouth."

Great, even Rick Arno wouldn't get himself into such a ridiculous situation.

I never realized until now how hard it is to stand without making a sound while hugging a tree for ten minutes. Just enough ambient light from the nearby porch let me see the backs of their arms and heads when I peered around the trunk. I couldn't shift my weight for fear of snapping an unseen twig or crushing a dried leaf. I closed my eyes and tried to relax, to control my breathing for the duration of their smoke break. An acorn fell near me with a loud, hollow plop. I feared the worst.

The guards paid no attention to the sound when another acorn dropped. The younger man crushed his cigarette on a chair arm and stood. "I'm going back. Ain't no harm in looking."

"Watch your six. He sees everything. He won't hesitate to call you out." The metal spring squealed when the second man rose. "Wait up."

They re-entered the estate and the porch light went out. I dropped to my knees and took deep breaths. The pecker image fresh in my mind, I hurried for the wall beyond a maintenance building and grabbed a double ladder. There was no brick wall to scale on this side of the mansion, only the tall iron grillwork fence topped with iron spikes. In my haste, one of the tree-climbing spurs kicked the ladder from the wall while I negotiated the iron spikes. The aluminum ladder clanged and bounced on the concrete walkway that ran parallel to and inside the fence. The sound shattered the silence. The Dictaphone slipped from my pocket and tumbled to the grass, inside the property. The porch light flicked on again. The same armed security men re-appeared on the landing. They fanned out, sweeping the grounds with flashlights. I jumped from the top of the ten-foot-high ironwork and tumbled to the ground while pain shot through my injured ankle. I fumbled blindly for my Dictaphone while I reached through the fence. The guards methodically worked their way toward the maintenance shed. There was no time to spare so I flicked on my flashlight to locate the Dictaphone. I stretched out in vain for it, but it lay out of my reach. I heard someone whistle and looked up. The guard from the party stood on point like a bird dog. He'd spotted my light and sent the younger security man running toward me like an Olympic sprinter. The only difference is this bolt of lightning carried a gun instead of a baton. I used a nearby fallen branch and stretched out, sliding the recorder closer. I grabbed it and ran, their flashlight beams tracking me. The man reached the fence, speaking into a walkie-talkie for mobile pursuit as he leaned the ladder against the fence and began to climb. I sprinted down the street, turned the corner, and ran flat out toward the Solstice, ignoring the pain in my leg. I jumped in, goosed the engine to 80 mph down Lindbergh. In my rearview I watched one SUV race south on Lindbergh and one follow me north. I hit the open road of Highway 40 going west and floored it, reaching 120. I constantly checked my rearview until I was sure I'd lost them. I doubled back on my route home several times until I was certain no one followed me. I hope they didn't get close enough to read the license plate.

I fancy my body parts right where they are. I've had enough gruesome mental images to deal with lately, I don't need any more.

Once home I locked the doors and shut the drapes. Every time I heard a noise I looked outside. I existed in a thick syrup of anxious dread—expecting to see Green's armed security force surrounding my townhouse or smug Detective LeMaster at my door, handcuffs at the ready, with a grinning Baker next to him flexing his biceps.

On the way to the bathroom to attend to my wound, I passed the hallway mirror and caught my reflection. A stranger dressed in black stared back at me. He had convinced me this was a good plan. He grinned at me and gloated that tonight we learned Warren Green is a criminal. Then the Stranger vanished.

Could I use the information I'd overheard? I'd found Steven Gray, reunited with his mentor Warren Green, but were they connected to Kris' murder? They seemed to suspect each other of some level of involvement in her death. Was Steven burying his head in the microscope a refusal to let Green read his expression or a sign of fear? If Steven's fears are correct, Green aspires to be a bio-weapons dealer on a global level, but the only proof I have is an audio recording of half-statements and innuendo. Had Kris arrived at the same conclusion? Had she shared it with the wrong people? Was she a whistle blower who needed to be silenced? Is this what she meant about not letting anything bad happen to me? Is that why she felt the need to break up with me, to protect me?

I decided to rest on it, but sleep came in fitful pockets, filled with dreams of falling, being naked in public, and of losing my teeth. I'd read enough textbooks on dream interpretation to know what those meant.

I JUST SIT IN THE CHAIR

After a restless sleep, I opened my eyes still a free man, for the time being not dismembered or disemboweled. I decided to leave the spy business to the tough guys with broken noses and big guns. Thankfully the stranger remained absent. My own face looked back at me when I made it into the bathroom. I showered and drove to work, taking the back stairs to avoid talking with Gus, our chatty, septuagenarian security guard.

How could I connect Green to Kris' murder after the cops had already cleared him? The lab would be dismantled and moved to a new location after my surprise visit. How could I leverage Steven Gray if I couldn't find him?

I needed luck and time but had neither. I didn't know where to begin when I sat at my office desk. My indecision near catatonic proportions.

I had to jettison some clients.

Get out of here now, leave the office, and go home. You're not ready for this. You can't help anybody right now.

Maybe so, but I have responsibilities, people count on me. And focusing on my patients should give me some needed space from my own problems. I should at least complete the work I agreed to first

I reminded myself that they've survived for years without me and can make it a month or two with another therapist. You've got money in the bank, live off your cut from the other therapists. Marilyn is a good therapist and wants to be her own boss someday. Let her run the business for a while and experience the extra hours of mundane paperwork.

I got up to leave several times, even made it out the door once, but sat back down to rummage through the thick stack of mail.

At last, I decided work will be therapeutic. I began preparing itemized statements for third party insurance payers, but images of Kris' cadaver kept appearing on the invoices. The stamp on a bill morphed into the flat birthmark on her shoulder. It looked at me, shouting "murder."

I can see clients and stay in control. Yeah, and maybe pigs will start flying outside my ninth-floor window, because I just saw a talking mole.

I dialed Marilyn's number and waited for the beep. "Hi Mare, it's Mitch. Thanks for your kind words about Kris. I'm going to take you up on your offer. I haven't decided how to dole out my clients to the others in the group, but I'll find the right matches by tomorrow. I'm heading home. Call my cell."

I grabbed my briefcase and headed for the door. My personal back line rang.

"That was quick," I said into the receiver, expecting Marilyn.

"HER DEATH WAS ANYTHING BUT QUICK," a mechanically altered voice replied, sexless, ageless, unrecognizable, robotic, not human.

My mind stopped. I felt turned inside out while the chloroform-soaked cotton ball landed near me again, ready to send me back to oblivion. Stunned, I forced myself to speak. "I don't know what you're talking about."

"YOU'RE A BAD LIAR. SHE'S ALL YOU THINK ABOUT, EVEN NOW."

The voice sounded like that of a twisted, wrathful God risen from a harsh, random electronic world to drag me back into the frog's slick glass coffin. I swallowed hard, focused on keeping my voice even. "You think you know something about me?"

"DON'T INSULT MY INTELLIGENCE. PERHAPS I SHOULD HAVE SENT YOU A TROPHY. I HAVE INTIMATE KNOWLEDGE OF HER LAST HOUR ON EARTH, HER FINAL THOUGHTS, AND WHETHER SHE BEGGED ME TO SPARE HER LIFE. DID YOU STARE AT THE MOLE ON HER LEFT SHOULDER WHEN YOU FUCKED HER, TOO?"

I felt the Stranger arise in me. "You're a dead man," I said in a low voice, full of emotion.

Harsh alien noises stung my ear. I held the receiver at arm's length until it subsided. The mechanical voice mocked me, laughed at my anger and pain. "YOU'RE THREATENING ME? THIS *IS* GOING TO BE FUN!"

He's using your raw emotions to relive the excitement of the kill. He's getting secondary gains when I lose control. Don't give him what he wants.

"You misunderstand. You must be dead inside to do what you did."

At last the angry robotic voice stopped laughing. "FOOD FOR LATER THOUGHT. IF SO, IT'S ANOTHER THING WE HAVE IN COMMON NOW. PAY ATTENTION TO WHAT I'M ABOUT TO SAY.

"I OWN YOU. YOU ARE ALONE NOW.

"TELL THE POLICE ABOUT ME AND I VANISH FOREVER.

"TRY TO TRACE ME AND YOU WILL NEVER HEAR HER LAST WORDS.

"IF YOU DO NOT COMPLY WITH MY DEMANDS, I WILL CONTINUE KILLING. I WILL SEPARATE YOUR CLIENTS FROM YOU ONE BY ONE."

Surprise him. Don't let him think he's in control.

"I don't believe you," I said and hung up the phone, my hands trembling. I found myself rocking back and forth, wondering if I'd pushed him too far.

Seconds later the back line rang again.

"NEVER DO THAT AGAIN!" I'd stepped on the hornet's nest, for every mechanical word sounded angrier than before.

"You disguise your voice. You're afraid of me."

More distorted laughter.

Keep him off kilter. "I know you. You're a client."

"YOU'RE THE THERAPIST. I JUST SIT IN THE CHAIR. PERHAPS THAT SUCCULENT, LEGGY STEWARDESS WILL BE NEXT. FOR SOME REASON, SHE WORSHIPS THE GROUND YOU WALK ON. WE CAN'T ALLOW THAT."

We? "I'm done talking to you."

"NO. FROM NOW ON, YOUR HEART WILL SKIP A BEAT WHENEVER THE PHONE RINGS. YOU WILL HANG ON MY EVERY WORD. YOU WILL COME TO LONG FOR ME."

"You certainly need a lot of attention. How do I know you killed her?"

"BECAUSE I CAN TIE YOU UP AND HAVE YOU IN POLICE CUSTODY ON A WHIM WITH A SINGLE PHONE CALL. CHEW ON THAT."

The line went dead.

I just sit in the chair.

Was this really the murderer? Is he a client of mine? Is Green is not involved in Kris' murder or is the call a red herring to throw me off track?

Why the sick cat-and-mouse game? The killer is an organized, intelligent sociopath. My head told me to contact the cops because he said not to, but wiretaps and traces would likely lead to a series of stolen cell phones or public phones. And irreversible consequences for my clients. He couldn't resist the need to call; the urge will strike again. In some twisted way this may be the break I'm looking for. Perhaps a part of his subconscious wants to be caught. Maybe his rage or sociopathy will trip him up and he'll underestimate me. My heart told me I couldn't risk never knowing who killed Kris. My head told me I could catch him without violating my innocent clients' right to confidentiality that would surely happen if I involved the police. I must think with my head, not my heart, and remain calm.

I'll do what he says, no police. I can't risk losing him and I can't risk my clients' safety. How does he know so much about my other clients? It's almost like he's been scouting them in my waiting room. My thoughts turned to Rick Arno.

If the murderer is a client of mine, I already know the irrational fears that haunt him and the dreams that drive him. Six feet away his complete psychological profile sits in my file cabinet among the others. All I need to do is find it.

Said the fly to the spider.

If that's not a rationalization, nothing is.

A TEN-MINUTE DESCENT

Night descended on the city with a gray pall as I sat parked around the corner from the police station, feeling like a felon. A sharp rap on the driver side window made me jump. Hairy knuckles and a gold wedding band pressed hard against the tinted glass, followed by the taut face of my friend Tony.

I powered down the window a third of the way.

"Christ on a cracker, you look like hell, Mitch. I couldn't believe it when I heard Kris was dead. Listen up buddy, if you don't return this to me, as is, I'll turn you in myself. I'm double mortgaged, Cindy has expensive tastes, and the twins are off to college soon. If I go down for this, I'll never get my practice back." He checked the street both ways before passing the thick folder through the narrow opening.

"Thanks, I owe you."

He kept a tight grip on the file. "You won't be thanking me later. Unlike our one-on-one games, there are no street rules here. This is one sadistic bastard. Change your mind, don't look at it. Nothing good will come of this."

"I have to. I can't tell you why."

"I shouldn't have caved, but you could sell swastikas to the Pope, if you wanted." Tony's mood grew more somber. "They've made you for this, Mitch. They're trying to pound square evidence into round holes and put you away. It just might work. Watch your back."

"I know. Thanks."

"I'm begging you as a friend, don't do this. Let it go."

I knew he was right. I tightened my grip on the file. "I have to try. You'd do the same in my position."

We stared at each other, both pulling on the folder. He flinched first. "Remember, I warned you."

I nodded. He let go.

A line of sweat appeared on his brow. "LeMaster and Baker keep odd hours. Those cowboys can show up anytime. They pound the streets day and night. I'm going on a break to the newsstand around the corner. Go nowhere; read it here." He looked at his watch. "I take it back exactly ten minutes from now."

I watched him stride, head down, along the tree-lined sidewalk under a threatening green sky, his briefcase and umbrella in hand. He faded into the ranks of others scurrying to beat the coming storm.

I powered up the window and stared at the plain brown jacket of Kris's murder file. I didn't open it at first, it felt like an anchor on my lap, ready to drag me to depths where humanity goes to die. I felt my stomach tighten; my hands grew sweaty. I looked in the direction Tony had walked, half hoping he'd circle back to reclaim it, but he was nowhere in sight.

What gruesome images lurked within the plain manila folder to burrow their tentacles into my brain?

To a certain degree, one must detach from clients to help them. I can do it again. Detach yourself now.

I had less than ten minutes to sift through crime scene evidence, review police procedures, interviews, and conjecture; then locate a thread that connected one of my clients to Kris. I hoped a clue would leap out and identify her killer. I took a deep breath and closed my eyes a moment.

A drop of rain hits the windshield when I open the cover and begin my descent.

Interrogation

While I read, an intense childhood flashback kept worming its way into my thoughts. When I was ten, my parents took me on a sweltering summer fishing vacation to Bull Shoals Lake. On the drive home a car packed with teenagers sped by us in a no-passing zone like we were standing still. Five minutes later we came upon their car. It had crashed head-on into a station wagon. Flames shot out from both mangled cars as my parents joined the bucket brigade, passing water from a nearby home in a futile effort to douse the flames. I saw the frantic pounding and heard the frenzied cries for help from those trapped inside the crumpled vehicles. I remember the bloody handprints smeared on the inside of the passenger windows and a tiny arm that clung to a teddy bear. The doors reduced to crushed hulls of twisted metal, the heat grew too intense at the crash site for the brigade. Somehow a boy and girl about my age had survived, along with their dog. They beat long odds when thrown from the station wagon before its roof collapsed like an accordion. Dazed, the kids sat on a grassy field near the cars when we arrived on the scene, their eyes goggled like they had landed on another planet. The short-legged mutt eagerly lapped water from a green plastic bowl. The open gash that ran the length of his spine didn't seem to bother him. My job was to tend to the kids while the grown-ups fought the fire and tried to rescue the trapped people. No matter what I did or said, I couldn't get the kids to talk or even tell me their names. I said inane things like 'it's going to be alright' because I had no idea of the right words to say at a time like this. They seemed gone, shipped off to some faraway place, oblivious to everything. I made small talk about the dog but couldn't draw the kids out of what I later learned were their protective cocoons. I felt like a failure.

Even though it was the hottest day that year, 104 degrees, the kids began to shake from cold. I borrowed blankets from the old man who owned the tiny A-frame near the country road. He said the kids were in shock. When I returned with the blankets, the little girl had rubbed her forearm so hard it bled. The boy rocked back and forth and made humming noises while he sucked his thumb. I put my arms around them, not knowing what else to do. Local rural fire department and EMT vans didn't arrive at the scene for another hour because they were battling a house fire on the other side of the nearest town. Minutes before the firemen arrived with water hoses and the Jaws of Life, all human sounds stopped from inside the doomed cars. The adults on the scene, my parents included, stood covered in sweat and soot, and most cried and held on to each other. Burnt flesh and smoking rubber polluted the air. More than one fireman and volunteer collapsed from the gruesome work in the oppressive heat. A fireman vomited. Another wept. The adults on hand helped the second responders carry the covered remains of twelve dead (there were eight teenagers in the car that passed us and four remained in the station wagon) on stretchers to waiting ambulances that doubled as hearses. The children acknowledged the procession with sidelong glances. The scratching and rocking continued. The police took the kids into protective custody. My parents later read in the Post that an aunt in Rolla adopted them.

No one said a word during the long, extra slow ride home. I remember my mother cried silent tears in the front passenger seat. When it was time for bed that night, I thought she'd never stop hugging me. I still see the teenagers' carefree faces as they rocketed past, especially one. He was sixteen, maybe seventeen, and sported a blond crew cut. Our eyes connected for an instant. He smiled and waved at me while leaning out the back passenger window, reveling in life, perhaps comfortable in the belief he'd live forever. Now that smiling young face existed only in my memory. I wondered by what monstrous miracle the younger kids had survived, how much they'd recall of the accident, and what the future held for them. I became a social worker in part because of that day when I had no idea what to say to those kids, on the day hell and earth collided and the devil claimed a dozen lives.

Reading the murder file was like reliving that accident, I couldn't avert my eyes no matter how I tried. At some point I realized I'd been pounding my fist on the dashboard, screaming. I frantically scribbled notes and took pictures of the crime scene photos with my cell phone camera.

I didn't see the figure approach through my fogged windows.

When the rap of knuckles returned, I reached to power down the window, but my arm hit the horn. I wiped away a patch of condensation and watched Tony swivel his head nervously up and down the wet streets. An unmarked police car glided silently through the rain-soaked intersection in front of us.

He made a frantic, hurry-up gesture with his hands while I fumbled for the right button.

"What are you trying to—" he said angrily but froze when he saw my face. The last of the blurry window disappeared silently into the door as water dripped onto my arm. He reached inside and said, softer, "I was a fool to let you talk me into this. I am so sorry."

I tried to speak and couldn't.

"Damn, I have to get this thing back. Stay here until you're sure you can drive. Take deep breaths. Go home." He reached inside the car and squeezed my shoulder. "I'll call you later, buddy."

I must have missed when the sky opened and dumped a torrent of warm rain that drove the filth of the city into the sewers. Watching the churning runoff seek its lowest level, I told it, "You missed some."

I don't remember driving home. The Stranger must have been behind the wheel.

II

I familiarized myself with police procedures after convincing Tony to steal Kris' file. I drank while I studied the writings of Dr. Edmond Locard, an early twentieth century criminologist. His Exchange Principal postulates that with contact between two items, there will always be an exchange. No matter how minute, the criminal will leave evidence or unwittingly take physical evidence with him from the scene. Locard also said that wherever the criminal steps, whatever he touches, whatever he leaves, will serve as a silent witness against him. This type of evidence does not forget and cannot be wrong. Only human failure to find it, study it, and understand it can lessen its value. Fingerprints, footprints, semen, blood, hair, cloth fibers, scratch marks, tool marks, and a world of other evidence can help identify a killer. Locard lived before the advent of DNA evidence, but his theories still ring true.

I can relate to this since transference and counter-transference occur in therapy.

At home I sat at the kitchen table with a Tanqueray bottle and organized the notes I'd scribbled in the Solstice.

By the time I got to the photographic copy of the autopsy report by the city Medical Examiner, I had a buzz. It laid out the physical evidence of asphyxiation, petechiae or pinpoint hemorrhages in the skin, conjunctiva of the eyes and deep internal organs in rational, clinical, detached form.

Just the facts, ma'am. Nothing less, nothing more.

Neck dissection showed evidence of internal hemorrhaging, a damaged larynx, and fractured hyoid bone. Inspection of the cervical spine revealed other fractures. The blunt force injury to the neck tissues and prolonged compression led to unconsciousness and death. Most of the multiple abrasions and contusions to the head, neck, and upper torso occurred before death, but some injuries were sustained after cessation of blood flow in the body, an indication of rage. The lack of patterned abrasions or uniform contusions on the neck led the ME to conclude that no ligature was used. The force vector of the assailant indicated pressure from an extremely strong assailant, several inches taller than the victim. The head and neck contained traces of latex and talcum powder. Trace fibers inside the oral cavity likely came from carpet or a towel. Examination of the genitalia revealed tearing and bruising of the vaginal walls. Trace latex was also present here but no semen. Routine combing of the pubis produced one non-matching pubic hair, complete with root follicle, that was logged into evidence. Swabbing under the fingernails produced grit and more latex, but no human DNA. The ME concluded the deceased was a victim of forcible rape, prior to death or at the time of expiration. The rapist likely wore latex surgical gloves and used a condom, apparently leaving the scene of the crime with these items as neither were found nearby. Cause of death was ruled strangulation by a pair of gloved hands. Liver temperature readings put the approximate time of death between four and seven o'clock the morning the body was found. Further speculation was reserved for the end of the report. The ME postulated that murder was the intent and the crime was one of passion or rage, likely perpetrated by someone who knew the deceased well enough to get close. If not, then by an assailant in a drug-induced or paranoid psychotic state, severe enough to account for immense short-term strength.

The how and when she died. Not why or by whom.

The caller taunted me about having had sex with her.

Was that hair mine from the last time we had sex? I had no way of knowing. When I gave LeMaster my samples, the nurse told them the preliminary report on the DNA would take a week. If my DNA was a match, LeMaster would use the physical and circumstantial evidence to arrest me. Worst-case scenario, I had seven days to find the killer before they jailed me for first-degree murder.

LeMaster lied to me about the prints at the scene. Techs found three additional sets of fingerprints other than Kris' that were lifted from the Dumpster at the crime scene. Two were smaller and assumed to be latent prints of small children, while one set was that of an adult. None of the prints so far had registered a hit in the known criminal offenders' database. None were found on Kris' body or anywhere else at the scene. A cataloging of the 214 separate items found in the Dumpster followed, but none seemed relevant to, or discarded from, the crime scene, except for two. For now, the unidentified fingerprints and Dumpster contents appeared to be dead ends.

Interviews with the Fed-Ex driver who discovered the body early that morning seemed fruitless. He said he saw no one else at the scene. His story remained consistent during repeated questionings. The driver had an arrest for burglary as a juvenile twelve years ago, but co-workers and a supervisor witnessed him prepare his truck at the loading dock during the time frame of the murder. Interviews with apartment residents living in the vicinity of the Dumpster led nowhere; no one saw or heard anything unusual that morning. Party guests corroborated Green's constant presence into the morning, giving him an alibi for the break-in. Green told the police he had no idea why Kris left the party when she did. He assumed, as his guests did, that she'd had an argument with me. Her work friends at the party told the detectives of her volatile separation from Steven Gray. The problem with the ex-husband theory was that they still hadn't located him. His paper trail ended, as LeMaster said, with his departure from the medical program at Gateway University. He wasn't using his Social Security number for work, taxes, or any other reason since he dropped out. He was into the wind, apparently by design. The report indicated that one major player at the party had no such alibi. She left at about ten o'clock, shortly after we did, claiming to have a migraine. She spent the rest of the night alone in her sister's home in Ladue while her sister and family were out of town. That person was Elizabeth Green.

The main person of interest the evidence kept pointing to was me, with Steven Gray a distant second. The circumstantial evidence led to me, the jilted boyfriend in an ugly crime of passion.

I was the logical choice based on the evidence here. I was their OJ. It sucks to be me right now.

I pushed the liquor bottle away when I arrived at the crime scene photos on my cell phone. They captured a brief snapshot of the agony of her last moments. I studied the crime photos in chronological order. They were beyond graphic; they were obscene. It was what I imagined the stills from a snuff film would look like, minus the perp. The first pictures showed what the Fed-Ex driver happened upon early that morning—a naked body sat propped against the green Dumpster, the face and upper torso partly covered by a grimy bath towel. The text of the report said the grime was consistent with smudge and grit from the Dumpster. The soiled towel seemed to be the only item taken from the Dumpster and used at the scene. Her clothes sat neatly stacked, cut off with a sharp instrument like a scalpel, and folded near the body. The next set of pictures showed head shots of Kris with the towel removed. I sobered instantly and felt sick to my stomach. Her hands duct-taped tightly over her mouth; her lifeless eyes open in a rictus of horror, a scream stifled.

Trace amounts of latex on her eyelids indicated the killer had opened her eyes to stage the scene. There were close-up shots of her bare chest. The killer had used her blood to finger-paint the following mark over her heart: II. Another photo showed a close-up of a bloody footprint at the scene with a ruler next to it. She must have sustained a scalp laceration during the struggle, for traces of her skin and hair were found on the edge of the Dumpster and blood pooled next to her body. The killer must have stepped in it while staging the scene, leaving a clear footprint of an old tennis shoe with a distinctive series of worn circular tread marks, size twelve. Same as mine. Examination of the footprints found at the scene pointed to a single perpetrator. If I can find the owner of the shoe, I find her killer.

She wasn't completely naked in the final set of pictures. A man's silk tie, fashioned in a perfect half-Windsor knot, hung around her mangled neck. The autopsy report confirmed that the killer did not strangle her with it, yet he took the time and effort to dress and pose her. What's the significance of the tie? Why pose the body? What's the meaning of: II?

The preliminary report indicated the fibers found in Kris' mouth likely came from the Dumpster towel, which was probably used to silence her screams during the attack. The duct tape was a common brand found in any hardware store in the Midwest. It yielded no trace evidence or saliva other than Kris'. The necktie contained no foreign DNA or usable prints. Both the tape and tie had trace amounts of talcum powder, likely residue from surgical gloves.

I had two sources of evidence, the murder file and the phone conversation with the man claiming to be her killer. It took time to do what he did. There was purpose to the staging, it meant something to him. He risked being seen, identified, and captured because he wanted to make a statement. This wasn't some psychotic stranger influenced by the full moon who randomly crossed her path. He probably followed her, learned her habits and schedule, and waited for the right time. He timed his attack before dawn and fled unseen, leaving no apparent witnesses. He likely knew her; she was a strong, assertive woman who would have put up quite a fight unless she had some level of familiarity with her attacker. He brought duct-tape, surgical gloves, the tie, and a condom with him, maybe more. The towel over her face indicated some level of shame for the deed; he staged the scene only to cover her face later. Maybe I can use that sliver of guilt against him.

Preliminary drug tests came back negative; he didn't subdue her with drugs. There was nothing unusual in her stomach contents, which were listed in detail. The taped hands over her mouth reminded me of the Speak-No-Evil monkey. Was she murdered because of something she knew? Because she posed a threat to share a secret? Is the symbol the Roman numeral two? Was she his second victim? It holds special significance to the killer because of its position, close to the heart. What is his message and who is it meant for?

I stared again at the final picture. Then it hit me.

The tie around her neck.

He staged the crime scene for me. I wished I was drunk again.

He wants me to suffer and keep on suffering, until there's nothing left of me for him to take. He wants to transform me into a modern-day Job. That was my silk tie around her neck.

I can tie you up and have you in police custody on a whim with one phone call.

The last time I saw the tie, I think, was in her apartment. Worse still, it was the one I wore to the television station when I decked the pimp, Frank DeLuca. That segment aired for three days on local television. If the cops connect me to that tie, I'm as good as gone.

I re-read my notes four times. No clue jumped off the pages or pictures to lead me to a client, Warren Green, or Steven Gray.

The killer knows he's smart. He's showing off. I hope he thinks he's smarter than I am. Somehow I need to use his hubris against him. He doesn't know I've seen the murder file and that I know about the tie. If I can cling to that scrap of hope, maybe I can somehow move one step ahead of him.

What does he think I've done to him? My gut tells me that's the key.

He's right. I already long for his next call.

Until the next exchange of evidence, Dr. Locard. Thanks for the help, but I'm gonna need much more than this.

CIRCLE THE WAGONS

I sat alone in the office that night, long after the other therapists had seen their last clients for the evening. I worked hunched over, prioritizing my list of suspects, focusing on recent males, violence-prone or those having the potential, when pounding shook my inner door. I assumed my two new best friends LeMaster and Baker had returned to fit me for my workhouse oranges, but a muscular young man dressed in a red plaid work shirt and faded blue jeans stared down at me. He could have been The Incredible Hulk's body double.

"You Mitchell Adams?" the baritone voice asked, while fingers soiled by oil and grease scratched at his full but trimmed beard. The telltale odors of gasoline and oil residue hit me.

Paul Bunyan of the grease monkeys.

From a belt loop near his right hip dangled a heavy set of keys. A swinging ivory skeleton head keychain with blazing red eye sockets grinned at me. A bulky leather tool belt forced his pants to ride slightly lower on his waist, revealing the lower section of a fully ripped six-pack.

Mike and Dave had to pull him off the poor guy or he would've beaten him to death.

"Guilty as charged."

"I thought about you a lot when I was locked in the nut house."

Neutral affect. This could go either way.

"It's good to finally meet you, Harold."

He stopped picking at his red-tinted beard and grinned. "I thought about what I'd say to you if we ever met. My thoughts on it changed while I did that time. At first, I decided I wasn't going to say anything, I was just going to pound you. Next, I was going to ask what gives you the right to play God and take away my freedom, then I'd beat the stuffing out of you. I thought about it some more and decided to ask if you were screwing my wife, and depending on how you answered, maybe bash in your head. When they finally discharged me, I knew what I had to do."

A muscular forearm shot out. "Thanks for doing what you did. I was too sick to get help on my own. I didn't know half the crazy shit I was doing. The meds have helped level me off and today I went back to work. Life's tough enough without thinking the whole world is against you."

My hand disappeared into his when we shook and I probably did a lousy job of concealing my relief at learning he hadn't come to pound me.

"That's great news, Harold. Are you back home with Lisa?"

His massive shoulders sagged and his eyes lost a bit of their light. "Just until I have enough money for my own place. I deserve better than someone who sleeps around with my friends and God-knows-who-else. I don't blame her for the way I am, but with Lisa it's all about her. Life with her is like being strapped to a bomb."

This was an unexpected twist, but c'est la vie.

"Harold, you're welcome to join the sessions. They can help make your decisions more amicable."

A cell phone on his tool belt chirped and he reached for it. "I might take you up on that, but my priority now is just staying healthy, keeping my job, and finding another place to stay. Thanks again."

With that, Hurricane Harold blew out as fast as he stormed in.

Late that night, I studied my client folders and called Marilyn at home to give her a partial client list and the therapists I wanted them paired with in the practice. I reminded her which stacks of paperwork on my desk needed attention and the mail that needed to be sent tomorrow for third party payers.

"That's interesting," she said, sounding tired, when I finished.

"What do you mean," I answered, knowing.

"All these clients are women."

I hoped she wouldn't notice that I turfed only the women.

"Yeah, funny how it goes in waves, isn't it?"

There was silence on the other end of the line, then: *What about that creepy borderline guy you've been seeing?*

"Back in prison, parole violation," I lied.

"The world's a safer place," she said, not sounding convinced.

I thanked Marilyn and told her to have a good night.

"Be careful and get some rest," she said, yawning.

I asked why she sounded so tired.

"Hello! It's two in the morning. Are you alright? I can come over."

"Sorry, I lost track of time. I wanted to give you the list."

She reminded me to be careful. This time it seemed more of a warning.

Intuitive Marilyn.

II   II   II

I drifted in and out of sleep, lost in a gray netherworld, the line between dream and reality erased. One instant I lost myself in Kris' dark tiger-eyes; the next I struggled to remember her face. How could I be losing her this soon? I despaired because we hadn't taken many pictures together. I saw myself burying my face in her clothes, taking in deep breaths of her, and rubbing the soft fabric on my face. Her scent moved through me and I caught a fleeting glimpse of her walking toward me and then she was gone. What will I do when the scent vanishes from her clothes? Like Gatsby with Daisy, would my memory of her recede year after year like a shoreline relentlessly pounded by waves?

I woke with a start on my office sofa. Six in the morning. Why was I still here? Maybe because we never had sex here. Maybe because I wasn't safe to drive home. Booze helped the first few nights. Last night I'd added Ambien to the alcohol, but nonetheless nightmares, flashbacks, and racing thoughts pierced the fog.

That dull ring again. My back line.

"HOW ARE YOU SLEEPING?" the mechanically altered voice demanded to know. The same angry, programmed voice, like the Darth Vader of my own private Death Star.

I pressed record on my Dictaphone, dying to ask a million questions, dreading the answers. My mind ran off in every direction this conversation could go. "Never better."

"ANOTHER LIE. YOU'RE MAKING LISTS AND CHECKING THEM TWICE, TRYING TO FIND WHICH ONE OF US HAS BEEN NAUGHTY AND NOT NICE."

I planted my feet to steady myself. "If you're a client, let's meet and talk this out like men."

No immediate answer, then: "YOUR JEALOUSY AND LACK OF TRUST DROVE HER AWAY."

"Who's lying now?"

"SHE RESENTED YOU FOR THAT. HER RESENTMENT WAS GROWING, FESTERING—"

"What makes you think you know the first thing about her, or me," I interrupted. This guy's an emotional terrorist.

The disguised voice seemed to grow louder, or maybe I imagined it. I couldn't tell if it was anger or impatience. "HER EX

TRIED TO CONTROL HER, TOO. SHE SAW THROUGH HIM, JUST AS SHE CAME TO SEE YOU FOR WHAT YOU REALLY ARE."

Does he know she broke up with me before she died? If so, how?

"Am I your rejecting, authoritative father figure? Have you replaced emotionally distant daddy with me? Was he abusive? Have you displaced your rage at him onto me?"

The silence stretched out for a five count until the Darth Vader voice slowly said, "WE'RE TALKING ABOUT YOUR DEAD GIRLFRIEND. SHE WAS ATTRACTED TO YOU INITIALLY, JUST LIKE SHE WAS DRAWN TO THE REST OF US. SHE WAS QUITE THE LITTLE WHORE, OUR KRIS, BUT YOU COULDN'T SEE THE FOREST FOR THE TREES. SHE REALIZED HER PATTERN WITH CONTROLLING MEN AND DID SOMETHING ABOUT IT. BY THE TIME YOU ACCEPT THIS, YOU'LL BE IN A JAIL CELL OR WORSE. THAT CHOICE RESTS WITH ME. I CAN HAVE YOU IN POLICE CUSTODY IF I PUT FIVE MINUTES OF EFFORT INTO IT."

The rest of us?

I'm not controlling! Stop it. Don't let him get under your skin. It's what he wants.

"You have quite the imagination and delusions of grandeur. Who abused you as a child?"

"WHO'S TO SAY I DIDN'T KEEP SOUVENIRS? I CAN PLANT EVIDENCE IN YOUR HOME THAT WILL LOCK YOU UP FOR THE REST OF YOUR MISERABLE LIFE, IF I WISH. I CAN DO WHATEVER I WANT TO YOU. YOU CAN'T STOP ME. IT'S QUITE THE POWER TRIP, TO BE SO DOMINANT OVER SOMEONE, ISN'T IT? ONLY NOW THE TABLES ARE TURNED.

NOT EVEN YOU CAN TALK YOUR WAY OUT OF THIS ONE. LIKE YOU TALKED YOUR WAY INTO HER."

He knows. *How could he possibly know so much about Kris and me?*

"If you're trying to scare me, it's not working," I lied.

"OH, I INTEND TO DO MUCH MORE THAN FRIGHTEN YOU. SHE SPREAD HER LEGS LIKE A JUNKIE FOR PEOPLE LIKE US. YOU DROVE HER RIGHT BACK TO ME."

I wanted to lead with my emotions but checked myself. If I mention the rape, he will taunt me with it. "Who are people like us?"

"SWEET DREAMS, SWINGER."

The line went dead in my hands, the floor spun and fell away from me.

I replayed the tape and made notes. Had I really known Kris or was the psychological torture part of his sick game of lies? Had she kept big secrets from me? Did she have an affair with her killer? Did our argument the night before drive her back to him? Is truth mixed in with his lies that somehow could help me catch him before LeMaster arrests me? Would my tie be the final piece of evidence needed to arrest me? If so, how long would it take the detectives to make the connection? Would the killer make good on his threat to plant more evidence, maybe the bloody shoes, in my townhouse for the final nail in my coffin? He contacted me, was he spoon-feeding information to the detectives? If so, I might have even less time than a week. One thing I knew, I couldn't believe a word he said and still maintain the will to hunt him.

The killer meant to eviscerate me. He'd shaken the firm foundation I thought I'd built with Kris. I had to find him before he completed his demolition work.

I was the sad character in one of my favorite oldies songs—playin' solitaire till dawn with a deck of fifty-one.

She was a junkie for people like us.

Sweet dreams, Swinger.

II   II   II

The next knock on my office door came at nine that morning. I let in LeMaster and Baker. "I'm going to have a spare key made for you two."

"Shit, you look tore up from the floor up!" Baker said. Seeing my couch hair, rumpled clothes, and empties, he said, "What the fuck you doin' sleepin' here?"

I'd rather die than tell him. "Lost track of time, I guess."

He got cut-eye with me. "Guess again, Doc."

"Never mind that," LeMaster said. He looped his thumbs in the front pockets of his dapper gray twill pants. "You had several arrests in college. You were quite the crusader—defender of the downtrodden, the poor, of criminals who claimed to be innocent. Care to explain?"

"Like you said, I was in college, in social work school. I took part in peaceful protests, sometimes helped organize groups against social injustices such as unjustified wars, inequities in the court system, and discrimination. I have no arrests for crimes against people or property."

"There's a first time for everything," Baker said.

LeMaster continued, "We interviewed women who knew you. Some were still quite angry and called you every name in the book; many said you hopped on to one woman as fast as you jumped off another."

"You talked to women I broke up with. I dated a lot before I met Kris. That's no crime. Now if you're done—"

"You're a Summa Cum Laude from Gateway University. Your peers hold you in the highest professional standing; they cannot imagine you capable of such a heinous act. We discovered a few past complaints directed toward your business but those involved another therapist in your practice that your company addressed and resolved to the mutual satisfaction of both parties, but there are no complaints against you in the National Association of Social Workers organization of licensed therapists or the Better Business Bureau. Your practice seems to be thriving financially as well."

I waited for the other shoe to fall, but it didn't. "Your point—"

LeMaster took a step forward. "You're a crusader. Sometimes the line between crusader and vigilante gets crossed."

Now I know where this is going.

"You offer your time and expertise as a consultant to the major local television stations to help educate the public on mental health issues. We watched old tapes from Channel Four. On one, you were fighting for one of your clients. Literally."

Baker worked a toothpick across his wide mouth and added, "Or maybe you just like to fight. Whaddaya say, *Swinger*? Bet that handle hasn't been too cool for the biz. We asked around in your professional circle. Some said the name is 'ap-ro-pos.' Wonder why that is?"

They referred to the punch I threw when I didn't know I was being recorded, but of course the film didn't detect DeLuca whisper his admission of guilt to me about Bob Vale's brutal assault.

Baker looked to LeMaster then quickly back at me. "We also got the fight at the Irish pub with the dead girlfriend and now this, two fights in a couple weeks. It's the beginning of a pattern, is what it tells me. Wonder what dirt we gonna find next, a little slap-and-tickle with clients, other im-pro-pri-e-ties?" Baker intentionally paused after each syllable of the word as he glared down at me.

It was pointless to debate the various connotations of the word swinger. I never *swung,* as in swapping sex partners at parties, but I dated a fair number of women casually for years before I met Kris. People can conflate casual dating with swinging. It didn't make sense to defend the punch because the camera captured it, our loud exchange of verbal taunts, and my ultimate loss of control. I hit DeLuca in the jaw. I assaulted him. Words in my defense would merely fall on deaf ears.

"Several things about that tape disturb us," LeMaster said. I will connect the dots and see the big picture. What will we find when we dig deeper—a compulsive need to control that drove her away, an obsessive rage that sent you over the edge? I know you're keeping something from us. Make it easy on yourself and tell me. If you refuse to cooperate and force us to learn the truth the hard way, I will throw the book at you."

Tell the police, I vanish forever.

The circumstantial evidence was piling up against me, threatening to put me in a deep, dark hole for a very long time. Could I find my way out of the darkness?

"I have nothing else to say to you, Detectives."

LeMaster appeared to do a slow burn as they walked to the door.

Baker spun around to face me. "Circle the wagons, Swinger. We be comin' and it gonna be soon. Maybe we toss you in a cell and scalp you next time. The man who did what he did to that woman deserves worse." Baker's grin exposed that shiny gold front tooth, and he whooped once like a wild Injun on his way out.

My heart, not my mind, agreed with Baker's last remark. As did the Stranger.

ALPHA MALES

I drove home, showered, made a cup of tea, and sat thinking.

If this was to be my last stand, I may as well quit feeling sorry for myself and keep shooting from the hip.

If....

I'd read it in high school. "If" was the first poem I ever really, really liked. I tried to live by Kipling's first two lines: *If you can keep your head when all about you / Are losing theirs and blaming it on you.* I've won most of these battles in my thirty-four years, but this is going to be my biggest challenge. It didn't matter that I faced disaster, knowing the killer was within reach comforted me in some odd way. I would not resign to my fate. I had to make sure the truth was not a casualty, and that meant bringing the killer to justice before the cops made me for the crime.

I had to fill each unforgiving minute with all my best deductive reasoning, good instincts, and years of training.

I poured over my client files for a day. Certain that my time as a free man was limited, I decided to take the caller at his word and focus on my clients. Tuesday was Wolf Paxton's regular appointment day, but I called and scheduled appointments with Father James, and Rick Arno as well. My trifecta of primary suspects—all Alpha males and current clients. I put Warren Green and Steven Gray on the back burner, focusing on a suspect priest, a borderline bass guitar player, and a ruthless millionaire businessman.

It took the remainder of the morning to dole out the rest of my clients to the other therapists in the practice, and after that I wanted to go to Kris's apartment to see if I could find any clues the police might have missed before I visit Bob in the hospital. After his assault and hospitalization, I'd blocked out our normal therapy hour to visit him and saw no reason to deviate from that routine now. Best to keep some semblance of normality to simply keep myself moving forward.

Normality. Nothing normal about this day, I thought, as once again the surreal gravity of the situation sunk in. One of my clients killed Kris. He somehow got hold of my tie, and he's going to frame me for her murder. I've got to outsmart him before I wind up behind bars. I knew I had some confessing of my own to do. There was no other way. My arrest eminent; I took a leap of faith and did what the caller was counting on me not to do.

I took a deep breath, and before I left for Kris's and the hospital, I picked up the phone and made a very difficult call, putting my life and freedom in the hands of another. If capturing the killer is the goal, not settling for a scapegoat, we needed each other.

II II II

I drove to Kris' place and used her spare key to unlock the new deadbolt. When I broke the seal of the police sticker on the door, the detectives would know the integrity of the apartment had been compromised. I ducked under the yellow crime scene tape, broke the seal, and entered. I wore latex gloves, like her killer. I knew what I wanted to find and hoped it was still here.

The apartment seemed stale and suffocating. I never thought I would not want to be here. The prickly pear and fishhook cacti on the kitchen window ledge were blooming and thriving, but the Vinca and spider plants had yellowed and browned, their leaves and tendrils wilted, curling to the hardwood floor. Ghosts roamed everywhere, on the worn yellow sofa and especially the mattress. For an instant I thought I heard her call my name; a past memory ejected itself from my mind. I went to one knee and reached under the bed, but it wasn't there. It wasn't in her closets or her chest of drawers. If it's in the evidence locker at the station, I'm screwed. I almost missed it because it was hiding in plain sight on her kitchen table. I grabbed the folder and a vial of lilac perfume, sneaking out with my tail between my legs, hoping no one had seen me come or go.

II II II

After the automatic double doors to the Intensive Care Unit at Gateway Hospital swung inward, I sensed a mood change at the nurses' station when I waved to a quartet of nurses and techs clustered around the circular chart rack. ICUs are all too often grim repositories for the most critically ill patients. Gallows humor in hospitals is more pronounced in ICUs, sometimes nicknamed 'The Valley of Death,' because many patients leave via 'Celestial Discharge.' Humor can be a way to cope with facing death every day, like whistling through a graveyard. Today the staff seemed more animated and carried an extra bounce in their step.

"Don't wait for me, honey. I'll be down soon. Go to him," nurse Patti told me, a smile spreading across her wide, kind face. Patti, a short stocky middle-aged woman and sole caretaker of her teenaged Down's syndrome daughter, exudes the steady patience and sheer force of will of a saint.

When I turned the corner and walked into Bob's room, an amazing thing happened. He turned his head toward me, clutched his throat, and in a scratchy voice said, "Hey, Doc."

The ventilator tube down his throat had been replaced by a tracheotomy collar, the butterfly bandages that covered multiple orbital fractures were gone and revealed yellowing bruises; he'd lost about twenty pounds, and his voice was raspy. Chest tubes still gravity drained to the floor, but he was extubated and, best of all, awake.

131

"Those two words just made my week. How are you feeling?" I said, returning his smile.

He looked at me as if through a fog. He clutched his throat again. "You okay?"

Is it that obvious? I nodded. "The question is, how are you?"

He closed the valve over his trach. "Sleepy. Throat hurts. Hurts when I breathe." He slowly nodded his head in the direction of the Pleurevac drainage system on the floor. "Patti says I have two drains down there catching blood—I see four with my left eye."

"It's good to have you back," I said, gently squeezing his hand.

He was already getting fatigued. My time with him lucid was short.

"Bob, do you remember details from that night at Dolly's Delight? Did you hear names called out or see any distinctive tattoos or earrings that could help the police identify the men who beat you?"

He began to drift off and I repeated the question.

He scratched the tip of his nose and plugged his trach. "Six guys big as Buicks … in the back of a truck … put a sack over my head … kicked and stomped me. Beat me with a tire iron … pissed on me … poured beer on me."

"Was a swarthy-looking man there—mid-thirties, jet black hair, well dressed, short ponytail—maybe wearing a gold cross with diamonds in his earlobe?"

Bob closed his eyes, plugged his trach, and grimaced. "Tired."

"I know. Was the dark man there with the big guys?"

He moved his head away from me and covered his trach. "I don't remember."

Then his brow furrowed and he inserted the valve. "He said we'd have a righteous ball at Dolly's with my disability check."

His eyes remained closed.

A righteous ball. My stomach turned. I knew someone who spoke that way.

"Who told you that?"

He fought a losing battle against sleep. I repeated myself, louder.

His hand trembled when he plugged his trach. He was exhausted. "Waiting room...."

"Who? In my waiting room or here?"

"Throat's dry, Patti." Crusty white matter appeared on his mouth while he slurred his words. He shook his head again, frowning.

I gently shook his shoulder, which must have hurt for his eyes bugged out and his body went rigid.

"What's his name?" I said, feeling like a jerk and wanting to put words in his head.

"Let me be, Patti."

"Describe him."

A minute passed and I thought he was asleep for good. Then with his eyes closed he fumbled one last time for the trach valve. "He used me."

He drifted off, where I hoped peaceful dreams awaited him that were free of big hairy guys built like Buicks and wielding tire irons.

Patti entered the room with an intravenous medication. "Isn't it something, Mitch?"

"More like a miracle. When did he wake up?"

She hung a fresh IV bag and examined Bob's trach site. "A couple days ago. If he'd been lucid then, I would've called your cell. You're the only person he asked about before the coma was induced. He adores you. You're a true friend."

You wouldn't be saying that if you'd walked in two minutes earlier. "Is he out of the woods yet?"

"The lung punctured from the beating and the vent probably caused the other to collapse. We call that a pneumothorax in the biz. I'll feel better when the chest tubes and Pleurevac drains can come out, but I don't like the way that eye looks. He can still be a dad with one working testis. Everything considered, I think we're gonna steal one back from the Big Woman Upstairs."

I smiled and said, "God's a woman?"

She looked at me like I just stepped off the ramp of an alien spacecraft. "Of course she is, honey. Life giving, Mother Nature, the Earth Mother. The Sacred Feminine, Gaia. I could go on. No offense, but if women ran the world, the planet would be better off."

"I believe you're right. How's Karen?"

She beamed like a beacon. "We learned to how macramé lace pillow fringes this week. She's my hero."

It was comforting to know that making lace pillow fringes still mattered somewhere in the world. A sudden pang of loss hit me. I grimaced.

"And you're my heroine."

I nodded toward Bob. "Nice save, Patti. Thanks."

She stood at the entrance to his room and pointed a stubby finger toward heaven. "Don't thank me, thank Her."

Before continuing her rounds, she must have sensed my inner turmoil, for I hadn't told her about Kris nor did the papers connect me to her since I wasn't family. Her mood turned sober while she assessed me. "Whatever you're wrestling with will work itself out. You will find a way." She looked in Bob's direction. "Take care of him and he'll take care of you. Our patients give so much of themselves. They remind us that life and love don't exist without pain."

Her first words oddly reminiscent of what I told Tony about the practice he may buy, the thought hit me that if everyone abided by that rule, the world would be a far better place. Patti for president.

Did Rick Arno's boundary issues extend beyond the waiting room and into my bedroom? He certainly gloated about spying on us, about seeing her kiss me before she got in my car. Kris excited him. He enjoyed trying to throw me off kilter. Had he followed us to her apartment? Was that his silhouette in the dark Escalade parked on Laclede the night before her murder? Did he return later, stake out her apartment, and follow her as she walked alone the next morning? I know he sees me as the Establishment, part of the legal/treatment system he loathes. Hate is a powerful motivator. Had I pushed him too far in our sessions? Did he feel compelled to lash out against an authority figure in his black-and-white, all-or-nothing view of the world around him?

II II II

Back at the office, I ran computer searches of potential clues found at the crime scene. My back line rang and I tensed, reaching for the Dictaphone, ready to salivate.

It was Tony, calling from the city police station. "Had to call in a favor for that unauthorized DMV search. You scored a hit on the Escalade—the plate ended in 820, this year's model, midnight blue not black, with all the bells and whistles, including tinted windows. Nice ride, but for 60K it better be." He paused and lowered his voice to a conspiratorial tone. "You're hunting him, aren't you? Is this the douchebag?"

"I don't know. The less you know the better. Tell no one about this. I hope to explain it to you soon over a cold one rather than through a Plexiglas window. Is the owner from the list I gave you?"

He repeated one of the names on my list. Surprise, surprise.

"Destroy that list. I owe you, my friend. Say hi to Cindy and the girls for me."

"Will do. Watch your six."

I disconnected and opened the pilfered Manila accordion folder, spreading out Kris's tax returns, bank and insurance statements, and her appointment calendar that dated back two years before we met. I made calls but none bore useful information, and I couldn't finish them all before my first appointment.

POUND OF FLESH

I could almost see the minute hand on the wall clock move as I waited for my first Alpha male client. I tried to remember the last good event happening prior to Bob's awakening when my back line rang.

"I KNOW YOU WANT TO HEAR HER LAST WORDS. WHAT SHE DID FOR ME AND HOW SHE BEGGED ME TO SAVE HER PRETTY NECK," the maniacal voice said.

I hit record on my Dictaphone and watched the tiny gray sprockets start to spin. My head followed suit as I weighed my response.

"No. You'll change the context and twist them to suit your needs." Please tell me, anyway.

"SHE SAID: 'YOU'RE RIGHT, I SHOULD HAVE STAYED WITH YOU.' HOW DOES THAT MAKE YOU FEEL, SWINGER?"

A tiny light bulb sputtered to life in my mind as I listened. It flickered but disappeared like a forgotten dream. I kept telling myself that he wants to talk to me more than I him. Maybe I'd eventually believe it.

Keep him talking.

"I don't care what you claim she said. Look, if these phone sessions continue, I'll have to charge you double. What'd you say your name was again? I'll need that and a copy of your insurance card."

"VERY FUNNY, BUT YOU'RE NOT LAUGHING NOW, ARE YOU?"

"No more games. Tell me who you are or turn yourself in. You keep calling me, you want to confess or be captured. Think of it, your name and picture all over the television, nothing but you on the front page for days. People will write books about you. You'll be famous, immortal—"

"YOU HAVE NO CLUE WHAT MOTIVATES ME," he interrupted. Then he said, "MY WORK ISN'T COMPLETE. YOU'RE THE KEY. YOU THINK YOU'RE SMARTER THAN ME. WE WILL SEE."

How am I the key?

Like with other jobs, there are victories and defeats in the career of a therapist. In some cases, working diagnoses evolve when more information is learned, some treatment decisions pan out while others don't. The client/therapist relationship plays out in the real world. Life happens. Shit happens. They often coincide. The human factor is the wild card that can trump the best therapeutic intentions. Therapy, like medicine, is part knowledge and part practice. There's an intuitive aspect to therapy that takes time to learn. School can only take you so far. I know I'm a better therapist now than after I completed my training because I've learned from experience and mistakes. Since the killer first called, I've racked my brain to think of every past treatment outcome that an unstable mind could perceive as failure. There are many possibilities. For each contested divorce I've mediated, both sides usually feel screwed. For every parental psychosocial evaluation I've completed to help a judge rule on a child custody hearing, the losing parent could be a suspect. If my involvement ended with the evaluation, I wouldn't even know which parent believed they became the ultimate 'loser.' I wouldn't be privy to the level of parental rights lost or how they're handling their grief and anger. Finding the killer could be like locating the right ant on a mountainside. I clung to the hope that the killer was a recent male client, one of the three men I was about to see today.

"Look, this is between you and me, but you have me at a disadvantage. What have I done to you? Tell me. I'll fix it if I can."

"YOU CAN'T REPAIR THE DAMAGE YOU'VE DONE, BUT I WILL. YOU THINK YOU'RE BETTER THAN EVERYONE ELSE, SITTING IN YOUR SAFE CHAIR MAKING DECISIONS THAT RUIN LIVES. THAT WILL END."

I was bargaining with the executioner. "Like you, I'm human and doing the best I can, but sometimes it isn't enough, despite our best intentions. I can help with your pain. Tell me about it."

There was silence on the other end that stretched out a minute. I thought he disconnected the line. Then I heard Darth Vader-like breathing through the disguising device. "IT'S TOO LATE FOR THAT. TAKE YOUR PICK—LIFE IN PRISON OR DEATH. I WILL EXACT MY POUND OF FLESH."

This was going to end badly for one of us. Or both.

"Neither. Which do *you* prefer, life in jail or the death penalty? I look forward to seeing you in therapy."

More silence. Had I been too aggressive, too confrontational?

Then finally: "YOU FORGET I CAN HAVE YOU ARRESTED WITH ONE PHONE CALL. OR PERHAPS I'LL FLY THE FRIENDLY SKIES WITH YOUR COMELY GROUPIE TO PUNISH YOU FOR YOUR ARROGANCE."

The line went dead.

I hoped I'd thrown him off balance when I told him I'd see him in therapy. Would all three show for their sessions?

I don't think he wants me behind bars because that would essentially put me out of reach, and he couldn't play his torture-by-phone game whenever the mood struck.

Lisa Carter was another story, though. I had a duty to warn that I couldn't ignore. I called her home number and Harold picked up. He said she'd just begun a six-day duty period, shuttling between Los

Angeles, Hawaii, Tahiti, and New Zealand. He didn't know why she was a no-show for her previous appointment. I thanked him and called her cell, but it went straight to voice mail. I warned about a general threat against her voiced to me by someone who could be a disturbed client. I asked her to call my office immediately, especially if she'd had any recent contact with another client, in the waiting room or anywhere. I reassured her she was safe while she was at work for the next six days, that the situation should resolve itself in the next few days. I promised to call back when it did.

'You're right, I should have stayed with you.' Had Kris really said that or was it a lie? If so, what did it mean? Don't let him get into your head. What grievous wrong have I done him?

Whether she knew her killer or not, and I think she did, Kris was smart enough to try to talk her way out of that alley first. She would have tried to mollify him, stroke his ego, and go along with whatever delusion he entertained if it helped her escape. Just long enough for him to drop his guard and leave her an opening.

I should have stayed with you. The light bulb remained off. Not a flicker. My head battled my emotions. Was it a reference to Steven, her ex, or someone else she knew? I only truth I knew is that the killer is a master of lies and misdirection.

I replayed every taped conversation with the killer in order and made more notes. Something wanted to take shape. I reached out my hand for it, but it came back empty.

He was the house, dealing all the cards. And the house wanted its take. I had to face a cold, hard truth. I could be going to jail for a long time.

II   II   II

Dark clouds gathered, threatening rain, as Father James Fogerty, the first of my three Alpha males, walked into my office and placed his umbrella in the stand near the door. He's the newest of my three clients, as this was only our second session. I'd reviewed his Church file in detail as well as my sparse notes from the first session, which was, for me, more of a feeling-out time and, for him, a muscle-flexing test. It seemed like that session took place a year ago, in another world, when I was someone else.

He appeared calm and relaxed as he settled into the client chair, the mirror opposite of our first session. He maintained good eye contact with no visible anxiety or tension. He even looked like he'd gotten some sun.

"Tell me about the young woman who filed the initial complaint against you, Father."

He raised an eyebrow. "Right down to business, I like that."

"We need to make up for lost time."

He cleared his throat. "Ah, if man only could. Jenny Marcus, a fourth-generation university pledge, filed the complaint. I was her advisor. She was a bright, inquisitive, energetic, sensitive, young woman eager to spread her wings but uncertain where she wanted to land. She longed for greater autonomy from her parents, whom she perceived as moderately suffocating, and sought a nobler purpose in life like most idealistic young people."

He painted a picture of an impressionable, malleable, neophyte woman desperate to enter adulthood. She seemed an ideal candidate for a mentor to guide her into the uncharted territories of college, careers, and responsible adult society. She was also perfect fodder for a manipulative sociopath.

"She claims you entered her room during a freshman retreat and tried to rape her. I quote, 'He kissed me and pinned me down on the bed, his erect penis up against me while he fought to undo my jeans. He covered my mouth but I bit his hand, drawing blood, and I screamed. He ran from my room minutes before people responded to my cries.'"

The report went on to say Miss Marcus waited two weeks before she told her mother of the alleged sexual assault. Jenny and her father lodged a formal complaint, but by then there was no physical evidence of any hand injury to Father James. No one who responded that night to her cries for help saw anyone enter or leave the building. A fellow student who answered her screams thought she might have had a nightmare. After the alleged attack, she was in shock and terrified. For whatever reason she didn't tell the first responders who attacked her, possibly out of fear or the wish to deny the alleged attack ever happened. She decided not to file a report that night.

"What happened that night, Father?"

He was the poster boy for control, blocking his non-verbals. "Nothing happened that night. Her story is fantasy, driven by her pathology. Earlier that day, she sought my counsel for a personal problem."

"Tell me about it."

"She came to me distraught over having to choose between her boyfriend and her parents, especially her father. For six months, she had been secretly dating an older man. She convinced herself she was in love with him. Her father labeled Romeo a pariah and, given the age difference and other factors, he ordered the boyfriend strictly *verboten* to Jenny. If she chose Romeo, she would kiss her inheritance of several million dollars goodbye."

"What other factors?"

"Differences in social class, life experiences, and skin color were like night and day. She's from a conservative, Mid-Western, Catholic, upper class, white family while Romeo hails from the inner-city projects, is a dark-skinned black man with a drug-dealing father serving five to ten years in federal prison. Romeo earned a full minority ride to the university and is finishing a degree in Physical Education." He allowed himself a wistful pause. "A mixed union is admittedly not all that unusual in these modern times, but certainly not what daddy envisioned for his only daughter."

"You learned a lot from one weekend retreat."

Unfazed, he said humbly, "I try."

"You said she sought you out. When and where did the meeting take place?"

"She asked to meet her on a park bench that rests in a more secluded corner of the retreat grounds. She said she wanted to talk about a private matter after lunch."

"Was there any physical contact between yourself and Miss Marcus during this meeting?"

"Yes."

I did not show my surprise at his answer. "Tell me about it."

In a calm voice he said, "Her anxiety level was so high she suffered a classic panic attack. I had her hyperventilate into the brown paper bag I'd brought my lunch in until her breathing normalized. I reuse lunch bags whenever possible to pinch pennies. While she did this, I rubbed her back and reassured her that she, with God's help, would make it through this difficult time. The tears finally slowed and she regained control. She hugged me and whispered into my shirt, 'I feel so close to you. You know just what to say.' The next thing I know she's pressing her lips to mine and her tongue is in my mouth. I broke the contact and told her this cannot happen."

"How did she respond?"

"She made an agonized reference to her father 'fucking her' again and stormed off. I called out for her to come back and talk, but that made her run faster. I considered following but chose not to; frankly, I was worried how it might look if someone saw the scene from one of the windows above the courtyard. It sounds petty now and I regret not catching up with her to process the transference."

"When did you see her next?"

"I didn't. I looked for her later that afternoon but couldn't find her. Nor did I see her that night or for the rest of the retreat. I called her dorm the following Monday, but there was no answer. Nine days later, the archbishop calls me into his office and I'm placed on administrative leave. I could face excommunication, forfeiture of my counseling license, and jail time. Church leaders have grown weary of paying hush money in the form of multi-million-dollar settlements for sexual abuse lawsuits, and of watching members leave the Church in droves."

It could have happened that way. 'He said, she said' stories are tough to sort out without corroboration from witnesses. "Your current attitude is quite different from a week ago."

"When we first met, I was angry, full of self-pity, and resigned to my fate. Now I'm ready to fight. What's so frustrating is that *I'm* the victim here."

OJ said the same thing.

"You don't seem to be the self-pitying kind, Father."

He remained silent.

"Okay. Why would Jenny Marcus make these false allegations against you?"

"When I described her earlier, I omitted the words troubled and disturbed. She confided in me about her history of sexual abuse from the ages of twelve to sixteen. While in high school, she made a number of similar claims against male teachers to the point that a pattern emerged."

"Knowing this, you still chose to meet with her alone?"

"Yes. I'm sure you've done the same in your career."

I thought of Lisa Carter. "Who does she say abused her?"

"The driving force behind the complaint against me, the same man who happens to be a prosecuting attorney for St. Louis County. Daddy dearest."

"Jenny didn't tell you of her alleged pattern of Crying Wolf. How did you learn this?"

A little muscle in his jaw worked overtime while he considered how to respond. "The city has a glut of professional investigators, a few willing to work for peanuts if it doesn't require too much leg or surveillance work. One happened to be a God-fearing Catholic who felt he owed the church a favor."

"You hired a private detective to delve into her past?"

"After she filed the complaint, yes."

"Do you have a written report from this P.I. that verifies your claim?"

"I do. I can bring it to our next session."

"You are a changed man since our first session."

He didn't respond. Push him.

"Last week you were cavalier about your punishment, resigned to your fate. Now you're preparing an aggressive defense that will put a troubled young woman on the witness stand and expose her abusive past. Your attorney will drag her character through the mud and try to break her."

He remained stoic, staring blankly at me.

"After the Marcus lawsuit, other young women stepped forward to register complaints." I referred to the Church file on the table. "Gloria VanZant, a past client; Trudy Jones, a former student in your religion class; Wanda Trudeau, another ex-client, among others. What do you say in response to the claims of these women?"

He rattled off credible accounts of young, damaged women who were: either in love or infatuated with him; sex addicts; in the manic, hypersexual phase of their bipolar illness; or jumping on the lawsuit bandwagon hoping for a quick, out of court, cash settlement from the Church. He provided plausible answers to every allegation.

Or he selected his victims very well.

"One particularly troubling lawsuit comes from Paula White, a former client who suddenly terminated her sessions with you. She claims you drugged and raped her during a session."

"Miss White has multiple personality disorder. Her father sexually abused her for years. She suffers from dissociative fugue states. During that session she had a blackout episode. I did not lay a hand on her."

According to the church file, Miss White did not seek immediate medical attention afterward. Like Jenny Marcus, Paula White's tardiness to step forward was understandable but didn't help in building a case against him.

Nothing in the file held definitive proof of his guilt. No victims remembered a distinctive mole, birthmark, or other identifying physical feature on Father James. If one of them had, she wasn't talking. Reading between the lines, these women could be living in fear of him.

The preponderance of the testimony raised big red flags, but a savvy lawyer would attack its circumstantial nature. Lacking a strong witness or incriminating physical evidence, I knew where this was headed.

I thought again of Lisa Carter and others. Of how easily I could be in his shoes. Alone with a young female client in crisis, her emotions run amok from her senses, her world in upheaval. She turns to you for help. In her eyes you're exactly what's missing from her life."

Clients put their trust in us; we see them in their weakest, most naked state. Their power and control shaken and tested, they charge us to safeguard and replenish both. Trust and power, lives shatter when either is abused.

It only takes one client.

But in his case there are several.

What bothered me was something he said earlier: I'm the victim here.

Did I believe him? No.

Could I prove it? No.

I tossed the file on the table next to me, at a loss how to proceed. "Tell me about your childhood, James."

He looked at his plain Timex. "Aren't we out of time?"

"Yes, but let's push on. A Baptist minister and his wife in Iowa adopted you and your twin brother at birth. Your adoptive dad died in his sixties from complications of a stroke. Adoptive mom developed Alzheimer's and currently lives in a special care unit near Ames. How does the son of a Baptist minister wind up a Catholic priest?"

He gave a brief smile and shrug. "I traded hellfire and brimstone for ritualistic tradition and dogma. Actually, the best local schools were Catholic and Jesuit affiliated and we both showed an affinity for learning."

Interrogation

He denied any history of physical, sexual, or emotional abuse, as well as any adoptive family history of alcoholism, depression, or psychosis. His biological parents remain enigmas since both infant boys were abandoned in baskets on a park bench near the entrance to a local hospital. He denied any personal history of depression or substance abuse treatment. He described growing up in a bucolic, Midwestern, extremely conservative, religious, sexually repressed, and somewhat guilt-focused family. He regularly dated girls, was athletic, social, and a good student who, like his father, gravitated to the study of religion.

I didn't know where to go with this. "It says in the file that your twin brother is deceased. How did he die?"

He maintained a stoic exterior but seemed to tense slightly. "He was the family superstar. Genius I.Q., handsome, outgoing, All-State quarterback and baseball pitcher, full ride to the major college of his choice. He existed on a higher plain than the rest of the world. He chose USC but walked away from campus his freshman year. We heard nothing from him until word of his death."

"You didn't answer my question."

"Mother received a certified letter regretting to inform the family that her son was dead and that a package containing his personal effects would arrive soon. The letter included an outstanding hospital bill and a number to call the morgue to make plans to transport the body home."

"What was in the package that came later?"

Emotion seized his face while he looked down at his hands. "A pack of Camels and a CD."

"That was it?"

"The world lay at his feet at eighteen, by thirty-three he had nothing."

"What was the cause of death?"

"Anaphylactic shock. He was admitted for cellulitis and fever, likely from an animal bite or skin tear on his leg. He came in malnourished, had lice in his hair, and maggots in his wound. Nobody knew he was severely allergic to IV Vancomycin and by the time the nurse checked him, his heart had stopped, and CPR failed. His body was a human pin cushion from insect and flea bites, but they found no traces of alcohol or drugs in his lab work."

Where am I going with this? What the hell am I doing?

"What hospital treated him when he died?"

"A community hospital somewhere between Wichita, Kansas and the middle of nowhere. It was so tiny you could pass by it if you blinked twice. I should know, I drove past it myself. I went there looking for answers, some sort of closure, especially for mother. He was admitted there as a homeless John Doe and died as one until weeks later when the hospital social worker finally tracked down his identity after a complex series of calls starting with the lone phone number found in his jeans. None of the calls yielded any useful information other than his identity. It's as if his last fifteen years was a *tabula rasa*. He left the world the same way he entered, dropped off at a hospital. They killed my twin, my best friend, and that killed our mother."

"Was the hospital found negligent?"

"No, but some of the records had been doctored to give the impression that my brother was checked more frequently than he was— additions in the margins of progress notes that pertained to nurse checks and notes ad nauseum saying that this patient couldn't provide an accurate history of allergies. The country hospital still used paper charts, believe it or not. Little CYA things like that."

"CYA as in cover your ass?"

He nodded once and lapsed into silence.

"How did you and your mother come to terms with his death?"

"Mother never did. She isolated herself from friends and family. She no longer ventured off the farm and stopped taking care of herself and the house. She gave up on life. Her mind's gone now."

"And you?"

"I was angry. Mad at him for turning his back on us. My perfect other half was destined for greatness and died a drifter. I'll never know why. I re-dedicated my life to helping young adults stay on the right path—in therapy, guidance and career counseling, or by leading university retreats."

It's plausible.

We'd run thirty minutes over, and I had research to do and case histories to check before my next Alpha male client. He seemed eager to leave. It was time.

"One last question. How did you know Kristin Gray before you raped and killed her?"

He met my stare with one of his own. "Who's Kristin Gray? Did she file a complaint against me, too?"

"That's hard to do from the grave. You're taunting me on the phone, with that disguised voice. What have I done to you?"

He rose from the chair and walked to the door. He paused for some time, hand on the door knob, looking down, seemingly lost in thought. "I have no idea what your problem is, but you're clearly not the right person to evaluate me. I will ask the archbishop for a new therapist. Someone less prejudiced and, frankly, someone more grounded in reality."

With that, Father James was out the door and gone, likely convinced that he was in treatment with a madman.

I'm not so sure myself anymore, Father.

The Stranger within me smiled.

Strike one.

LOOSE LIPS

I heard the outer door swing open and my appointment light came on. Wolf Paxton arrived right on time for his session. He wore gray lizard-skin cowboy boots, faded stonewashed blue jeans, a darker blue denim shirt with a Mustang embroidered on the back, and topped off the bucolic ensemble with a white cowboy hat.

He grinned like he'd just eaten a pig at a barbecue.

The Stranger wanted to wipe that smirk from his face. We settled on a compromise.

"You look happy. Did you just strike black gold in the back yard, Sam?"

He stretched out his powerful legs. "You're not far off, son. I just closed a business deal, a big one. My skin's still tingling from the verbal punch and counterpunch, drawing the proverbial line in the sand. Feels like I just had sex with a beautiful woman who wants to keep coming back to the Wolf den for more."

I crossed my arms and stared at him. "I'm your therapist. I'm not your son or your friend. Does this business deal involve Warren Green?"

Ears pricked, he sat up in the leather chair as if to steel himself. There was a new hardness in his voice. "I told you before he was a man with a vision. He's a winner—if you're not with him, you're on the wrong team. I stand to clear a million dollar profit the first week on my original investment once delivery is made." He puffed out his barrel chest.

He looked ready to come on my carpet.

"Which unfriendly country did you and Green sell out to? What enemy water supply is about to be contaminated? Chemicals developed here in St. Louis that cause permanent sterility in women, marking the end of an enemy's next generation of soldiers."

His mouth formed a perfect circle. "How did—?" Then he composed himself. "You overheard a great deal that night you trespassed."

I said nothing. I wouldn't give him the satisfaction.

He leaned forward and smiled, baring his capped front teeth. "You didn't see the security cameras throughout the estate during your little mad dash out of there. Only blind luck prevented you from apprehension on the way in; a bank of cameras malfunctioned that night. They have many nice close-ups of you leaving. You're in over your head. You're damn lucky to be alive, *son*."

That didn't get a rise out of me.

He crossed one leg over the other, smoothed the sharp crease in his jeans and continued, "Go to the police if you like, but you better have proof. Your word as a trespasser and murder suspect, won't amount to a pile of horseshit next to the fine word of Dr. Green, a respected businessman and pillar of the community. The police will find an actual functioning stable with some of Elizabeth's riding ponies eating the hay you hid under. Security found threads from a pair of black jeans snagged on a nail in the trough and drops of what I'm sure is your blood. None of that matters, the police will arrest you soon for murder.

"So, continue with your little questions, if it makes you feel better."

I met his gaze. "What are you hiding? It was you who followed her in your blue Escalade the night before her murder. You staked out her apartment. I know you made a quick U-turn and sped away from me that night as I walked toward your midnight blue Escalade. Why were you following her? You could have easily returned later, followed her in the morning, and raped and killed her. You've had affairs since your wife got sick, maybe you liked what you saw and forced yourself on her. The police will want a sample of your DNA now." I picked up the receiver on the table and punched in a number. "If you don't want to explain it to me, I can have Detectives LeMaster and Baker of City Homicide here in ten minutes."

The smirk vanished and he squirmed in his chair, red-faced, while a thin bead of sweat appeared on his brow. "Stop. Put the phone down. Damn, I can't tell if you're full of shit or not. You'd make a hell of a poker player. I doubt this will stop the deal, but I value my own neck more."

I returned the phone to its cradle just as a computerized message spit out the local time and temperature in my ear. "Go on."

He rubbed his hands together much like he'd done in past sessions when frustrated and angry over his wife's health. "I followed her a few times. Both of you."

"Why?"

"Warren wanted dirt on her. He was afraid she may have overheard talk of the deal at work. He was concerned her knuckleheaded ex-husband might compromise the project. That he'd say anything to her to get back in her good graces, like brag he was about to come into money. Loose lips, you know. He wanted leverage, just in case. I never laid a hand on her."

"Who broke into her apartment?"

He hesitated, looking away.

"You know. Tell me." I reached for the phone again.

He held his hands out. "Hold your horses. Green hit the roof when we couldn't dig up anything. He decided to put her on tilt at the fund—at the party. After that, he wanted it taken to the next level."

I couldn't see Green himself doing the dirty work. "You said 'we,' who smashed in her door that morning?"

"His name's Jonathan Blue, one of Green's long-time security men. They call him Mr. Blue. You probably saw him at the party. Intense looking, wears a conservative dark suit, always carries a piece, and doesn't mind when people see it."

"The man in the dark sunglasses?"

He nodded. "I wouldn't want to be on his shit list."

I had been hiding in the dark hugging a tree trunk not five feet from Blue, trespassing on his employer's property while they were busy perfecting a covert killing machine to sell to the highest bidder.

The Wolf's brow furrowed. "Did she show you the note he left?"

That crumpled piece of paper I never got to read. Damn.

I hid my surprise. "Yes, but I want to hear the message from your mouth."

He seemed to shrink within himself when he said: *If you value your boyfriend's life, keep your fucking mouth shut.*

It sat between her legs while the cop took her statement. She chose to stuff it in her pocket and dispose of it.

Images of her lifeless body propped against the green Dumpster, her eyes frozen in horror and her hands duct-taped over her mouth, flashed before me. I wish she would have shown me the note; we could have dealt with it together. I felt sick.

Jonathan Blue. He's not a client. Were these calls a smokescreen?

If so, why the uncontrolled rage, the bludgeoning, the rape, and staged murder scene to protect a clandestine business deal? Why the cryptic symbol, II, over her heart in blood? My gut told me Mr. Blue was impersonal, all business.

"The detectives will want to know who perpetrated the attempted break-in. It's an important clue." I reached for the phone again, but he waved his hand for me to stop. "Blue could have easily entered her apartment, killed her, and stolen a stereo. Make her murder look like yet another senseless robbery in the city gone bad, but he didn't. His orders were to jimmy the door jamb a little, make enough noise to wake and scare her, and leave the note. He overdid it but didn't kill her."

"How can you be so sure, if Blue is as over the top as you describe?"

He stared at his boots, reluctant to answer. "I was the driver. I watched from the street below. It was just before dawn, but I saw everything he did on that second-floor landing. He never went inside."

"What else?"

He thought for a while. "Blue came back to the car and said the scare job gave him a boner. He embellished the break-in. After his assault on that door, a stiff wind could have knocked it down. She must have been terrified. I had no idea he was going to take it to that extreme. He cut it so close the cops that arrived at the scene passed us in their cruiser when we left."

"Green gave the order to scare her?"

He didn't answer.

"How do I know you didn't go back and kill her? Both of you are quite eager to please your master. Maybe to get a bigger slice of the pie for doing his wet work."

His eyes narrowed. "Look, I've been up front with you. I don't know who killed your girl. All I know is we left her scared, but alive. We didn't want anybody dead from this."

"Then you should have invested in golf courses. Why are you calling me, disguising your voice with a machine, bragging that you killed Kristin? Why frame me for her murder?"

His hat spun between his powerful hands. "If someone is doing that, you have bigger problems than me. I was just asked to keep an eye on a potential fly in the ointment," he said, staring at me.

"You have your own problems now, Sam."

My accusation seemed to embolden him. "I've told you everything I know. Why I said anything at all was in deference to you and a healthy respect for the police. You got some bull balls, accusing me of murder."

The Stranger entered our session. "You and your master have a lot of explaining to do to the police. Give my regards to Rita. Remember her?"

He bared his teeth again. "I'm going to let that slide because of what you've been through." His eyes narrowed again. "If I were you, I'd watch my back from here on out."

He's the second person in less than an hour to tell me that. "Are you threatening me?"

In a singsong country voice he crooned, "Mr. Blue."

The Stranger smiled. By all means, let's meet Jonathan.

Wolf donned his cowboy hat and quickly ran his fingertips along the wide brim before he walked out, leaving me just as befuddled. In a fair world, he wouldn't have the chance to ride off into the sunset to howl at the moon again.

Strike two.

GREAT WHITE SHARKS

Would these be the last therapy sessions of my career?

The Wolf's premature departure gave me extra time before my final session to run more computer searches. I called the rest of the phone numbers in Kris' appointment calendar and searched through her insurance provider statements. I replayed the recordings of the killer in search of a thread, a connection that might click from the past.

The light bulb started to sputter to life again when the phone on my desk rang.

"YOU WARNED THAT JUICY STEWARDESS GROUPIE OF YOURS," the Darth Vader voice said.

"What if I did?"

"AS PUNISHMENT, A CONFEDERATE CALLED LEMASTER AND BAKER."

A confederate? Does he have a partner in crime?

"NOW THEY KNOW YOUR BIG SECRET."

I closed my eyes and waited for the blow.

"THEY KNOW KRISTIN WAS YOUR FORMER CLIENT."

He paused, waiting for a response that never came.

"THEY KNOW THAT WAS YOUR TIE AROUND HER NECK. THEY KNOW YOU WORE IT THE DAY YOU PUNCHED THAT MAN DURING THE NEWS SEGMENT."

The Stranger wanted to scream, to hit something.

"YOU'RE FARTHER ALONG IN THE GAME THAN I EXPECTED YOU TO BE. I SUSPECT YOU CHEATED SOMEHOW ... BECAUSE THAT'S YOUR NATURE." Angry robotic laughter filled my ear, then: "THIS IS TOO EASY. NO WONDER SO MANY MURDERS GO UNSOLVED."

"I'm going to enjoy tearing you apart," The Stranger answered.

"MY JUDGMENT IS FOR YOU TO LIVE OUT YOUR DAYS IN DISGRACE IN PRISON. I WILL SEND NEWS CLIPPINGS OF MY FUTURE *WORK* WITH YOUR CLIENTS, STARTING WITH THAT LEGGY FLIGHT ATTENDANT. THAT UNFORTUNATE SOLDIER BOY IN THE HOSPITAL MAY HAVE TO RELIVE HIS INJURIES WITH ME. YOUR PARENTS, TOO. THE WORLD IS GROSSLY OVERPOPULATED. I WILL DO MY PART TO THIN THE HERD."

"You know where I am. Come get me instead."

"YOUR CLIENTS WILL LEARN THEY WOULD HAVE BEEN BETTER OFF IF THEY'D NEVER MET YOU. THAT WILL BE YOUR LEGACY."

"You'll regret you were ever born. More than you already do," The Stranger told him.

"I WILL CONTACT A BROTHER OR COMRADE IN PRISON TO MEET YOU. HE WILL REIGN DOWN PHYSICAL DEGRADATION ON YOU. MAYBE ONE DAY, BEFORE LONG-TERM INCARCERATION HAS TURNED YOUR MIND TO MUSH, I WILL TELL YOU WHY I DID THIS—"

"I like this story better," I interrupted, "You gave the cops old news. I already told them about Kris. I told them about the tie that you stole from her apartment. The detectives know I didn't kill her. They know I've recorded every phone call you've made to me. Soon they'll isolate your real voice. If you don't want to die in prison, let's settle this once and for all. Quit hiding and come to me."

Darth Vader paused. "YOU'RE BLUFFING."

I hoped I'd shaken his tree enough to cause him to act impulsively. "Suit yourself. Wait for them to break down your door. You have a few hours of freedom left. Start searching for a good rock to crawl under or a cave to hide in. Your life is over."

The Darth Vader voice continued undeterred. "YOU WILL NEVER FIND ME NOW. I'M GOING UNDERGROUND. FOR THE REST OF YOUR DAYS, YOU WILL NEVER KNOW THE TRUTH. LIVE WITH THAT."

I pushed him too far. He played his ace in the hole. "No. Please don't go. Tell me what she said that—"

The line went dead.

I will contact a brother or comrade in prison….

Is he an ex-con like Rick Arno?

The Great White shark of psych patients was up next, the last of my Alpha males, and I wondered if he would take me down, if this would be my last night as a free man.

<h1 style="text-align:center">II   II   II</h1>

Rick Arno strode through the doorway straight to the leather chair, as if doing so could speed the passage of time in my office and return him to the streets faster. He wore a black Harley-Davidson shirt, faded jeans threadbare at the right knee and boots with pointed steel toes. He had his customary three-day growth of beard, today his stringy hair was pulled back into a ponytail. He wore a shark's tooth around his neck that dangled from a plain brown leather cord.

A wary look appeared on his face. "Why did you request the extra session? Is my p.o. pissed at me or something?"

"Your name surfaced again in a criminal matter. You will tell me the truth or go back to jail. A client of mine nearly died. You were a witness. I want to know what you know about it."

His restless leg immediately stopped shaking.

"I've told you when our sessions are over you are to leave through the privacy door. You are not to return to the waiting room and talk to other clients. This is to insure confidentiality for all. You met Bob in the waiting room. You took him to Dolly's Delight massage parlor the night a group of goons beat and robbed him. He's been in a coma since. Now he's awake and talking. I know you were there and that the trip was your idea. You waited until his disability check arrived on the first of the month. Explain yourself. If you lie, I'll know. Consider me your parole officer before you answer."

He sat stunned. "You're right. I met him in the waiting room. He liked my stories about life and playing in a rock band. He looked up to me like a big bro—"

He looked to see if I was going to interrupt or challenge his claim. "—ther. He suggested we do the town one night. He was a lonely, dorky guy who wanted to meet a girl. He kept talking about your woman, the heartbreaker I saw you with. He saw some picture in your office and wouldn't shut up about her. It was getting old. I could tell from the get-go he was a sandwich or two shy of a picnic, so I said, 'Trust me, where we're going all the girls are nice,' and if he wanted to get lucky, then we had to drive out to Dolly's. He can dress up like Napoleon Bonaparte there and act nutty as a fruit bat, long as he has the green."

"How noble of you, Rick. Go on."

He cleared his throat and shifted in the chair. "I drove us there in my cherry-red Camaro. He loves my ride—"

"I know all about your car and its gravitational effect on female barflies and orgasms. What happened next?"

He closed his eyes. "We each chose a babe. Mine was Amber. She has these ginormous fake—"

"Stick to facts about Bob."

He seemed to be chewing the inside of his mouth. His hands took turns balling into fists. "We went into separate rooms in back. Afterward, I ran into the hooker he chose. She asked what the hell was wrong with my friend. I told her he was just a little slow, and then she laughed and said all he wanted to do was talk and get a massage. She'd never given a real massage before so she winged it. When his time was up, he asked her out on a date. A date. Can you believe it?" He tried to contain a snicker but couldn't.

"Dolly's advertises itself as a massage parlor, does it not?"

Rick slowly regained control over his laughter. "Sure, and I hear the people who go to strip clubs on the east side go for the room temperature, ten-dollar beers."

"Did you see Bob get into a fight at Dolly's? Did you see him hauled into a truck by a group of men?"

Rick scratched old pockmarks on his nose and shook his head. "I never saw the dude there again. His hooker thought he left when me and Amber were upstairs."

"What did you do then?"

"I waited for him until three in the morning, drinking and chatting up the girls. Then maybe I heard one of them say that the bouncers had escorted a guy out earlier because he was bad for business. Asking customers all sorts of questions. Duh! Clients like their privacy. I cruised the parking lot and when I didn't find him, I split."

I glared at him.

He caved. "What was I supposed to do, end up bleeding in the same ditch with Forrest Gump?"

Maybe I heard. You heard plenty. If only real life was as kind to the Forrest Gumps of the world as the movie was.

"How did you know Bob was bleeding in a ditch if you weren't involved?

He was stalling, trying to invent an answer that never came.

"Déjà vu all over again. You abandoned Bob forty miles from home at a brothel, like the young woman with asthma you ditched along a roadside. What do you do to your enemies, like me?"

Rick looked perplexed and on the defensive. "I looked for him and he was gone. The dude had no phone." He raised his voice, fists balled. "Who the fuck doesn't have a cell phone these days?" He'd reached fight or flight mode but made no effort to leave.

"Did you see or hear from him again?'

"No," he said, looking at me sideways.

"You're lying."

"I called his house the next day." He shrugged. "No answer, no machine, of course."

"You witnessed the beating, didn't you?"

He closed his eyes and turned away. He didn't answer.

"DIDN'T YOU?" I shouted.

Startled, he looked down. After a minute, he nodded.

"Did you take part in it?"

He looked me in the eyes. "No, I swear."

"You can connect names to faces of those who did?"

He nodded again, nervous. "I had to give him to the dark man."

"That makes you an accessory to first degree assault. You'd return to prison for that."

He sat stiff in the chair. I could tell he was scared.

"You have a prior relationship with DeLuca or you'd be in the hospital bed next to Bob."

In his silence I read the expression on his face. "You do, don't you? Tell me about him."

He fidgeted with the bottom of his shirt and scratched his stubble. "This goes nowhere? Not even my p.o?"

"If you tell me the truth."

He massaged the bridge of his nose with his fingertips like he had a migraine. "I worked for him the week he moved Dolly's from the boonies to Jefferson County. It was in the hot summer. I drove a rusted U-Haul van at the tail end of a convoy of trucks and ate a ton of dust. Helped his crew set-up and organize the counters, magazine and video racks, massage tables, beds, sex toys, peepshows, and trailers out back for the girls."

He made eye contact with me. "Punching him on television made you a marked man. He's a righteous badass."

"Does he know you see me in therapy?"

"I don't think so, but I wouldn't underestimate him."

"What else can you tell me about him?"

"During the set-up, this twitchy little tweaker got nabbed on a five-finger discount. DeLuca's right hand man KC caught him in the act."

"What did he steal?"

"Half a trunk load of sex flicks, skin rags, feather boas, lotions, condoms, strap-ons, and cock rings. Penny ante crap, but the dark man wanted to make an example out of him. We had to watch while the bouncers tied him to a chair and beat his face bloody. Then the dark man poured gasoline over him while he eyeballed us individually. He struck matches around him, coming closer and closer. The tweaker started to cry and bargain with him, then peed his pants when DeLuca didn't answer. The dark man quoted Bible verses about stealing. He had this calm, detached look on his face like when a cat toys with a mouse. The dark man patted his head, reassured him it would all be over soon. He smiled and cut his hands free. We looked at each other, thinking the big scare was over. A glimmer of hope returned to the little dude's face. The dark man tossed him a towel but the tweaker didn't know his upper body remained tied to the chair. DeLuca tossed one more match and lit him up like a Roman candle."

He appeared to relive the scene and shudder. "Meth freak's hopping up and down on the chair like a flaming Mexican jumping bean. Screaming and crying, all the time he's trying to put out the fire on his face and body with the towel." Rick tried but failed to stifle a nervous laugh. "The bouncers laughed so hard their sides ached. Meth freak overturned the chair. His head hit the floor, hard. The jerking and twitching stopped and the place grew quiet. KC finally turned a hose on the poor bastard and then collected winning bets from some of the others. The tweaker had either passed out or was dead. They left him tied to that chair, smoking. He wasn't moving. The dark man looked each of us drivers in the eyes and said: *This is what happens when you fuck with my business.*"

"What happened to the man after that?"

"I don't know. KC and the dark man ordered us all back to work to finish the set up. The next time we had a chance to look, meth freak was gone. I guess the bodyguards disposed of him."

I imagine Rick laughed his ass off along with the others, grateful it wasn't him in the chair.

There was nothing of substance to immediately pursue in Rick's story. Though there was a victim, there was no body, and no one to back up Rick's claim. Nevertheless, I said, "Would you testify to this in court?"

Rick looked at me as if I'd grown another head. "And wind up worse than that meth flambé tweaker? No way, Jose. Jefferson County is to methamphetamine as Columbia is to cocaine. The dark man is well connected in Jeff. Co. I'd rather do hard time and don't even think about using my p.o. against me."

I believed him.

"You saw what DeLuca did to the thief. You had a good idea what Bob was in for, yet you did nothing."

He sat quietly seething.

Where was I going with this anyway and how does it help me find Kris's killer? I didn't think DeLuca or his muscle-bound monkeys killed her, but I wanted to put the dark man away. I need more from Bob to accomplish that. Time to shift gears.

He hates you. Use that.

Kris' duct-taped death scream flashed before my eyes as I returned my attention to Rick.

"How clever of you to invent Bob's fascination with my girlfriend, but Bob was in a hospital bed fighting for his life when you attacked her. You saw us that evening outside her apartment. She turned you on. You followed us, didn't you?"

"What? No, I—"

"Why did you kill her? Why are you calling me in a disguised voice, promising to ruin my life even more? What have I done to you?"

He sat as still as a partridge in high grass about to be flushed. At last he said, "Your girlfriend ... somebody snuffed her?"

Not the response I expected.

I nodded.

"Bummer, man," he sniffed. "She was hot."

"I know how you feel about me. I've also lobbied to shut down DeLuca's prostitution ring. You admitted you worked for him. Is he your drug supplier and fence, too?"

He didn't answer.

"Was it your idea or his? Did he hire you to kill her as payback for me blowing the whistle on Dolly's? Did you rape her as a fringe benefit of the deal?"

He sat rigid in the client chair; his hands gripped the armrests so tightly his knuckles turned white. "I don't know what your game is, man. I've done a lot of things I'm not proud of, but I never snuffed the life from anybody."

"You killed Kris. WHY?"

He stood and strode to the door. "You're the one who needs help. You're crazy as that goofy dude who asked a hooker out on a date. Try to send me back to prison on this bogus charge and you're in for a fight. You won't find me hanging around the waiting room in this cuckoo's nest anymore."

He slammed the door behind him.

I exhaled and rubbed my aching forehead, feeling defeated.

Great, now the clients are calling me nuts to my face.

Thanks to in part to The Stranger, all my practice needs now is a bare light bulb swinging from the ceiling and a water boarding area. I've started the Dick Cheney School of therapy, where recidivism is zero because no one survives the treatment. What have I done to my three clients? And it didn't lead me closer to the killer.

What to do next? A dive into a giant Tanqueray swimming pool sounded good.

Strike three, I'm out. I failed. The killer will get away with murder. I'll be in prison while the killer plans to target my parents and clients.

If that pubic hair matches my DNA, I'm going to jail. Too much time has passed. I need a miracle—an eyewitness to step forward, a startling new evidence find, or the killer to get drunk in a bar and brag about the crime to an off-duty cop.

Get ready to be arrested, Mitch. You're in for a long hard road.

I'd gone all-in with my chips; certain the killer was one of my three Alpha males. They called my bluff each time. Had one of them misdirected me down the wrong rabbit hole?

I wanted to scream, but instead let out a strangled groan which, like a prayer, went unanswered. I fell to the floor, defeated.

I missed something. Deductive reasoning hadn't led me to the killer. I'm trying too hard. I've got to let it go. Let Kris go. I must free my mind. Listen to the world around me, focus. Achieve a higher level of consciousness.

I sat and rested with my legs crossed. I thought of the Buddhist practice of mindfulness and their belief that life is pain and suffering. I'd meditated before, but it had been a while, so I struggled at first, to let go of all my anger at the unfairness of life. But in time I began to feel more at peace. I rested in the bare awareness of new thoughts, feelings, and perceptions while they occurred to me. I allowed new neuronal connections to occur. If I observed every thought that passed through my mind, my limited self would dissolve and be replaced by a more serene and spacious sense of awareness. I don't know how long I sat this way, but out of the emptiness I achieved what Buddhists call the clear light of mind.

This clarity called to me and I listened. My stream of thought flowed to my birth, to everyone I'd met in my life or heard about in history. This seemed to last forever but may have been an eye blink. I lost track of time. A rapid-fire hodgepodge of images and thoughts appeared before me: Adam and Eve, the Ying/Yang symbol, pictures of Buono and Bianchi, the duality of good and evil, police sketches of the Zodiac killer, a Schwarzenegger and DeVito comedy, the infamous law students Leopold and Loeb, the actress Julia Roberts, the grim faces of LeMaster and Baker, and the shy, smiling face of my first crush, a little grade-school girl. These images and thoughts repeated in my mind like a continuous film loop.

There had to be some connection between these diverse things—the first couple on earth, the duality of male and female, the Hillside Stranglers, good and evil, the Zodiac Killer who was believed to have been one man and was never caught, the movie *Twins*, two sociopathic lawyers in the early twenty-first century who murdered a fourteen year old boy in a plan to commit the perfect crime, a famous current movie actress, my detective antagonists, and a nice, cute former classmate.

The light bulb flickered and went out.

Couples, duos, duality, male/female, criminal and comedy pairs, and twins. Singles that didn't fit were the Zodiac Killer, Julia Roberts, and the girl from grade school. But they had to, somehow.

Julia Roberts has an actor brother Eric. A twin brother.

Rochelle, the cute little girl with the nice smile, has a twin sister Michelle.

Only the Zodiac Killer didn't fit.

I thought of the signs. The light bulb flickered.

The symbol Ⅱ. Gemini. Close to the heart. Twins.

The light bulb stayed on.

The pieces suddenly fell in place like Tetris blocks. It made perfect sense, to a sick mind.

I had to journey all the way back to the beginning. My neophyte theory jibed when I thought back to how I first met Kris and even further back, to the first days of my graduate practicum.

I should have stayed with you. He couldn't resist running his mouth. His hubris betrayed him after all.

I quickly ran computer searches with a more focused direction. I recalled every memory I could of my first River City State Hospital psychiatric patient ten years ago when I heard a knock on my office door. No wonder I missed it the first time. He's a clever, cunning killer as well as an accomplished liar and actor. He twisted the story enough for me to be unable to piece it together earlier. Without access to the murder file, the clandestine tapes of our phone conversations, her insurance records, and a long memory of my early years as a fledgling therapist, I would have been helpless against him. The worn paper in Kris' Manila folder further sealed the mystery.

A decade old chart gathering dust in the Medical Records Department at River City State Hospital on Arsenal held the key to begin to understand the motivations of a killer. The knocking grew louder.

The world appeared a bit brighter and more balanced than a minute ago. I should have meditated earlier. The answer came to me when I quit trying so hard. When you stop searching for something is often when you find it. When you don't think about hitting a home run is when you do.

The person was pounding now. Insistent.

Knowledge is power, and I was certain the man who killed Kris stood outside, banging on my door. I knew who he was. One way or another this ends tonight.

THE MOON WILL TURN TO BLOOD

The pounding rattled my office door. I composed myself, flipped the switch on my Dictaphone to "on," and opened the door to find the Alpha male I expected staring me in the face. He glided into my office and closed the door behind him.

"I hope I'm not interrupting. I forgot my umbrella."

"Let me get it for you. I thought you were going to beat my door down for it," I said, not taking my eyes from him, but he reached the stand before I could. The palpable tension in the room sucked the air from my chest.

Where was The Stranger when I needed him?

I approached Father James. "Why did you kill her?"

He reached into a fold of his umbrella and produced a small handheld device of some kind Velcroed to its inside. He pointed it at my chest.

"Not another step. This is a police issue Taser X26. It is an electroshock weapon with a range of thirty-five feet. It causes instantaneous neuromuscular incapacitation. This pulse model will bring down a subject wearing a level three body armor vest. It will penetrate your clothing with ease, should you get any more bright ideas. People occasionally die when tased, but they usually had prior health issues or were children." He smiled. "A fringe benefit is that it really, really hurts." He locked the door to the outside world and jammed the back of a chair against the knob. "Walk around the desk. Sit in your chair." I took my time, thinking. He followed a cautious three steps behind and ordered me to walk faster.

I sat in the leather chair as instructed while he yanked the nearest phone cord out of the wall. I pointed at the Taser. "Between that and the voice scrambler, it appears you enjoy weapons and spy toys, Father. Is this standard issue for the priesthood now?"

He laughed.

"The Boss Voice Changer is not a scrambling device. It provides complete control of timbre, tone, reverb, and pitch. The human voice is made up of two components. The first is pitch-sensitive waves and the second is non-pitch-sensitive fixed harmonics, which vary with the vocal cords and the actual size and shape of the vocal tract. The BVC cloaks everything. I could have chosen Mickey Mouse, a cute little girl, or a kindly old man. Even multiple voices to make you believe a gang of killers was framing you. Darth Vader seemed apropos. Anyone with seven hundred dollars can buy one of these beauties on eBay—you d be amazed how simple it's been for me to obtain anything I want for my … avocation."

"I must admit you thought of almost everything."

He frowned upon hearing my qualifier and leveled the Taser at my chest. "When I was in practice full-time, I had a panic button to press in case a client became violent. I looked for one as I walked around your office during our first visit. Too bad you opted not to have one. Empty your pockets."

I reached into both front and back pockets as commanded. He confiscated my cell phone and left the change and wallet on my walnut desk.

"This answers my question from our first session."

"What was that?"

"The different meanings of grace. You're in need of the third one."

He smirked. "You are the clever one but look where it got you. I wish I could have been in the morgue to see the look on your face when you identified her. Leaving your card in her pocket was a nice touch."

"If you're the Marquis de Sade."

I chewed the inside of my mouth to conceal my budding anger and fear. "I assume this confirms your guilt of the sexual harassment charges filed against you by Jenny Marcus and the other university students."

"Guilty as charged, but you suspected that from day one." He pointed behind me. "Your iPad on the desk over there, hand it over."

I complied.

"Don't think about screaming for help. If you do, you experience the Taser. When you awake with a gag, your punishment will multiply exponentially."

"Now I know why you paused at the door earlier. I wish I'd checked your umbrella. You considered grabbing your weapon. Why didn't you?"

The smirk on his face widened to a grin. "Does it matter? At first I wanted to see you publicly disgraced and sent to prison, but I'm flexible. I decided to let fate decide."

He produced a thick roll of gray duct tape from a back pocket and tossed it in my lap.

"Tape your right wrist to the armrest, tight as you can. Refuse and I will tase you."

I wanted to maintain a dialogue because the more we spoke, the longer I delayed whatever he had in mind.

"I know why you murdered Kris. She's payback for the death of your brother."

He failed to check the surprise that played briefly on his face. "Impressive. How did you make the connection so quickly, given the red herrings and limited accurate information I supplied?"

"It wasn't that difficult," I lied. "The symbol II you drew over her heart in blood is the Gemini sign for twins. You carry a torch for your dead brother. You harbor an idealized vision of his memory long after his accidental death—"

"Accidental? You and the quack turned him into a walking zombie. You ripped out his soul and left an empty shell," he interrupted, a sudden fierceness in his eyes.

"You left other clues. We'll discuss them later. It's common for people to idealize a loved one after their death, even amoral people with delusions of grandeur such as yourself. It's much safer for your fractured sense of self to compartmentalize and repress the negative memories, remember only the positive attributes—"

"You're stalling. Secure that wrist now," he said with a snarl. He looked ready to spit on me.

"But you can only do that for so long until some trigger clicks in your black-and-white world and you explode. You harbor intense hatred toward women. What did mother do to you?"

"Shut up and do as I say!"

My question seemed to vex him while he paced and made furtive glances at the door, even though the H-shaped suite of rooms was silent as a catacomb. No other therapists occupied the offices at this time of night. Maybe I'd planned this all wrong, being alone. My office was at the back of the layout, too isolated for my liking now.

He watched intently as I cinched the tape ever tighter around my right wrist. "Someone helped you. The police didn't release the Gemini symbol to the press."

When I didn't answer he said, "You may be smart, but you're the one who's incapacitated. I'm the only murderer in this room who'll walk away a free man."

"Nobody killed Jack—"

"You fried his brain!"

I struggled to work the roll faster while his pacing intensified.

"That's enough tape. Put your left arm on the chair rest. Resist me with your free hand in any way and I tase you." He grabbed the roll from me and began taping my left arm to the chair so tight it hurt."

"Why are you tying my arms to the chair?" I said, as if someone could hear.

He smiled and said nothing, staring through me. His eyes were vacant. "No one can hear you."

The duct tape spun rapidly off the roll with a shrill *skree skree* sound. Now my words were my only weapon. I thought of the unfortunate wannabe thief DeLuca tortured and fought to block the image of me flopping to the floor with a fiery chair strapped on my back. My heart skipped some beats and my mouth went dry. I started to sweat.

I'm at the mercy of a man who has none.

Now that I was secured, he seemed to relax a bit and sat on the edge of my desk, assessing me. He placed the Taser on the table and crossed his legs like we were two colleagues discussing a challenging case.

Under no circumstance could I let him cover my mouth. Keep him talking.

He said, "You should be groveling before me, begging for your life, but even now you're smug. Why is that?"

"That's the way I am. I rub people the wrong way. I don't think I was breastfed. Were you?"

"You do realize what's about to happen to you?"

"Why don't you provide me with the gory details? I know you want to."

He said, "Not yet. You can't phone for help and you're restrained. Why *are* you so confident?"

I smiled at him. "Knowing you murdered Kris has lifted a weight off me. The truth has set me free."

He waggled a finger at me. "I don't believe you. You should be losing your wits by now. Crying, wetting yourself, bargaining, begging for mercy. Giving me the respect I deserve, for I hold your life in my hands. I am God to you. I have mastered the wrath of God. I have become the Will of God. To be God is the ultimate rush. To reign and destroy as He pleases."

"You're right. You've been right the whole time. Do what you have to do. Just do it quick."

He looked skeptical. "No. First we have to talk. Like Mendez, you must acknowledge your sins and repent or the retribution's not the same." He paused and smiled. "You and I are very similar."

"No, we're not. You delight in hurting others. I try to help people."

"You get off on the power of your chair. You use it when it serves you."

I looked up at him. "So, crazy Jumpin' Jack Flash was your twin brother. You know what they say about the apple and the tree."

His jaw muscles tensed. He slapped me hard with an open hand. "He is Jumping Jack Parks, All-American quarterback and National Merit Scholar, not this Flash caricature you and the mental health system concocted to dishonor him."

His punch packed a wallop. My lip bled and I tasted blood as it trickled down my chin. "You're right. At one point Jack was all that and more. But he stopped being Jumping Jack Parks, USC golden boy, long before fate blew him to a state psychiatric ward halfway across the country. By then he was a John Doe, whose only coherent words were the lyrics to the Rolling Stones' song *Jumpin' Jack Flash.* You dishonor him by your actions—"

"Liar!" He hit me again. Harder, this time with a closed fist. I saw stars. This time he loosened a tooth.

"Interesting. I'm a liar yet you spoon fed me a yarn about Jack dying in a rural Iowa hospital from an allergic reaction."

He smirked. "If I provided a closer version of the truth, you would have figured it out. Where's the fun in that? I must admit you had me going for a moment on the phone when you claimed to know the killer's identity. I considered not showing, but when the session began, I could tell you didn't know. You bluffed your way this far, farther than I ever imagined you could, but your luck ends here. Bully for you that you figured it out; too bad, so sad it's too late for you to do anything about it."

Talking buys me time. And so I kept talking.

THE WILL OF GOD

"A cop brought in a John Doe one winter morning. It was my third day as a practicum student on the psych unit. As far as the cop could piece together, John Doe must have hitched a ride east from Colorado with truckers along Highway 64 when he became psychotic at a city diner. He began screaming and throwing silverware at other patrons. He stripped off his clothes and ran naked into an nearby yard to make snow angels. The manager called 911 and John Doe was brought to the psych ER. He was the first patient I ever treated."

Just lucky, I guess.

"He was agitated and paranoid, not oriented to person, place, or time when he arrived. He couldn't provide any history or tell us his name. He carried no identification. He constantly sang that Stones song, so some of the staff took to calling him Jumpin' Jack Flash. River City State Hospital gets more than its share of transients and homeless, especially in extreme weather. He was a danger to himself and others when he arrived. Dr. Mendez admitted Jack—"

"Ah, hapless old Dr. Mendez. I wonder whatever happened to him." He smiled as if bathing in the afterglow of a happy reminiscence.

Mendez was the on-call psychiatrist the day John Doe came through the ER doors of River City. Any shrink worth his salt would have been ethically and professionally bound to admit him. He was delusional and malnourished—his body a tapestry of contusions, superficial scrapes, and old track marks. He had needle marks between his toes and under his tongue. His front teeth showed decay, most likely from poly-substance abuse, poor nutrition, and bad hygiene. His discolored and raised fingernails the telltale signs of chronic alcoholism.

Interrogation

When I started my practicum at River City, Mendez had one foot out the door to retirement. He was a competent doc when not on his high horse. He took his role as gatekeeper in the ER seriously. He harbored a deep-seated resentment for those who feigned suicidal thoughts to hideout from the law or a gang, for homeless people looking to get out of extreme weather, for poor people who'd run out of food, money, and medication between disability checks, and for the non-compliant, mentally ill who missed appointments. He considered health care a privilege and not a right, even though most of our patients had no insurance or Medicaid. I think he believed the ever-shrinking amount of money our red state allotted for the indigent and disabled came right out of his own pocket.

By now Jorge Mendez, the reclusive little River City State Hospital shrink from Brazil who wore over-sized glasses that seemed to wrap around his entire head and magnify his eyes to fly-like proportions, had retired years ago. His wife died a year before he retired and, with their grown children scattered across the country in residency programs, he lived alone in St. Louis. A former colleague who still works in the state system told me Mendez had passed away not long ago. A heart attack, at home alone.

"From the delight in your voice, I gather you already know Mendez died recently."

He smirked and folded his arms. "The detective force in this city is consistent, I give them that. People say getting away with murder is hard. Is there no one to challenge me? Who out there is worthy to be my foil? Not the police. Certainly not you."

My eyebrow rose. "You're saying Mendez didn't die alone?"

He stared at me with what I took to be scorn or pity. "Do you remember the amount of hair that myopic old quack had? Didn't the police wonder why a nearly bald man would use a hair dryer in the bathtub? I even left the box and receipt in the house. Like most people, Mendez was a creature of habit. He drew his bath at nine every night. All I needed to do was buy the blow dryer at a nearby Walgreen's. The chain is so darn convenient. There's one of them or a CVS on almost every other corner in the city, isn't there? Anyway, he liked to leave his back door open to catch the breeze coming through the screen. I forced the screen door latch and walked into his bedroom. He drank half a bottle of Merlot with dinner every night and liked to finish it in the tub. No doubt trying to wash away his past sins and shut out the demons of memory. His feeble attempts at absolution failed, he'd developed quite the drinking problem over the years. He was content to anesthetize himself to his crimes against man and God. I wasn't about to let him forget that easily. We had a spirited discussion about Jack and his own salvation. Regrettably, we didn't see eye to eye."

I've fallen into the hands of a multiple murderer.

"You must be very proud of yourself, Father."

He ignored my comment. "I offered him the Last Rites before I reunited him with his dead wife, but he said he no longer believed in God, and he never once begged for his life. He knew he'd misdiagnosed and mistreated Jack. He saw the light and agreed that ECT had been the wrong treatment for Jack. By the end of our consultation, the sad little man *wanted* me to toss the dryer in the water so I could reunite him with his beloved Imelda. Tub electrocution is not always a sure thing, so I brought along a box of Epsom salts for better conductivity. He had also urinated in the tub while we spoke, which upped the voltage. There was no dramatic burning of the skin or smoking hair like you see when it's portrayed on television. He thrashed and jerked; he foamed at the mouth and nostrils some. His bowels emptied. The voltage may have killed him or maybe he slipped into ventricular fibrillation. He slid down into the water so maybe the cause of death was drowning. The flesh on his flank that had been parallel to the water level appeared paler than the rest of his body and I noticed some mild blistering. No fuse blew, no circuit breaker tripped." He paused while a look of bemusement came over him. "I fished the hair dryer out and, to my surprise, it still worked! I pay attention to and learn from the trivia and minutiae of my craft. I turned it back on of course and tossed it in the tub."

He laughed sardonically. "Mendez allowed the soft science of his chosen profession to take precedence over his Catholic faith. I restored peace and dignity to his Golden Years. I even cured his alcoholism and depression."

What a horrific way to die. I sat dumbfounded in silence, wondering what awaited me.

"There's a certain symmetry to their ends, wouldn't you agree? It doesn't restore order to the universe, but it's a start," he said, making certain I saw him glance at the nearby Taser on my table. My stomach did a slow barrel roll.

"So," he said, as he rose from the desk and paced. "Let's talk about *your* role in Jack's treatment at the State Hospital." He put a hand up to his face and stroked his square chin, reminding me of a former anatomy professor who liked to pose before grilling his class on the functions of the medulla oblongata and hypothalamus.

"You don't have to tie me up to discuss Jack's care," I said. "Unless you've already judged and sentenced me, too. How about we dispense with the kangaroo court, already?"

"This is your trial. Defend yourself."

"Who did you kill before you became a priest?"

He waggled his finger at me again. "Don't change the subject. We're here to address your sins. Being an important member of the interdisciplinary treatment team, you obviously concurred with Mendez' decision to proceed full steam ahead with a course of bilateral electroconvulsive therapy."

He looked once again at the Taser and back to me.

"May I remind you that this happened nine or ten years ago?"

He nodded impatiently as if he was speaking to a child. "Continue."

"As I recall, Mendez first treated Jack's presenting problem with anti-psychotics. He went by the book. The staff provided a safe environment and did their best to get some nutrition and vitamins in him while he frenetically bounced around the ward strutting like Mick Jagger on stage, singing that song over and over. Sometimes he enlisted other ward patients to act as back-up singers, with varying degrees of success. Other days he was so out of control he required five-point restraints in addition to chemical ones to protect himself and others. When the delusions stopped, he lapsed into a profound catatonic depression. He refused to eat and, as I said, came to us already malnourished. He remained a blank slate, we had no health history to work from and the only words he uttered were those damn song lyrics while he puffed out his lips like Jagger. You admitted that Jack walked away from being the Big Man on Campus years ago. Who knows what traumas and abuse he endured during those lost years to become the homeless psychotic who eventually entered our ER? Everyone tried to help Jack and work with him because he was a human being in crisis who needed help. The profound depression Jack fell into didn't respond to trials of the latest anti-depressants. There's nothing unusual in how Mendez treated Jack. On some level you must know that.

"You weren't there nine years ago. If you've carried out this vendetta relying on information coerced from Mendez or gleaned from Jack's old chart, you are in no position to judge the people who did everything they could to help your brother. Am I getting through to you?"

His facial muscles grew taut. "You and Mendez went before a judge and conned him into authorizing the electroshock. You turned him into a walking vegetable. First with the drugs, then with a 'course' of fifteen shock treatments, as if it's a menu item one indulges in with friends."

James's delusions seemed well-developed, fixed, and unshakable. His behavior was escalating. He was blinded to the fact that his brother's catatonia put him at risk of dying. ECT can be an effective treatment, even as a last resort.

If he expected a new doctorate practicum student to dissuade a board-certified psychiatrist with thirty years' experience from treating his own patient with ECT after numerous medication trials had failed, talking my way out of this chair was doomed. I attended the involuntary commitment hearing as an observer, I provided no testimony. The image of Rick's drug-addled co-worker on fire and bound to a chair while DeLuca and his goons looked on and laughed once again intruded into my thoughts.

Let's see if I can sell swastikas to the Pope today, Tony.

"You and I share an ingrained professional prejudice against Electroconvulsive Therapy. We help others with our words, not by strapping them to a table and passing enough electricity through their brains to induce a seizure. Jack's psychosis didn't respond to medication and he'd slipped into a severe catatonic depression that put his life at risk. ECT was not used as a form of punishment like it was in *One Flew over the Cuckoo's Nest.* Jack needed quick symptom relief after other treatments had failed. Mendez gave the logical next step a try. It eventually snapped him out of his catatonia. As a clinician, you know this."

Father James looked at his fingernails as if he was unhappy with a manicure. "Don't waste your last words trying to bond with me—"

"You read his chart, but you weren't with us a decade ago. A paper chart crudely encapsulates a patient's stay, it doesn't begin to show all the hard work of the staff. It can't describe the severity and depth of Jack's illness—how the disease stole his self from him, how it executed him before he came to us, forcing him to stand and look down at his own living corpse. Laymen can't comprehend this, but with our training we can."

"Enough! You're postponing the inevitable. You're about to feel what Jack experienced."

I ignored his threat. "Jack ceased being Jack long before he was wheeled through those ER doors. ECT didn't kill Jumpin' Jack Flash."

He hit me hard on the jaw again. "His name is Jack Parks!"

I shook off the cobwebs while I scrambled to think of a way not to die. To keep driving home the point that Jumping Jack Parks had ceased to be and morphed into Jumpin' Jack Flash long before he arrived in St. Louis only stoked his rage.

Before I could think of one, two wires exploded from the Taser and imbedded in my chest. Every muscle in my body locked like a giant cramp. It felt like someone beat me up and down my back with a two-by-four while someone else tightened a wire from my forehead to the base of my neck. My shoulders hunched to my ears. My toes curled, my jaw locked, and if I hadn't been taped to a chair I would have fallen to the floor. It was the longest five seconds of my life. I lost all physical control but remained conscious.

I watched him remove the leads and set about loading another charge.

He smirked until that handsome face clouded over again. "The therapist in me can't resist asking: how did that make you feel? Was that barbaric enough for you?"

Something he said earlier made me think. When in doubt, delve further into the past.

"Thanks for the memory jog. Why are your last names different?"

He shrugged. "Some of what I told you is true. We *were* left on a bench near an Iowa hospital on a twenty-degree morning. Our birth mother let fate decide whether we lived or died. A passerby found us. She left a note in the basinet saying the voices in her head commanded her to kill us because we were evil. The note also said the birth father wanted nothing to do with us and had left her. It ended with, 'Don't bother to look for me, because I plan to kill myself. Evil begets evil, Wanda.'

"Your birth mother suffered from post-partum psychosis."

He nodded. "Probably, or schizophrenia or a psychotic depression. We'll never know. I tracked Wanda Fogerty down, though. She was sixteen when she jumped off a roof a month later." His face darkened. "Back to Jack. Tell me about his response to ECT, your work with him, and the day he escaped."

There was much more to his childhood story, but could I maneuver and cajole him back to it? I watched him reload the Taser.

"All food intake stopped when Jack became catatonic. It was either ECT or a feeding tube but the medical team agreed ECT was the preferable option. During the treatments, the catatonia lifted, his mood began to improve, he ate enough food to stay alive, but he still didn't say a word or sing a lyric. I tried individual therapy, group therapy, play therapy, biofeedback, introducing various stimuli into his immediate environment such as music, radio, television, art, cartoons, video games, and pictures of hundreds of subjects. A football game came on television one day while he sat in a community room. He became agitated and charged the staff. It took four orderlies to keep the other patients safe and place him in five-point restraints. I asked him about it later but of course he never answered. Pictures of football games and family scenes at times provoked similar turmoil, but he remained mute. It was clear he harbored great shame or fear over some traumatic event. You've obviously read my notes in his file. You already know my suspicions that Jack had repressed severe physical, emotional, or sexual abuse."

James looked me in the eye and calmly Tasered me again, in almost the exact same spot on my chest. The pain and spasms were worse and lasted longer. I passed out briefly. When I came to, my teeth ached from grinding them together.

I felt hands grab me by the shirt. "My, you're getting hot under the collar. I bet a nice drink of cold water would taste good about now. What do you say, Swinger?" He held a cup of water in his hand. As he brought it close to my mouth he spilled it on my chest, soaking my shirt.

I'm alone with him and about to die. This must be how Kris felt. Keep your wits about you. Let the cobwebs clear before you speak. Don't react to him. I never did get Jack to open up to me. Just like when I was ten with those two kids when hell and earth collided. Practice never makes perfect, but it does make a better therapist. Classroom theory only takes you so far, you learn by observation and doing. Armed with experience and what I know now, I could have helped those kids, but Jack was a different story.

He finished reloading. "You may continue with your defense."

"The day of his death, Jack slipped through a door on the locked unit. I think he finally felt ready to return to life on the road. Staff saw the elopement and chased him onto Sublette Avenue, where a postal service truck idled unattended while the mailman walked a package to a front door. Jack stole the truck and hospital security called the cops. He made it all the way to the Poplar Street Bridge, going east into Illinois. He wouldn't stop for the cruisers that tried to force the truck into the guardrail. Ramming into the cop cars, the taller blue and white postal truck jumped the guardrail and plunged into the Mississippi with Jack behind the wheel. It was the dead of winter; twenty degrees with ice floes drifting downstream."

He splashed more ice water on my shirt front and in my panic I remembered the fate of Dr. Mendez. Keep talking, keep him talking.

"Divers searched and dredged the river for days, but the water level was high that winter and the current too strong. Massive amounts of driftwood and silt hindered recovery efforts. Days later and miles downstream, rescue workers fished the truck out of the water, but no Jack. Experts figured the body would eventually be found weeks later even farther south. Police at the scene estimated the truck left the bridge going ninety miles an hour and plunged the equivalent of a ten-story building before it hit the icy water. They put the odds of anyone surviving such a concussive force of impact and the freezing temperatures at a thousand to one. Witnesses corroborated his elopement, including a visitor who was near the door to the ward. People living near the hospital saw Jack drive off in the postal truck. The hospital treated Jack's escape as a sentinel event, one involving the death or serious injury of a patient.

Independent state agencies launched a full-scale investigation. No criminal wrongdoing or negligence was found, but double doors were recommended and installed on all the locked units."

He shook his head. "More lies. You cover for one another. The hospital bribed the visitor and neighbors in order to keep their accreditation. Mendez manipulated and altered Jack's chart to cover up his incompetent care, nurses and techs added notes after the fact to whitewash the record for the review board."

"The bloated and decomposed body of a man matching Jack's body type was pulled from the river miles downstream months later, but dental records were not a match."

He pointed a finger at me again. "You couldn't even get my brother to talk. You weren't there for him when he felt he had no choice but escape your torture chamber. You're all accomplices to murder. You and Mendez drove him off that bridge."

I was assessing another patient when I heard of Jack's elopement, but James was beyond reason. My presiding judge and jury will not abandon his pre-conceived conspiracy theories. This decompensating psychopath entrenched in a fixed delusion will soon be my executioner. How many more Taser shots was he planning? Jack had eight ECT treatments. How many more shots could my heart take?

My hands tingled, then turned numb and ashen from the tape cutting off the blood flow. I had to play one of my aces in the hole. "I know Kris saw you for one session after she separated from her husband. I know she stopped seeing you because you hit on her and thought you were, in her word, spooky. Did you kill her out of revenge or fear she would expose you?"

His face registered surprise. "I'm impressed. She told you about our session?"

"No. I found records of old appointments. Like I said, it wasn't that difficult," I lied. I had to know. He was right, I was salivating to know the truth. "Did you kill her out of revenge?" I heard the desperation in my raised voice.

His smile morphed into that creepy leer. "There's more than meets the eye. Back then I provided on-campus counseling to students and, as you know, I have a certain predilection to beautiful young women. At the end of our session, I tried to schedule a second one but she declined. Years before, I learned of my brother's commitment and murder. My Roman Catholic collar helped me gain access to his hospital file. After all, who turns down a grieving priest whose brother has been pronounced dead? That's where I happened upon your name and that of Mendez. Imagine my surprise when your name resurfaced years later with Kristin. You had a vested interest in seeing her marriage end. How dare she reject me for you, the man who helped destroy my brother?"

We'd met by chance a year after her session with him, but I was in no position to split hairs.

"When I'm done here, I will make an anonymous call to the police," he said. They will be shocked by what they find. Thanks to me, Swinger, you will be front page news. You will be famous—no, infamous."

A picture was beginning to take shape.

He turned to the computer at my desk and pulled up a chair in front of it.

I took advantage of his activity to speak. "Upstanding parents with strict, conservative religious and family values adopted you and Jack. Why did you go before a judge to change your last name to that of the birth mother who left you both for dead and later killed herself?"

The blank white screen of my word processing program appeared and he began to type. His fingers stopped in mid-air, was he pondering my question?

"Away from the watchful eyes of his congregation, my Baptist minister father was a … different man. We never knew what would happen when he came home. Until late at night. Whispered voices would grow louder, harsher, then an insult followed by a cruel remark. No matter how softly they were spoken, we heard them through the thin walls. We never saw the bruises; he'd hit her in places covered by her long dresses. Appearances and family order must be maintained, he always said."

I had to take my shot. "It didn't stop there, did it James?"

"When we disappointed him, we felt the switch or he forced us to kneel on marbles and jacks for hours. If we talked back, dinner was a bar of soap. Jack and I had a nickname for him that we never uttered to another soul, except once. We called him the Wrath of God. When we turned eleven, the Wrath of God first took Jack into the basement at night. I cannot describe the animalistic cries, pleas, and grunts that rose from below. They still keep me up at night. Jack changed after that—"

"He was the sacrificial lamb—"

"SILENCE!" He raised his cocked fist, eyes wild, then lowered it to run his hands through his hair. "He rescued us. He bore God's Wrath. Father ordained our futures—Jack was the Chosen One, destined to be the scholar-athlete at an elite college, while I was to remain home and follow in his footsteps as a minister. Things happened according to his design until the Wrath of God suffered a massive stroke, a large subdural hematoma deep in the left side of his brain. He lay helpless in his hospital bed: the right side of his body flaccid; he was unable to speak or swallow; and a nasal gastric tube down his throat kept him fed and hydrated."

"That event must have caused a myriad of conflicting feelings in you."

James smiled. "You would think so. He was fully alert and oriented after the stroke," he said as the twisted smile returned, "but helpless as an infant in a basinet."

"And you did what you had to do."

"I told you we are alike. I was alone with him one night in his hospital room, listening to the monitors beep and hum and whirr. I watched his vital signs scroll across the screen. I experienced an epiphany. If he was the Wrath of God, I would become the Will of God. I woke him. I told him our secret name for him."

"What did you do then?"

"I told him I planned to convert to Catholicism (how he detested the hypocritical Catholics!) and join the priesthood, after I made sure he was dead. I'd also change my name to Father James Fogerty, a stereotypical Irish-Catholic name. The look on his gaunt, rage-filled face clouded over with fear for the very first time and it invigorated me. I lowered the bed rail and positioned his limp body upright on the side of the mattress, aiming the left side of his head at the floor." He paused and closed his eyes, as if reliving the memory.

"Then what did you do, James?"

"I whispered in his ear: *I'm doing you a favor*. Then I pushed. The sound of his head hitting the floor was like a bowling ball knocking down a pin. I looked down on him and waves of power rolled into me. I watch him jerk once or twice, then go still. I slipped out the door and walked home. I slept the sleep of the dead and woke to the happy news."

While he relived this memory, his taps on my keyboard became stabs and jabs.

"Your adoptive mother knew about the abuse and did nothing." It wasn't a question.

He stopped typing, leaned back, and closed his eyes. "I hate her for that." His eyes hardened again. "Don't flatter yourself and think you have a prayer of talking me into releasing you. That's not going to happen. We are on an irreversible course here."

The idea was tops on my list. "After you killed your father, why enter any religious order, especially one that practices celibacy? Why not rebel all the way and join Al Qaeda? At least you'd get your seventy-two virgins when you died."

He chuckled to himself while he typed. "Glad you've still got your sense of humor." He turned to me. "You're going to need it."

"I aim to please."

"A priest is in a position of trust and authority, even with the recent negative publicity. I counsel young women for a reason. I remain viewed by billions worldwide as God's shepherd moving among His sheep."

More like a lion in sheep's clothing.

His tongue poked out from between smiling lips as he pecked away on my computer. "When his skull hit the floor, I was no longer His slave. I became the Will of God."

"But the feeling didn't last, did it?"

He glared again. "I returned to his hospital room and stared at the spot, reliving the sights and sounds that night."

"The Will of God intervened again with Mendez. You had the opportunity and the experience to make this one last longer, didn't you?"

The smile broadened. "I drank in his fear and fed on his terror for hours, much as he enjoyed dehumanizing Jack. Mendez welcomed death."

"Kris didn't. She fought back."

The sly smile morphed into that sick leer again. "She dismissed me. For the likes of you."

Keep him talking about himself. Something he'd just said about being a slave....

The restraints stung my arms, like they contained thousands of needles. "You had to be terrified that you were next. After all, you and your brother were twins. I bet you breathed a sigh of relief each time he took Jack downstairs instead of you."

He abruptly stopped typing. "Nobody can understand abomination if they haven't lived through it. To the rest of the world I'm a monster."

Yes, you are. "People with training like you and me understand. Each woman you've been sexually attracted to since eventually disappoints and becomes equated with your adoptive mother who failed to protect you and Jack from God's Wrath. Their level of punishment depends on how badly they rebuffed you. You're exacting revenge on your mother with each woman who enters your world. You couldn't have stopped Jack's abuse. You were a little boy."

He looked away, but his jaw muscles tensed with emotion. I waited minutes, hoping he'd crack on his own.

He pointed the Taser at me and I cringed in my sopping wet shirt. Am I wet enough to be electrocuted?

He paused. "But *she* could have stopped it."

"Yes she could have, but instead she sacrificed Jack to the Wrath of God. Both mothers, birth and adoptive, rejected you. The young women you were attracted to eventually rejected you so you stalked, demeaned, and sexually abused them. You chose the most vulnerable victims, ones most susceptible to psychological manipulation. You developed sophisticated techniques to prolong the abuse. You even used drugs to manipulate some of them. Then Jenny Marcus had the courage to speak up. Once she did, the rest came forward like dominoes. This shook your ordered world, but even so your plan to discredit them might have worked. Until I came along."

He listened intently, looking my way but at an angle so his face remained mostly hidden. He seemed to hang on my every word. I ignored the burning pain in my arms.

"Kris rejected you years ago, but not to the point she had to experience your wrath. When she resurfaced later, romantically linked to me, the therapist you were assigned to see, you snapped. Your need for revenge overrode the need to lay low and ride out the Jenny Marcus storm, but this time you chose the wrong victim. Kris was emotionally strong; she fought back. She refused to bow to your will. You took risks because you made this personal. You left evidence at the scene."

"I did not!" he said, his voice disbelieving.

"You were very conf—"

The leads imbedded in my chest a third time. I smelled my skin burn while puffs of smoke rose. The cramping and the two-by-four to the back of my head feeling crushed me again. My head snapped back; I bucked in the chair. My jaw locked; the world went black.

I heard a voice from somewhere, all around, nowhere … the bottom of a well?

"You mentioned evidence," he said, yanking the leads from my wet chest.

I rode out the pain behind closed eyes until my panting subsided. "He called my bluff. You liked Kris, at least enough to cover her face with a towel. In your rigid belief system she had to die, but you felt remorse."

He didn't respond. I forged on.

"You loved your brother, but also resented him. You painted the Gemini symbol over Kris' heart in remembrance of Jack—"

"In *honor* of him," he interrupted, then lapsed back into silence.

"By destroying my reputation and killing me, you're murdering your father again. The psychological torture was to break me down, isolate, and control me. Lining me up like you positioned your father in his hospital bed. But Kris' murder was too impulsive. You needed a fall guy."

I'm sure he plans to kill my other clients one by one; he's decompensated that much.

He remained quiet, brooding, but his face looked ready to explode. Amp it down a notch, switch topics.

"How'd you come across my tie?"

The smirk returned. "The power of the collar strikes again. After I learned I'd been assigned to you for therapy and that you two were a couple, I studied her habits. One day I positioned myself to be walking the same way when she returned from the Laundromat. I offered to carry her baskets. I let fate decide what happened next. The Will of God almost took over and forced His way into her apartment. Until I saw your tie in her living room. That gave me the idea. When her back was turned, I slipped it into my pocket. That it was the same one you wore on television was an added gift from God's bounty. I followed the two of you several times. Even climbed the tree to reach her second-floor patio. You were going at it in the bedroom like rabbits. What a show!"

"You're making mistakes. You want to be caught. The high after 'the Will of God' strikes never lasts long enough. Your needs are escalating beyond your control. You chose the wrong fall guy in me. I will not beg or bargain with you."

He looked over at me. "You're hardly in a position to gloat."

"The church will never let you skate on the charges."

"I provided believable clinical responses to every allegation. Innocent until proven guilty, beyond a reasonable doubt. Jenny will be alone on the witness stand. Daddy cannot save her."

"The church will make an example of you."

"The church remains society's moral compass, despite her problems. I have sympathetic, even understanding, friends high up in the church. Those who believe our obligation is to show the world God's path, to convert infidels. It's time to return the church to its former position of dominance. Powerful brethren are pushing to abolish the separation of Church and state."

Great, he wants to return society to the Middle Ages.

"You skipped a few Commandments on the way to world domination. I didn't get the memo that says walking God's path includes rape and murder."

"Don't be so naïve. God smites whenever He wills, often through us." He moved the mouse on my computer, clicked the print button, and a crisp white sheet with my company letterhead spilled out on my desktop. "Here's your suicide note. Hope you like it."

"How thoughtful," I said, as he held the paper up to my face.

I Remember Smells

I can't bear to live with this guilt any longer. I've been a failure and a fraud for so long, I can't recall when I lost my soul. I can't help anyone, much less myself. I never meant to hurt Kris, but I couldn't bear it when she left me. When she refused to take me back, something inside snapped and I went berserk. I don't remember beating and choking her. I don't know why I taped her hands over her mouth near the Dumpster, but I covered her face with that towel because I was so mortified. I hope she and her family can eventually find it in their hearts to forgive me. I don't deserve to live a lie, and they deserve the truth.

Mitchell Adams

"Not bad for a first draft, you definitely have talent. You should address it to Kris, though. Suicide notes are almost always written to a particular person or group. I don't use the word 'berserk.' Change it to 'lost all control.' Mention my parents at the end. Something comforting like they were always there for me, urging them not to blame themselves or that I alone am responsible for this tragedy. Throw in that they're vacationing in Africa on safari, for a nice touch of realism. You also overlooked the obvious fact that the note is typed and unsigned. Anyone could have typed this. Free my hands and I'll write and sign it for you." I looked up at him and smiled. He did a slow boil.

His face contorted when he stood up. The face of an old man appeared before me. It was not that of Father James. It reminded me of a vulture. "It's time to put an end to your arrogance. The sun will be turned to darkness and the moon will turn to blood on this great and awesome day, your beginning of sorrows. I will feed off your destruction for days."

He's paraphrasing Bible verses. The day of reckoning, my Judgment Day, has come.

He produced a length of thin rubber tubing and a syringe from his pocket.

"Why the syringe?" I asked, my voice rising even though I was trying like hell to control it. I squirmed in the seat and tried in vain to back away. I could feel my chest tighten, my skin crawl.

Where is everyone?

He dug an empty soda can from a waste basket and bent it back and forth until he tore off the bottom. "You know what this will be?" he asked, cleaning it with an alcohol swab.

I groaned. "It's curved inward, like a spoon."

"Very good. Have you done this before?"

"A few of my clients have."

"I'll adjust the dose for you. Give you half a chance." He produced a Bic and a small vile of brownish-white powder. He carefully measured some of the substance and squirted water from the syringe into the soda can bottom. He heated the can over the Bic until the drug dissolved, stirring the solution with the plunger.

"The note is fine." He smirked again. "Have you developed a new perspective on ECT yet? At first I planned your suicide by shooting you full of cocaine and throwing you through this ninth-floor picture window so you could experience what Jack must have felt, but your pain would have been over too soon."

Satisfied with his drug prep, he drew the liquid into the syringe. "I've chosen to let fate decide. China White is a pure form of hercin that looks more brown than white. As you see, it is liquid soluble and, as you are about to experience, it rapidly crosses the blood-brain barrier. I don't believe this is enough to kill a novice user of your size, but with China White you never know its purity. Many die from accidental overdoses. You get high, I make another anonymous call, and the police find you passed out here with the note."

"Won't it look suspicious if I'm duct-taped to a chair?"

"The tape will be gone by then. They rush you to the hospital, pump you full of Narcan, and try to save you for the trial and public humiliation. If you survive, you go away for first degree murder. I take your place with that leggy stewardess who used to worship the ground you walked on. I will send cohorts to defile you in prison. Eventually I will arrange for an amoral Neanderthal to toss you from the prison roof to see if you've learned how to fly. I like that plan best. What do you think?"

"I'm more of a New Testament kind of guy."

His smirk became a frown. "You are quite the accomplished bull-shitter. As an added bonus, I added the HIV virus to the heroin. Got another smartass comeback for that, Mr. Funnyman?" He moved closer, ready to wrap the rubber tubing around my arm and raise a vein. "You're about to lose that smug attitude. The second this needle's in, your life is over."

I had to think of something, anything, fast. I'm missing something.

"China White? I'd expect that from Jack."

He hit me again so hard my nose bled. "Say my brother's name again and I tape your mouth."

"You were right about everything. I feel at peace like poor Dr. Mendez. Thank you for telling me about the Wrath of God and the Will of God."

He wrapped the rubber tubing below my bicep and tapped my arm in spots, probing for the right vein. Making a face, he said, "What?"

I was on the verge of blacking out again. I spit blood onto the carpet. Sweat stung my eyes.

I stared at the syringe. "You got an air bubble in there."

"Does it really matter? If you're done stalling, it's time. Enjoy your last pleasant feeling of well-being. It's like a Vicodin high, only much stronger. You'll feel warm, sleepy, maybe a little itchy. After that, it's all downhill." My vision blurred again; the vulture face moved toward me like the black hand of a clock.

I struggled for breath, trying not to hyperventilate as I faced head on the terrifying presence of the Will of God. I was about to die. The needle hovered over my skin, about to puncture my vein. He was enjoying it, dragging out the taunt. I thought of Kris and how she must have felt. I thought of everyone who'd ever been brutalized by someone they knew. I thought of two innocent twin boys at the mercy of a father, a man of God who turned out to be a monster.

Then everything fell into place. "Daddy forced you down into that dark basement, too. Didn't he, Jimmy?"

He stopped. The vulture leer stared at me, then through me, until his eyes glazed over.

"Your father took turns with you and your brother. You repressed the memory. You've conflated sex with control and power ever since. The needle wavered in his hand while he weighed my words.

I had one chance to guide him through this before he regrouped.

"I can help you. Look at me." He turned away. "Look at me, Jimmy!"

When at last he did, I spoke in a calm voice. "You have me bound; you are in complete control. Focus your attention on my left thumb and index finger. When my fingers touch, you will allow yourself to fall into a deep, restful state. You will be able to hear my voice and talk with me during this restful time. You will allow yourself to remember past events in your life while in this relaxed state."

I usually place a pen and a light source close to my client's face to try this, but I had no choice now. And it wouldn't work at all unless some part of him wanted to know, wanted to remember, to fill in the memory gaps of his childhood trauma. It was my only chance. No one was coming to save me.

"Imagine yourself resting peacefully on a secluded tropical beach, you've just had the best deep body massage of your life, the bright sun feels warm on your relaxed body, a cool breeze is at your back while a faint mist reaches you from the bluest ocean you've ever seen. Allow yourself to be at complete peace with the world while you watch my fingers." With what little strength remained in my aching wrist, I had been slowly diminishing the space between my fingers while I set the scene.

I said a silent prayer as my fingers touched.

He closed his eyes. His chin lowered to his chest when my fingers met.

So far so good.

"Can you hear me, Jimmy?"

"Yes."

"Open your eyes now."

He did as I said and raised his head.

"You are safe here. No one can hurt you. Allow yourself to see your boyhood home. Take a tour through the living areas on the main floor, revisit your room and the backyard you played in. Can you see it all?"

Silence, then: *Yes*.

"What are the earliest childhood memories of your mother?"

He paused, then: "Sitting on her lap … tugging on her apron when I wanted something. Licking the batter off the spoon. The smell of her chocolate chip cookies baking."

"What are your earliest memories of your father?"

His brow furrowed and he grew anxious.

"You're safe. He cannot hurt you."

"Sometimes he let me steer the car from his lap. He was strong … his voice sounded like it came from everywhere. He knew God. He talked to Him."

"You're doing fine, Jimmy. Remember, no one can hurt you here. Allow yourself to remember going down to the basement when you were eleven. Allow yourself to remember what happened there with your dad. He can't hurt you anymore. He's dead."

He closed his eyes and made small, jerking head movements like he was having a nightmare. Behind the lids his eyes moved rapidly, and I feared the hypnotic induction would be broken. Then: *Smells. I remember smells.*

"Which ones?"

"Mold, coal, licorice, almonds, sweat…." His eyes goggled; I saw fear in them. "And copper."

"Allow yourself to remember why you smelled them."

He pursed his lips. "Water would seep in through cracks in the basement foundation when it rained. Over time the drywall got moldy from it. I could almost taste it in the air after the water receded. The water ruined Jack's old set of plastic-coated weights, tiny chunks of concrete always on the floor for us to step on. The house had a coal furnace when it was first built. Part of the original basement was an old coal bin. The bin area later became part of the crawl space under the house. It was full of spider webs, bugs, and shadows. Jack and I thought monsters lived in the black depths of the crawl space. We were wrong." He stopped and swallowed hard.

"Allow yourself to continue, you're doing great, Jimmy."

"He liked licorice candy. I smelled it on his breath downstairs."

"Who?"

"Him."

"Your father?"

A brief head nod.

"He'd give me a piece of candy after we were done … before we went back upstairs. The almond smell came from a bottle, some type of liquor. He only drank it in the basement, away from mom."

Amoretto liquor?

"Allow yourself to continue remembering, Jimmy. You're safe here, no one can hurt you."

His eyes narrowed as he stared into the past. "I remember him in a white shirt. His thick, black curly hair poked out of it from the front and back. The sweat poured from his chin onto my back when he forced his way into me. I always went face first into the dirty sofa cushions. I didn't want Jack to hear my screams."

"You're doing great, Jimmy. Why do you remember a copper smell?"

He bit his lip. "He had a special chair, beyond the padlocked door next to the coal bin. At first it was just an old wooden chair with wooden arm rests and a high back. He added a footrest like wheelchairs have, but these also were made of wood. He pounded hundreds of sixteen penny nails through the back, the seat, the handrails, and even the footrest. The jagged heads stuck out past the entire surface area. If I disobeyed, he'd force me to sit naked in it while he reprimanded me. He'd strap me in with belts around the waist and arms, my forehead and ankles. My own body weight caused the back half of my body to bleed. If I cried out he doubled the time in the chair. Sometimes when it was my turn I'd see the shine of Jack's blood on the nails under the bare bulb. The chair smelled of copper. I see the blood on me, to this day. He raped me. And Jack."

"He's dead. He can't hurt you anymore, Jimmy. Now I want you to focus again on my fingers."

He looked at them, apparently surprised by the color. "They're blue."

"They sure are. When my fingers touch this time, you will awake refreshed and remember everything that happened in your past with your father." I slowly brought my trembling fingers together. When I did, he looked up at me with the eyes of a lost little boy and began to cry.

"I HAVE TO TELL HIM!" he screamed between sobs, staring beyond me.

"It's okay. Untie me, Jimmy."

He looked at the syringe in his hand as if he were seeing it for the first time. He dropped it and began wiping his hands together and on his pants. "The blood! Look at the blood! Help me get it off!"

The room spun. I had to act fast before I blacked out. "I'll help you wash it off. Help me out of this chair. You can just be Jimmy again. No more blood on your hands!"

He studied the floor-to-ceiling window in my office, the Taser, the syringe, my taped wrists, and suicide note. He reached into his back pocket and a glint of steel flashed in the air. He walked to me, a scalpel extended in his right hand and paused. A shadow of the vulture leer of the Will of God returned to his face. What was I thinking? I should have tried to have Jimmy free me while he was hypnotized. I shut my eyes, then thought better of it and opened them to show him I wasn't carrion yet. The scalpel came closer to my face, then my heart.

Was he about to cut a II into the singed flesh over my heart?

In one swift motion the scalpel swung to my left wrist and sliced through the layers of tape like paper. Then he freed my other wrist.

My arms were on fire and I nearly passed out again. He stood over me, scalpel in hand. I asked him to help me stand when the door exploded inward and flew off its hinges with a deafening twist and shriek of metal, and the chair James had bucked against the door splintered into kindling. A black battering ram clanged to the floor. Four burly SWAT members in full gear, guns drawn, rushed in two-by-two formation through the door. They quickly disarmed a confused Father James, pinned him face down on the carpet, and cuffed his hands tightly behind his back. He offered no resistance while they searched him. His face looked like that of a frightened eleven-year-old boy. I sat there shaking and pleading for them not to hurt him, promising him he'll get the help he needs.

I have a crazy job in a crazy world.

SWAT searched the remainder of the offices and pronounced them clear.

COOL BREEZE

"Where the hell were you?" I croaked.

Baker tried to help me to my feet but my muscles were locked so tight from the Taser hits I couldn't stand. It took some time for the feeling to return to my arms and legs. LeMaster slowly made his way to my leather chair. He inspected the syringe on the floor, the overturned vial of China White, the cooked soda can, and the rubber tubing Baker had taken from my bicep and thrown on the desk.

LeMaster looked at me. "After all he's done, you tell us not to hurt him?"

I shrugged, feeling light-headed. I tried to regain control of my breathing. "What took you so damn long? You were supposed to take him down long before it got this far."

LeMaster picked a miniscule fiber of lint off his suit and looked at his partner.

Baker placed a meaty hand on my shoulder. "There was a perfect shitstorm of events. Broken transmission on the SWAT van. A fiery car accident with multiple injuries that snarled traffic. We called for Clayton police backup until we arrived, but there was a miscommunication and they went to the wrong address. Good thing you made your confession to us earlier, if we were sure you'd smoke out the killer this way the two of us would have been nearby in the building, instead of having ears only on you. Sometimes it's hard to follow the sheep and catch the wolf."

"You were supposed to be outside!"

"Sorry, my man."

"You could have called Gus the doorman and told him to press the fire alarm."

Hair matted to my forehead; my arms began to sting as the feeling returned to them. I looked down at the priest, face down on the carpet. "It doesn't matter now. I had him under control."

LeMaster rolled his eyes.

"If I had use of my arms right now, I'd punch you both. You first, LeMaster."

Baker grinned. "I'd give you one."

"I think I can stand now. Help me to the bathroom."

He sniffed the air, uncertain what he smelled. "That your shirt smoking?"

I feel lucky to be alive. "It's the latest fad. *Caliente* is the brand."

By now a small army of people had entered the scene, a bevy of forensic techs and a police photographer. LeMaster shook his head. "Dr. Adams, you're part of a crime scene. This was kidnapping and attempted murder; everything must be by the book. First, we take pictures of you in your disabled state and inventory his weapons to prove he could carry out his plan. We caught him, now we have to make sure we can make the charges stick."

"*We* caught him? I really have to pee."

"He should have taped your mouth. Sit." LeMaster said as he waved in the photographer for quick pictures. He shook his head and a hint of smile appeared.

"Ah, now we're buddies? I don't think so."

"That's it," LeMaster called over his shoulder. "Anybody got a roll of duct tape?"

While LeMaster helped me to the chair and lightly reaffixed the tape, Detective Baker manhandled Father James off the carpet with one hand and Mirandized him. Baker got nose to nose with him after his rights were read. "You a rapist, murderer, and a Catholic priest? My Momma and auntie go to mass every Sunday. You lucky they not here right now because they would kick yo' ass back to me-dee-E-VIL times, but we got something almost as bad. The brothers in lockup got a thing about rapists. Some of them know people been diddled by priests. Some of them been diddled by priests themselves. You gonna learn what vengeance feels like—"

I turned to Baker. "He's had plenty of that, Detective."

Now I'm shielding him from Baker's anger. Amazing.

He ignored me and kept his cold glare on the fallen priest. "Go ahead. Say those four little words I know you itchin' to say."

The frightened little boy now gone; Father James stood toe to toe with Baker. "I want my attorney."

Baker grinned. "You a fast learner. He better be Johnny Cochran, F. Lee Bailey, and Perry Mason all rolled into one." He grabbed him by the shirt and tossed him to a uniformed officer. "Get this piece of shit off Dr. Adam's carpet."

Baker saw the look of concern on my face. "What? Want me to dial it down? Too over the top, too black?"

Father James fixed his vulture eyes on me. "First round goes to you, on points. We are not done here." Two cops escorted him from my office to a waiting squad car below.

Baker shrugged. "What? You think I hurt his feelings?"

"I helped him recall his childhood. Prison can't be worse than it."

Baker looked puzzled.

"Listen to the tape."

He looked more confused.

I'd fantasized so much about what I'd do to the man who killed Kris that I was becoming someone else. Now I felt sorry for us both.

I fixed a blank stare on the photo technician. It felt like a mug shot. I took the Dictaphone from my pocket, turned it off, and handed it to Baker.

"It's all here. He told me to empty my pockets, not turn them inside out. So I gave him what he expected to see, my wallet and change. I turned on my Dictaphone and left it in my pocket. Maybe you'll understand why I wanted you to ease up on him after you listen to it."

If you figure it out, maybe you can explain it to The Stranger. I wondered what he meant when he said we are not done here.

Baker and LeMaster logged the Dictaphone into evidence while I staggered to the bathroom, peed like a racehorse, and splashed water on my face. My hands still shook and my head throbbed, but a little less. The armpits of my shirt were soaked through. I rechecked the veins in my arm to make sure there were no puncture marks and cleaned the marks and burns on my chest. My arms felt like they were bleeding but weren't. By this time an EMT arrived and examined my chest. The gravity of what happened hit me all at once. The walls closed in. I rode out a series of dry heaves.

The phones in the outer offices, except my ripped out one, were flashing non-stop, for who knows how long. As police and forensic people moved in and out of the offices, I was surprised to learn that Marilyn and Gus were in the hallway at this late hour, badgering the cops for information. I smiled at the sound of Marilyn's shrill voice and the cop's growing impatience with her. One threatened to cuff and haul her to jail if she didn't shut up. I shouted to them that I was okay and would see them after the police had finished with me. Marilyn couldn't enter the office earlier in the evening for her client's appointment due to the chair blocking the outer door and, dedicated therapist that she is, found another office in the building that offered privacy for her client and they had their session. Then she set about to the mystery of the door that wouldn't open and paged Gus, who was on-call that evening. Once Marilyn sets about to fixing something, she doesn't quit until it's fixed, and she protects the office and her work like a mother bear with her cubs.

While the rest of the police unit examined, scraped, lifted, collected, dusted, and photographed the crime scene from every possible angle, LeMaster and Baker took my statement in one of the adjacent offices.

LeMaster handed me a cup of coffee. "It was a good thing you called earlier to tell us about the phone calls and the tie. I know it was hard for you to admit you withheld evidence. You should have told us sooner so we could have been better prepared. If you hadn't called at all, though, you would be dead or on your way to jail."

I put the cup down because I don't drink coffee. "I almost died because you were late." I was glad I wasn't in the throes of a heroin overdose or thrown through my ninth-floor picture window, but I'd have been more grateful if LeMaster and Baker had been on time. I never anticipated a Taser Velcroed to the inside of an umbrella. "I'd already made the appointments with my three suspects. I couldn't back out to buy you time. That would have tipped off the killer. Was Father James ever a suspect for you?"

LeMaster took my coffee and shrugged. "We weren't aware of the connection between Miss Gray and the priest. We wanted to question the ex-husband but never found him. We *were* about to arrest you for murder."

"Why today?"

"The preliminary DNA report on that pubic hair. It came back as a highly probable match."

"But she was my girlfriend." My voice cracked. That simple word—*was*—threatened to overwhelm me.

Baker handed me a bottle of water. "We had a world of circumstantial evidence against you. I noticed the tie you wore at the studio was the one around her neck...."

"But?"

"Some things didn't add up. Anonymous calls pointing us to you. They were too convenient, too neatly packaged."

LeMaster looked up at me. "I was convinced you were guilty, even with the anonymous calls."

Baker shook his head. "The calls were untraceable, from phone booths and prepaid cell phones. My gut told me the killer was calling us to frame you. Now we can compare voices. You weren't the type to kill his girlfriend and leave trails Stevie Wonder could follow, at least not without having a rock-solid alibi."

I stood up, less wobbly this time. "I'd like to go home."

LeMaster cleared his throat. "Not so fast, Dr. We didn't listen to the whole tape, but we heard enough. You knew about the Gemini symbol. You knew exact details of the positioning of her body at the Dumpster. How?"

Busted. I was so close.

Tony risked his job to get me the murder file. Time to improvise. Once I knew what the folder looked like, I knew I had seen it earlier. "When you escorted me to the station for my samples, the desk officer called you away. The file was on your desk. I looked at it then." Why start telling the truth now?

LeMaster eyeballed me with skepticism. "Seeing those pictures would have been traumatic. You weren't fazed at all when we returned."

I met his gaze. "I can keep things bottled up when I need to. It's a therapy trick." One I just invented.

"Why don't I believe you? You must be quite the speed reader, we were gone a minute, two at the most. You and our police psychologist are thick as thieves. Did Tony Martin have a hand in this?"

Less is more when you lie. Creating a diversion helps, too.

I shook my head. "No, but I can help you solve another crime. Now I know where to find Steven Gray. You'll want to question him. He's involved in something illegal and potentially dangerous."

LeMaster braced himself and kept his eyes on me. "Fine, I'll bite. Why?"

"He's living in seclusion at Warren Green's Frontenac estate, on Green's payroll. He's conducting research involving the development and sale of some sort of biochemical weapon that may cause permanent sterility in women. Green may have recently brokered a deal with a foreign military power to purchase it. There may not be much time to prevent this weapon from being used against a civilian population."

"Who's your source?"

I said nothing.

They looked at me, incredulous. LeMaster's mouth hung open. "I'm not going to like the answer or you're not at liberty to tell me, right?"

I nodded. "Door number two. I'm morally obligated to tell you what I've learned, but for reasons of confidentiality I can't reveal my source. Pressure Steven Gray and he'll roll over on Green in exchange for immunity and the chance for a fresh start."

LeMaster looked at his watch and dialed a number on his phone as he started to walk down the hall.

Once LeMaster left, Baker grinned and extended his massive right arm for a fist bump. "You were one Cool Breeze alone in here with that whack job."

"Thanks."

He chuckled softly. "Shit, brother. You look like twenty miles of bad road. You want to go to the hospital for tests on your heart?"

"The EMT cleared me and said if my condition worsens to call my doctor." I double-checked—again—the vein in my arm to make sure Father James's needle hadn't punctured the skin.

The toothpick quickly moved to the other side of his mouth. "Pretty slick, you changin' the subject from the Voice. Wave the carrot of another big collar in my ambitious partner's face and he chases it like a draft horse hooked behind a plow."

I said nothing, repressing a smile.

He grinned. "Your secret's safe and so is your friend. You helped us get a psycho off the streets and now maybe collar some corrupt high rollers. So, whatcha got on this uppity doctor who mixes and barters the plague from his fancy west county mansion?"

I walked between the forensic techs as they gathered their equipment, preparing to leave, found the cassette I recorded while hidden in the trough of Green's converted stable and handed it to Baker. I told him what it contained and admitted to my trespassing. I did this to save lives, possibly generations of them. I kept what Wolf Paxton told me in therapy to myself. I'm mandated by my Code of Ethics to go to jail rather than surrender Paxton's name or confidential treatment history. If the cops connect Wolf to Warren Green, they must do so by their own police work. Green's the driving force behind the research and development of the bioweapon, and he's the one who must be stopped. Wolf is merely an investor and lackey. Nonetheless, I anticipated some restless nights for telling the cops what I knew.

Baker scowled. "We can't use this to get a warrant, but now that we know some of the players and where they at, we turn over a rock or two and see what scurries away from the light. Then we turn the screws."

"I know how that feels."

Baker patted me playfully on the back. "Man, we didn't cuff you or throw you in a holding cell downtown. You only got the one barrel, Doc."

"Thanks for going easy on me," I lied.

"How the hell did you hypnotize that crazy dude who was hell bent on destroyin' you, then convince him to let you go? I thought no one could be made to do somethin' they don' wanna do under hypnosis."

"It fit his comfort zone. He had me under his thumb. Part of him longed to remember the motivation behind his behavior. His delusional rage came from his subconscious. Abusers were often victims of sexual abuse as children. Abused kids often repress gruesome memories for years to cope with a chaotic and dangerous environment."

"How many years you been doing this hypnotic voodoo practice on your clients?"

I looked at him. "That's only the third time I've ever tried to use a hypnotic induction on a client." And only the second time it worked. I was suddenly cold and clammy. "Thanks for getting here when you did."

"Happy to. That's the cool part of the job, watchin' their faces when they know it's all over." He shook his head. "Weird takin' down a priest for murder, it's usually pederasty and even then the system don' get its hands on them most of the time. The church takes care of its own. Times like this make me wish there's a hell."

"He grew up in hell. He needs to be in a place now where he can't hurt any more innocent people."

"Amen to that, brother. He gonna lawyer up and cop an insanity plea."

"He needs help. A forensic psych hospital may be the best place for him, and they can study him. He's educated and physically healthy. We should find a way to make some use of him rather than warehouse him in a cell or execute him," said the man who wanted to kill him earlier.

LeMaster remained engaged in an animated conversation on his cell phone, but soon motioned Baker to join him.

Baker shifted the toothpick in his mouth a final time. "We gonna need you to come to the station, get your complete and signed statement on record. We better get a move on, that gonna take some time. You the man, Cool Breeze."

In the lobby, Gus the elderly security guard saw me and pushed his way through the crowd. He called my name and waved me over. Then he said, "Was that young man who just left able to speak with you?"

I looked at Gus, confused. "Who?"

"He didn't tell me his name. In his thirties, maybe forties, I'm not good with ages anymore because everyone's younger than me. He had a thin build and wore a baseball cap low over his eyes. He paced by the elevators and, you know me, I went over to chat, it helps pass the time on the job. The young fellow didn't like chit-chat; he kept looking at his watch like he wanted to leave but couldn't. I thought he might be one of your patients who got scared off by all the excitement."

"Why do you think he was my client?"

"After the SWAT team entered, he asked me if you were okay. I said I think so, and he left in a hurry."

"Thanks, Gus. You remember anything else about him, call me on my cell. I don't care what time it is, call."

His look of concern seemed to ask if everything was okay. "I will, Mitch."

Outside the front door to my office building, a large crowd pressed up against police barricades along the street, a buzz ran through the throng after a handcuffed Father James was escorted and helped into the back of a police cruiser near the SWAT van. People pointed while Baker and LeMaster escorted me to their unmarked car, most likely wondering if I was in custody. As we walked past the barricades, rumors ran through the crowd about a hostage situation inside and dead bodies.

It was after four in the morning when they finished with me. Baker drove me back to Clayton for my car. I was so drained I was slap happy. "How'd you get that scar?" I asked.

"What scar?" Baker said and winked at me as he dropped me off at my red Solstice, the last car left in underground parking. "Get some sleep, Cool Breeze," he called over his shoulder. His grin revealed the shiny gold tooth again. "We heroes now."

A SPIKE RIGHT THRU MY HEAD

In the old days—a mere week ago, before my life turned upside down—I used the drive home after a day at the office to decompress from the sessions, so I wouldn't take my work home. That wasn't going to happen this time.

I thought about what Gus had said earlier, that a mystery man was asking about me, wanting to see me. What if he wanted to make sure that I was dead? Did Father James have a confederate after all? Rick Arno fit Gus's description and I'd already established that he met with other clients in the waiting room. Had he somehow hooked up with Father James to form a sinister alliance? Steven Gray, Green's goon Jonathan Blue, and even Wolf Paxton fit Gus's general description.

I should have felt better. Kris' killer was in custody. Bottom line though, I was back where I started. Kris was still dead, and I was alone in the dark with wild thoughts running through my head.

It seemed like I was missing something. Nearly everything Father James had said surprised me but saying things for shock value was his style. Yet there were things that still didn't make sense. Maybe I'm overthinking it. I'd been under the most intense pressure imaginable. Bits of what had transpired remained a blur. But still....

Gus never called.

First round goes to you, on points.

I thought of my tie around Kris' neck. I thought of my parents on safari. Family ties. As I walked from the garage into my kitchen, the revelation took my breath away like *I'd* fallen through a frozen pond. I knew the identity of the man asking about me at the office.

I could make a run for it in my car but looking behind me for the rest of my life isn't living. I've never believed in guns for home protection. Too many tragic, accidental shootings. I parked the Solstice and grabbed a baseball bat from the garage and a knife from the kitchen. The living room seemed clear, undisturbed. Then I saw it—a glint of reflected light from the foyer floor. One of the vertical glass panels parallel to the front door had been broken from the outside. The front door was slightly ajar. I stood behind a living room chair, bat in one hand and knife in the other. In a loud voice I called out, "I know you're here. Show yourself, Jack Parks!"

When the lights went out and blackness surrounded me, I nearly came out of my skin. A famous voice howled from my surround-sound system; the volume amped so loud it rattled the windows. *Jumpin' Jack Flash!*

My grip tightened on the knife. I took rapid gulps of air to oxygenate my blood system while I prepared to fight or flee.

The lights flashed on and off, then at last remained on. A thin figure appeared from the hallway leading to the bedrooms. Six foot one, wiry build, feral-looking, brown hair long and wet, a pack slung on his back, the camouflage muscle shirt he wore revealed a myriad of tattoos. Up and down his right arm were the lyrics to his signature song, on his left the famous Rolling Stone's tongue logo. A writhing, fire-breathing dragon head poked from the upper part of his chest. Syringes and skulls adorned his arms and upper torso while a pack of Camels were rolled up in the sleeve of his shirt. The tats were all new since I last saw him. He held a .38 in his right hand and my bottle of Bombay Sapphire in his left. He tapped his foot to the music as he stared at me, then turned down the song with my stereo remote.

"You always liked dramatic entrances, Jack."

His voice came out raspy and raw. "You bring a knife to a gunfight?"

I placed the weapons on a nearby table. "I never would've guessed those would be your first words to me."

He fired up a cigarette and blew a smoke ring. "My brother told me that if anything happened to him last night, I was to kill you. Make your death painful and slow. If I could figure a way to disgrace you at the same time, so much the better."

Please, no more duct tape.

"You've been on the road ever since the escape."

He nodded.

"That's where you want to be. Even now."

He took a long pull of gin. "Beats the hell out of being a sober, frightened, little boy molested for years in that pissant town. Dear old mom liked when it was our turn, it kept him off her for a while. The college scene? I never wanted it."

"You created your own inner world, to survive."

"You could say that." He cranked the volume as the music built up to the next lyrics and he sang along off-key, in a voice coarse as sand.

I para-phrased some of the lyrics. "Straps across your back, crowns and spikes. You sat in the chair, too."

He looked surprised. "Jimmy told you about the chair? I'm impressed. We never told another soul about that locked room. The old man's hobby was torture devices from the Inquisition. His favorite was the interrogation chair, the iron chair, whatever you want to call it. He built one in the basement from pictures he'd researched in the library." A hard look washed over his face. "Sometimes he'd lean his weight on us in the chair. There's no going back to the real world after that. My ink helps cover the scars, the memories of that room. Jimmy still wears his."

"That's why you'd rather get high on the open road, isn't it?" I took a step toward him.

He pointed at the sofa with the gun barrel. "Sit. Some people don't want to be saved. I'm one of them. Accept it. I have."

I crossed my legs. "How did you survive the fall into the river?"

"The fall broke my wrist and nose. I nearly blacked out and died from hypothermia once I swam to shore. I stole a pickup to get outside the search area. I lived on the open road, hitched rides with truckers, and did what I had to do for my ink and chronic. While passing through St. Louis last winter, by pure chance, I sat in a soup kitchen downtown and saw my twin wearing a Roman Catholic collar. I thought I was coming down off a bad trip. He thought I'd died years ago and he begged me to stay in town. Seeing him brought back memories I don't want." He shook his head. "If I had to look at his face much longer I'd lose it, but he insisted we keep in touch. He gave me a pre-paid cell phone, made me promise to answer it whenever he called. I almost threw the damn thing away a hundred times. Then he contacted me and said he wanted me here this week. He instructed me to bring a vial of China White and supplies. He grilled me about technique and dosing. I assumed he wanted to get high, to feel the experience. I knew nothing about all this until he told me to kill you if he didn't. Then I bummed a ride to your office."

"He electrocuted Dr. Mendez."

He nodded, emotionless. "If it helps, you and the staff did everything you could to save Jack Parks ten years ago, but he died when he was a little boy. Jack Parks never made it to St. Louis, but Jumpin' Jack Flash did. I'm living the life I want. You know the saying: live free and love hard, die early and leave a beautiful corpse."

"Your brother also created an inner world to survive. It's never too late to learn more about yourself."

"I know me, I can't stay in one place for long.

"Jimmy conformed, or at least put on a good front. Following the old man's career path further warped him. Maybe seeing me sent him back into the chair. I know reliving that will screw with your head. Maybe he's cut from the same cloth as dear old dad and likes to give pain more than do anything else. Either way he needs to be locked away where he can get help from people like you. But if he's the old man reborn, they should put him down."

He finished the Bombay, wiped his mouth, and tossed the empty next to me on the sofa. "I haven't had the good stuff in a while. I used your shower—they can be few and far between on the road. I left a mess and some wet towels on the bathroom floor. I also helped myself to some food."

He tucked the gun into his waistband. "Here's the deal. I see no reason to kill you. I am going to walk out the front door. I will not hurt you. I don't want your money or your car. What I want from you in return is your silence. Don't tell a soul I was here. Do not tell anyone I'm alive. For all you know, Jack Parks the mental patient died nine years ago in an icy brown river. Agreed?"

I nod. "He may have died, but he remade himself. Jumpin' Jack Flash can do the same."

Jack grinned. "You never know. Maybe someday, but I doubt I'll live long enough."

"You have my word."

"Sorry about the window. And my brother." He left without a sound.

I closed my eyes and slept for thirteen hours, curled into a ball on the sofa. When I woke, I thought I met Jumpin' Jack Flash in a dream. Until I saw the broken glass by my open front door.

SINGING LIKE A CANARY

For the next two weeks Marilyn and the other therapists in the practice continued to see my female clients. I screened hundreds of phone calls from friends and acquaintances while I shunned local and national media. Once the basics of my confrontation with Father James became public knowledge, a couple of agents left messages, touting book or movie deals. It was the last thing I wanted and they left a sour taste in my mouth, so I passed on my fifteen minutes of fame.

My parents arrived home from Africa. We talked and cried about Kris and my ordeal until we couldn't anymore. At the end of the visit mom teased me for being unable to stay out of trouble while they were away. At that point I realized everything was eventually going to be okay, though I still can't imagine life without Kris. I took the good times for granted amid the daily routine, the drudgery, the disappointments, the pain, and suffering that makes up life. I will not do that anymore.

I threw out the rest of the alcohol and felt on edge for days as my body detoxified. I drank water or green tea and returned to eating healthy. Life without Kris felt wrong and a little terrifying, but some days less so than others. I went to an occasional dinner with Tony and Cindy or caught a movie with other friends or co-workers. Long autumn bike rides along the Katy Trail for the fall foliage and biking across the Grafton Ferry to Pere-Marquette State Park and along the Great River Road helped clear my thoughts. I worked out at the gym, played one-on-one with Tony and let him win a few. I made an appointment with a colleague named Gary Peltzer to see where I stood with my grief. We can all use a little help and a window into our psyche now and then. I remain a bit of a mess, but am on the right path.

One morning the doorbell rang. I opened the door and saw a giant fruit and wine basket with skinny legs swaying unsteadily. A human voice huffed and puffed behind it. Debbie Macklin, the blonde television reporter, sans cameraman, struggled beneath it to stay upright. The basket was wider than her and looked like it weighed almost as much.

She blew a bang from her face. "I'm sorry to drop by unannounced. Is this a bad time?"

"This isn't going to change my mind. I will not agree to an interview."

She started to sway under the weight of the basket. "Can you grab this before it crushes me?"

I did.

"It's a peace offering. No strings attached, I promise."

"In that case, thanks and come in. Can I get you anything—a double cheeseburger, a can of Ensure?"

She adjusted her clothes and straightened her hair. "Very funny. It's rabbit food only for this working girl. When I see a juicy medium rare steak, I drool and then cry. The program director can cut my airtime if I exceed a certain weight, porcine mutant that he is. He reminds me all the time that the camera adds ten pounds." She took in the living room and seemed nervous. "I want to say how sorry I am for your loss. I can't imagine what that must be like. I also want to apologize for what happened at the station, it wasn't planned. I hope you believe me, but I understand if you don't."

I accepted the apology but apparently she wasn't finished.

"I value you as a consultant to the station and consider you a friend. You're smart and funny. You're one of the good guys." She offered her business card. "My home number is on the back if you feel like going out to dinner some night. My treat, I can watch you eat real food. Not to wrangle a story or ask questions about what happened. I'm a pretty good listener."

That'd be a bad idea for both of us. "I'm flattered, but I'm afraid I wouldn't be good company."

She squeezed my hand. "If you change your mind, call me." She kissed me on the cheek and then she was gone.

The biggest surprise came in the afternoon mail one day—a certified letter from the National Association of Social Workers, the governing board for over 150,000 Social Workers in the United States, serving notice of a pending investigation into allegations of sexual misconduct between me and a client. The letter did not name an accuser or victim, but their next correspondence would so I could prepare a defense. If found in violation of the Social Work Code of Ethics, I could lose my license and practice. I tensed at the thought of losing everything I'd worked so hard for. Where was this coming from?

I spent the rest of the next afternoon on the phone with board members of the state NASW chapter in Jefferson City, Missouri, who referred my case to the local board. The St. Louis board insisted I respond in person, and promptly, to the serious allegations made against me. We set a day and time.

That evening, I settled down on the sofa with today's Post-Dispatch and a plate of cheeses and fruit. The front-page headline immediately caught my eye.

SCANDAL ROCKS CAMPUS

Dr. Warren Stirling Green, chief of the Gateway University Medical School on Grand Avenue, was arrested late last night in a shocking raid of his Huntleigh Hills estate for the alleged attempted sale of chemical weapons. Initial sources claim the weapons were designed and researched under Dr. Green's supervision on the grounds of his estate and later mass-produced at an Illinois lab he leased that the FBI has now seized and shut down. The Center for Disease Control and ATF also participated in the joint sting.

St. Louis City detectives, acting in conjunction with the St. Louis County Crime Task Force, have learned from multiple sources that Dr. Green had allegedly been shopping the chemical weapons to several potential suitors, foreign and domestic, in search of the highest bidder. It is rumored Dr. Green recently brokered a deal for the deadly chemicals with an unidentified suitor.

This breaking news is particularly disturbing due to the magnitude for possible loss of life if these allegations are proved true. The delivery system for the chemical weaponry was deceptively simple—to incorporate enough of the deadly liquid into the water supply of a rival country, rendering the female population of that country sterile, thus eradicating the next generation of an enemy force or an entire culture, pending the discovery of an antidote. It is rumored that Hamas and Israeli representatives were engaged in a fierce bidding war against each other for first strike capability. An ancillary segment of Dr. Green's alleged research was the development of an abortion pill, possibly meant as a diversion from his covert research.

Dr. Green and his attorneys declined comment. Father Cummings, the president of Gateway University, expressed shock and dismay upon learning of the charges filed against one of the University's most prominent leaders. When interviewed Father Cummings said, "I want to go on record and say Dr. Green is innocent until proven otherwise and he will have our full and complete support during what I'm certain will be an extensive information gathering process. Dr. Green has been a valued member of the St. Louis community for many years.

He's a good man and friend. Our thoughts and prayers are with him and his family during this difficult time.

"That said, Gateway University, being a Catholic institution, would never condone or approve such research and development. Gateway University would never green light the study of an abortion pill based on moral, ethical, and humanitarian grounds, and we abhor the concept and use of chemical weaponry. Gateway University categorically disavows any knowledge or sanction of these projects and if Dr. Green is found guilty of these charges, rest assured you have my word the University will act surely and swiftly to sever all ties with Dr. Green."

St. Louis City Police Chief Joseph Moreno reported that Detectives Francis LeMaster and JoJo Baker recently broke the case after questioning one of Green's assistants about his potential involvement in a separate, seemingly unrelated murder. Assistant Chief Rhymes said, "Only their skilled interrogation techniques brought this matter to light. City and County forces quickly mobilized to take Dr. Green and several key staff into custody. The FBI also detained a visiting foreign arms dealer. We will also be questioning other prominent St. Louis area businessmen regarding their possible involvement in the funding of this alleged illicit operation. If this plays out as expected, the number of local investment suitors will continue to grow and stun the public with its scope. Several major company names and reputations may be tarnished in the fallout."

Dr. Green hails from a wealthy family originally from the south. His father, Dr. Stirling Green inherited the family fortune from his father Winston Green, a land baron and tobacco plantation owner who was also rumored to have done business with the Nazis during World War II. Dr.

Green's great-grandfather Zebediah Green purportedly made the initial family fortune as a rumrunner and later as owner of several distilleries.

After dinner the bell rang, I opened the door to find Detectives LeMaster and Baker.

I showed them in. "Just like old times."

LeMaster said, "Have you read today's paper?"

I smirked. "I did, Francis."

LeMaster's expression hardened.

"What brings you two back?"

"You withheld information from us. I can level charges against you for obstruction of justice by not informing us of the threatening phone calls that promised future murders. You obtained unauthorized access to a confidential murder file, either on your own or with assistance. You trespassed on private property without reasonable cause. The last two actions are serious."

I was too exhausted to stifle a groan. "If you're here to arrest me, just do it."

"Given what we've learned recently, had you been detained by their security force that night, they would have killed you and dumped your body. Then you would have been the presumptive killer on the run, your reputation in ruins, and the subject of an intense but fruitless manhunt. Family and close friends at first would refuse to accept your guilt. With the passage of time, they would begin to have doubts about your innocence. That, or they would have to face the most unbearable grief of never knowing the truth. Your legacy would have been that of a murderer. A hunter or hiker might have eventually discovered some of your bones in a remote woodland burial site years later if you were lucky. The public would reach the conclusion that you received the violent death you deserved and the world is a better place for it. Your behavior was irresponsible, reckless, impulsive, and driven by emotion."

I couldn't argue with him. "If this is meant to make me feel more like an idiot, you're preaching to the choir."

"I just have one more thing to say. Job well done. I wanted to screw with you one more time."

I shook his hand. "I'm not going to miss these talks."

Baker handed me a cardboard box. "Your answering machine, in working order."

Kris' voice.

"We're keepin' the tapes of the priest and the earlier ones with his disguised voice, for court. Missouri allows one party to legally tape conversations without the second party's knowledge. Another nail in his coffin."

"Is he talking? How's he doing?"

LeMaster shook his head. "He lawyered up with a church attorney and has been quiet as a silent movie star until yesterday. We found tennis shoes hidden in a storage locker he rented, size twelve, with trace evidence of Miss Gray's blood on the soles. The tread pattern is an exact match to the bloody footprint found near the Dumpster. He's on suicide watch, sequestered from the other inmates. He seems to have … what's the word you shrinks use? Decompensated. He fired his attorney and announced that God will defend him in court. An insanity plea is in his future."

"What about Green?"

"He hired a big-time national attorney that heads a team of six others, who are working the media like preachers, telling anyone with a microphone or notepad what a saint he's been for the community and a pioneer in the medical field. He's out on a massive bond because of his pull and no prior record, but they're keeping close tabs on him. It's funny that he never filed a complaint against you for the trespassing. I have a theory on that. When we arrived at Green's estate, his security chief assaulted two officers. Baker took him down. We're leaning on Jonathan Blue but so far he's not talking. We think Green planned to sic Blue on you.

"What about Kris' ex?"

"Steven Gray is singing like a canary. He's smart and cocky, with a big mouth." LeMaster looked at me. "He reminds me of somebody I know."

I'll give him that one.

Baker cleared his throat. "Green put him on the payroll sometime after he washed out of med school. He claimed to be broke, strung out, and alone after some redhead left him for greener pastures. He's confident they planned to leave him holdin' the bag on this operation that he swears Green told him was legit when it began. He cut a deal—he's givin' us names of investors and descriptions of potential buyers, everythin' he knows about the operation, in exchange for leniency. Green tried to screw him, so he's rollin' over on them all, but we've found no evidence that anyone in Green's group had any involvement in your girlfriend's death."

I cut in. "My source says Jonathan Blue orchestrated the attempted break-in at her apartment. Green ordered it to scare her, but I'm inclined to agree Father James acted alone."

"Why the scare tactics?"

"She worked as Green's executive secretary. He feared she may have overheard enough at work to put two and two together. Control freaks don't like loose ends. After the break-in, she shared some vague suspicions with me, but she didn't have a clue what Green was working on. That's why I went over the wall at Green's estate." Part of it, anyway.

"Gray says he made a big mistake leavin' his wife and bailin' on medical school, that he regrets ever workin' for Green. He gave us a Sad Sack story of watchin' her from afar, kickin' his coke habit, and cuttin' back on weed. He hoped for one big financial score with Green, then to try and re-enter her life."

LeMaster motioned for me to follow him down the hallway, which I did. "One other thing and I will turn you over to Baker. I have a daughter who looks like your Miss Gray. She has a drug problem and chronic underlying depression. She's checked in and out of every drug rehab program in the metro area with no success. Can you help her?"

That explains the faraway look in his eyes when he held Kris' picture that day. I had assumed he was searching the photo for some arcane clue.

Outwardly he maintained his stoic front, but emotion overtook him. His taut face and clenched jaw carried the desperation and heartache of a parent who's afraid they may lose a child. He waved his arm stiffly in the air. "She's all I have … aside from this job." I consoled the lonely little man who tried his best to put me behind bars.

"I'm not ready to see clients again, but if she's open to talking, I know good therapists who specialize in addictions."

We shook hands. He gave me his business card before he left.

Baker wore a bright red Hawaiian shirt with swaying palm trees and smiling blue parrots. He tilted his head toward LeMaster and put a meaty arm on my shoulder. "Us two gonna be he-roes and get a pay upgrade because of you. We won't forget that. My little partner over there got his eye on the po-lice chief job one day, but his clock be tickin'. Little man with big dreams."

Baker leaned forward conspiratorially even though no one else could hear. "You want one more crack at this priest in the interrogation room? For *any* reason—see if you can get him to talk or just fuck with his head. That's our gift to you, if you want. Perps in leg irons trip all the time and smack their heads bloody on the metal desks in those rooms." Baker's sclera bulged white as eggs as he stared into my eyes.

Something stirred in me. It whispered and called to me. For an instant I thought I felt hot air on my ear.

I'd spent two weeks purging myself of The Stranger. He threatened to consume me and I still wasn't free of him. A primitive part of me wanted to make Father James hurt as much as he hurt Kris. I hated how Father James made me feel. How he manipulated me, how I had to become and think like him to catch him. I didn't want to give him the slightest chance to exert his power over me just to mess with his mind. To do so, I would become like him again. It wasn't worth compromising my values for the satisfaction of rubbing his nose in his capture or breaking it on a metal table. Neither would bring Kris back. I'm glad Baker hadn't approached me earlier with this.

I met his gaze and shook my head. "Skilled forensic clinicians should study him to learn how his mind works. Not me."

He nodded. "Fair enough, Doc."

A moment of silence passed until I looked at him. "How do you check your anger on the job and stay sane?"

"Simple. Every so often I get to beat up the bad guys. I was about to ask you the same question."

When I didn't answer, he worked his toothpick around and pointed briefly to the serpentine scar on his face. "This is what can happen when you try to play by the rules. I tried to break up a bunch of gangbangers rapin' a dancer outside a club one night, I got six of 'em down on the ground but the last one cold cocked me from behind. Woke up chained to a tree trunk and they started slicin'. Turned out the lady, Simone, had a piece in her purse. She did what I should've done. She capped two of 'em while the others ran. After that whole mess, we took care of one another while we healed. We still do, five years later. Most people don't know nothin' about that, but you not most people, Cool Breeze."

"I like the sound of that nickname better than the first one."

He nodded and we shook hands. "Swinger just don't suit, I guess. Anyhow, I got your digits when we get any news on the killer priest."

"I appreciate it. Simone's lucky you were around."

Baker started to walk away but stopped. "Shit man, I'm the lucky one. We cover for each other. The department has your friend The Voice as a consultant, but is it okay I call you if I ever get stuck on a case and need an expert psych-o-logical opinion?"

"I'm not sure I'll be up for that for a while. I plan to take a break from the police for a while. No offense."

"None taken. It'd be a non-paying gig, anyway." He smiled, revealing that shiny gold tooth one more time.

I never told a soul Jack Parks is still alive or that someone broke into my townhouse that night. I never mentioned Jumpin' Jack Flash again, although I think about him and wish him well. You can never escape the past, but the circle finally seemed closed.

Life will do that to you. Sometimes.

MINUTE AND FAR AWAY

I kept a low profile well into November—exercising, reading, and taking long hikes—it felt good to become yesterday's news with each passing day. I kept abreast of the latest about Father James and the Gateway University scandal. While the days passed the number of phone messages diminished. I returned a select few. My few minutes in the limelight completely faded. I met with Dr. Peltzer once a week; he helped me better understand the role The Stranger played in my life. Everybody has got one whether you know it or not and how we handle him (or her) helps define us. Violence and hate are like ripples in a pond after a stone is thrown into it, the effect seems to never end. My friend Tony likes to say, "We all start out the same. How we handle what we experience makes us unique." Father James wasn't born a multiple murderer. Some take the *it's all about me* path while others help those around them.

One November day I drove downtown to meet with the NASW board and face the anonymous complaint. The board kept me waiting thirty minutes. I was brought into a room before five social workers, four women and one man, who looked down on me from what looked like a judge's bench.

An older African American lady sat in the middle of the panel. She wore a dark blue power suit and had lavender highlights in her hair. She looked to me. "Thank you for meeting with us today. I will call you Dr. Adams and you may address me as Miss Washington." She referred to her yellow legal pad. Her lavender hair didn't move with the rest of her, apparently welded in place by hair spray.

"I see before me extremely serious accusations, charges of such a grave nature that, if true, could result in the immediate forfeiture of your license and practice, Dr. Adams. Do I have your attention?"

I nodded my understanding. "Yes you do, Miss Washington."

Miss Washington pursed her thin lips. "When, and under what circumstances, did you first meet Kristin Marie Gray?"

I rattled off the date of our session and passed her copies of the dated invoice and my progress note. "As the note reflects, Miss Washington, Miss Gray had decided to divorce her husband before she made the appointment with me. She was not clinically depressed, psychotic, or schizophrenic. Her goal was an amicable divorce and, since her husband at the time was not present and she did not know how to reach him, I made suggestions, most of which she'd already thought of on her own. She did not discuss details or her feelings about the separation. She wanted a sounding board, to make sure she was on the right track. I spent fifteen minutes with her. I didn't plan on charging her, but she insisted. She paid her co-pay and I submitted a bill to her insurance. She thanked me. She didn't want to schedule another meeting unless she made contact with her husband and he agreed to come. I didn't hear from her again."

Miss Washington looked to others on the panel, then back to me. "Did you have any further *professional* interaction with Miss Gray after the follow-up session?"

I noted the emphasis. "No, Miss Washington." In therapy years, fifteen minutes is an eye blink.

The chairwoman made a harrumphing sound. "I see, but you *did* have later contact with your client, didn't you? When did you begin a romantic relationship with Miss Gray?"

I referred to my notes. "One year and six days after our first meeting, I was in the Gateway Medical Center cafeteria visiting a colleague who worked second shift. I sensed eyes staring at me from the table next to ours. When my colleague's break ended and he returned to his floor, the woman approached me and apologized for staring. She said I looked familiar. She looked familiar to me as well but I couldn't place her. She said her name, I said mine, and then we remembered. She asked me to stay for tea. We became friends, found out we had a lot in common, and started to date a few weeks later."

Two compatible equals. End of story, or so I hoped.

Miss Washington frowned. "Our profession has strict standards about dating clients. Once a client, always a client. Psychologists and MDs can date and even marry their clients and patients, but not social workers." She removed her reading glasses and leaned forward. "Did you date Miss Gray when she was married?"

"No, Miss Washington."

"Do you use or deal illicit drugs of any kind, Dr. Adams?"

"No. If I may ask, where are you going with this, Miss Washington?"

"Did you use drugs when you treated Miss Gray?"

"I did not treat Miss Gray, nor have I ever dealt illicit drugs. I smoked pot occasionally in college."

"Did Miss Gray use drugs?"

"Not to my knowledge."

"When did you last see Miss Gray?"

"Months ago, when I identified her body in the city morgue."

For a moment I thought I saw her lavender hair move ever so slightly out of place.

"Excuse me, Dr. Adams. Did you say the morgue?"

"I did, Miss Washington. One of my recent clients, a sociopath, had a fixed, paranoid delusion involving me. He finagled his way into becoming my client. He killed several people before he murdered Miss

Gray, then tried to frame me for her murder and kill me. He's behind bars now, awaiting trial."

Has she been living in a cave?

She covered her microphone as a council member whispered into her ear. "Dr. Adams, would you mind waiting in the hallway while the panel convenes?"

Thirty minutes later they summoned me back.

"Dr. Adams, this is a highly unusual case and, I believe, requires special consideration. This grievance was not filed by Miss Gray. The complaint was scathing, dramatic, at times rambling, and it mentioned specific criminal activities that did not pan out when we checked your police record. The complainant named you as the cause of Miss Gray's failed marriage, claimed you used and dealt heroin, and that you forced Miss Gray and other female clients to work the streets to supplement your income and support their drug habits. The letter we received was signed, 'Respectfully yours in Christ, the Honorable Father James Fogerty.' Is this your sociopathic client, the man in jail for murder?"

"Yes." A chill went through me. Had he injected me and if I'd survived and been sent to jail, no one would've believed me.

She nodded to the panel. "I am from Jefferson City. I want to thank my St. Louis colleagues for informing me about the uniqueness of this case and your involvement in this tragic local story. On some levels, it places the grievance in a whole new perspective."

On every level.

She took a sip of water and pursed her lips again. "That said, I still believe you violated our Code of Ethics, Dr. Adams. You made an egregious error in judgment. You probably don't feel lucky right now, but you are. Had your relationship with Miss Gray ended in a bitter break-up, if she had deeper psychological scars, or harbored a lingering antipathy toward men and wanted to hurt you, *she* could have made your professional life a living hell. You could have lost everything."

I did lose everything. Please don't take my practice too.

"Our profession lost a promising young student. You may have helped catch a bad man and attain some degree of notoriety for yourself and our profession, but Miss Gray would likely be alive today if not for your actions. In light of this new evidence, the extenuating circumstances, and given the source and motivation behind this complaint, it is the decision of this board to allow you to return to practice with our stern reprimand. I'm sorry for your loss, sir. I hope to never see you before this board again, Dr. Adams. You are free to practice. Consider yourself lucky."

You don't know half of what I've done, Miss Washington. If I'd done everything by the book, Father James and Warren Green would be free and I'd be in jail or dead.

I swallowed my pride and bit my tongue. What she said was true, given our Code. Sometimes it's best to keep your mouth shut and take your lumps like a man. "Thank you, Miss Washington, members of the board."

During Thanksgiving week, I saw a few established clients. Bob Vale had returned home from the hospital, progressing in outpatient physical rehab while I helped him with post-traumatic issues. He's undergone a series of surgeries to hopefully restore full vision in that eye. Before discharge, Nurse Patti turned matchmaker and set him up with a cute young lady volunteer at the hospital. They've enjoyed dinners and movies together. I've never seen him smile so much. My efforts to put the dark man Frank DeLuca behind bars failed, but the negative press and public outcry forced him to pull up stakes and move Dolly's Delight deeper into rural Missouri, away from the metropolitan area. I saw Lisa and Harold Carter in a joint session; they decided to work on their marriage. Rick Arno was back in jail awaiting arraignment on a statutory rape case involving a sixteen-year-old girl. Wolf Paxton and Father James of course had more pressing legal matters.

The first kiss of winter hit early this year; cold northwest temps and winds froze the ground and blew snow flurries that amounted to nothing but nevertheless drove anxious residents to the stores to empty the shelves of bread, milk, and eggs. Do St. Louisans hunker down during winter storms and make nothing but French toast?

The day before Thanksgiving I received a surprise visitor in the office.

I didn't recognize her at first as her lustrous black hair flowed unencumbered past her shoulders. She wore a simple white denim shirt over form fitting tan jodhpurs. She held a lush sable coat in her lap. The first time we'd met her long legs and athletic body remained concealed by a full-length gown. The rosy glow to her cheeks made her look as if she'd just come from a long ride on one of her stallions.

Elizabeth Green extended her hand. The left was sans wedding ring.

We offered condolences to each another; I made her a cup of chai tea.

"Before I tell you why I'm here, I want to apologize for my husband. I've known of his unfaithfulness for years and heard a litany of rumors involving him with many women, including your Kristin. I know what you're thinking, but I will not go down that path. I don't know anything about the two of them and I don't want to know. He married me for my money and my presentability. Warren squandered the lion's share of his family fortune before we met. At least I had the foresight to insist on a pre-nup. I was unaware of this horrid business venture. I want to start to repair the damage Warren has done to the community and to my name. *That* brings me to you."

"I'm sorry, I don't follow."

She crossed her legs and looked me in the eyes. "I plan to divorce my husband and build a comprehensive women's health care center in St. Louis. It will be the finest, state-of-the-art facility in the bi-state area. It will have medical buildings, a mental health clinic, and an on-site shelter for women and children. I would like your involvement in the planning and organization of the mental health facility. You can be the director, a consultant, or therapist. Whatever you wish if you're interested."

I had received a gracious rejection letter in today's mail from the CEO of a downtown marketing firm I'd met with in October. My heart wasn't in the presentation and the CEO chose to go with a cheaper offer from a bigger counseling agency to provide EAP benefits to his company.

One door closes....

"I'm surprised and flattered, but why me?"

"I have many contacts within the mental health field and the police. I'm aware of the break-in that my husband apparently ordered at Kristin's apartment, your nocturnal visit to our home, and of your trials with the police to find her killer. You protected the confidentiality, well-being, and safety of your clients throughout it all. Even the more odious ones. My understanding is that you challenge your clients, but you also go to bat for your people and fight for them. I'm looking for qualified professionals with integrity like you to run my center."

It's a good thing she didn't consult Miss Washington or Rick Arno or Wolf Paxton.

She had me investigated and tactfully acknowledged my Channel Four fight with DeLuca over Bob.

"I'm not back to work yet, but I will consider it. If I agree, I'd rather be involved in the treatment aspect rather than an administrative or consulting role." I thanked her and we exchanged cards.

II   II   II

That night I sat in my toasty living room with a fire blazing and printed out a boarding pass for a flight. Next to the printer sat Kris' unopened fortune cookie from the Chinese delivery we had the night after Warren Green's party. I put down my hot chocolate and popped open the crinkly cellophane wrapper. I tore the thin folded cookie in half and read the message: *Your spirit will live forever among the stars.*

Try telling that to Jay Gatsby, Confucius.

With Father James in custody and the case against him taking shape, Kris' remains had been released to her parents, Joseph and Marie Gray, who next have the horrific task of burying their oldest daughter the day after Thanksgiving. I'd talked to Kris' mom on the phone a few times after the murder, but not as much as I probably should have because at the time we sounded like two open wounds.

I finished boxing her belongings and photos to ship to her parents and younger sisters when I told myself now was the time. I had a decision to make. I'd found something when I moved her belongings from the apartment after the detectives gave the okay for me to do so. The cops had overlooked it; I stumbled upon it by chance only after I removed the mattress and box springs and dismantled the bed frame. I stepped on an uneven area of carpet near the baseboard previously covered by the bed. The carpet was pulled up slightly from the tacking strips. Hidden underneath lay a small bound book. I held it now, turning it over in my hands like Wolf Paxton with his fedora. I really wanted, and really didn't want, to read it.

I'd nearly turned the latch a hundred times—I had caved and played the answering machine tape those nights I really missed her on those nights that ended with a visit from The Stranger—but left it unopened. So far.

I told myself that inside may contain more evidence for the police to use against Green or Father James. It would obviously reveal much more about Kris.

I toyed with the latch. Kris had taught me how to love without condition, without measure. She showed me that love never ends. For that I will never forget her. I'd become too cynical and judgmental, too self-centered, less forgiving, and too hard on myself and, at times, with my clients. I owe people apologies and need to ask for their forgiveness. When we think we have everything figured out, life reminds us that we're never too smart or too old to stop learning. It was obvious she'd hid the diary from me, from everyone.

Should I give it to her family, along with the rest of her belongings?

I sipped hot chocolate and opened the latch to Pandora's Box.

I exposed the pages and tossed it into the fire without reading a word. The corners of the pages curled and turned brown well before the spine of the book broke down. The logs beneath popped and sputtered.

Never in my dreams did I ever think burning a book would feel so right.

"Keep your secrets, Kris." I watched the flames reach out and consume the cover. Green light and smoke swirled and rose, turning the lines of written words to black ash that drifted up the flue, through the chimney, and into the darkness, where they would live forever with the stars.

The End

ABOUT THE AUTHOR

Scott L. Miller is a retired, former licensed clinical social worker who earned his MSW at St. Louis University. He worked extensively with adults, children, families, and the elderly in state and private hospitals in St. Louis City and County, which allowed him to see and work with most every psychiatric diagnosis in the DSM as well as experience a taste of city life while doing home visits.

Long fascinated by the power of the written word and an avid reader, he utilized his acquired psychiatric and medical knowledge to write the Mitchell Adams series, as well as numerous stories and works in progress.

He lives in Chesterfield, MO with his pocket beagle Juliet, the greatest dog ever.

ACKNOWLEDGMENT

This was my first foray into the world of traditional publishing. Since then, I regained the rights to this novel but still want to thank Kristina Blank Makansi for giving me my initial break. I don't forget those who help me along this journey and also want to thank my deceased second wife Beta, who provided insights into the world of Intensive Care treatment in hospitals from a nursing perspective for this story.

Many thanks to Dr. Felix Vincenz for his insights on private practice.

I want to thank my Mom, Virginia Miller, for being my biggest supporter. She's looking down from heaven, smiling.

Forgive my anachronistic license re: certain buildings in St. Louis, some of which are no longer there or I changed the shapes and sizes along the way for the story.

To those in psychiatric and medical professions, you make the world a kinder and gentler place with each life you touch. You have hard jobs. Remember to laugh. To people with mental illness, try not to be hard on yourselves.

I want to thank the trusty workers at New York Book Publishers for their steadfast work in re-releasing Interrogation. Thank you for the new cover, for the formatting, and for all you do. Specifically, Lisa Smith (aka: Tokyo!), Logan Walsh, Jeremiah Hofsted, Jessica Cohen, Emma Beker, and anyone else associated with this project.

www.ingramcontent.com/pod-product-compliance
Lightning Source LLC
Chambersburg PA
CBHW041048310726
48978CB00011BA/471